Peregrination Series

Book 1

PEREGRINATE- V. TO TRAVEL THROUGH OR OVER; AN EXTENSIVE VOYAGE

Earth

Peregrination Series Book 1
S.G. Boudreaux

SG Boudreaux

2nd edition

ISBN 978-1-7339636-6-4 (paperback)

ISBN 978-1-7339636-7-1 (digital)

SG Boudreaux

PO Box 12936

Lake Charles, La. 70612

Printed in the United States of America

Sgboodro2@yahoo.com

www.SGBoudreaux.com

I would like to dedicate this book, first of all, to my husband Chris who believed in me enough to have this book published. My beta readers which include my sister Faith who read every page several times and gave me great feedback and editorial advice. My sisters Vanessa and Anita who encouraged me with their great compliments, and my pastor Glenn, who also encouraged me through the writing of my novel series.

SG Boudreaux

Peregrinate: Leaving one's homeland and
wandering on foot, usually for the love of God.
(v.) to travel, especially on foot, to travel over or through.

<u>Glossary</u>

Capped letters are the annunciated parts of the word while **bold** letters receive the long sound.

Peregrinate or Peregrination (PER-e-gri-na**t**) - To travel over or through something. An extensive journey usually for the glory of God.

*Dragoman (*DR**A** -go-mun) – was, or is, an actual profession. They served the kings of empires as interpreters in Turkish, Arabic, and other Persian speaking countries. They were men who were skilled in many languages and political information about other countries and served as a sort of consultant. In my books, they serve to lead the Peregrines on missions.

Peregrine (PER-e-grin) – Noun derived from Peregrinate - Made up for the book. A person who travels over time, through storms for the glory of God.

Scroll of Rubric – made up for the story. Rubric means red and is simply a code or instructions.

Staff of Moses – This is an actual item from the Bible, used by Moses, whom God used to perform many miracles. My research concluded that it has never been found.

Goddelikheid Crucible or Divinity Crucible – the name Goddelikheid is a translation of divinity in a foreign language. However, a crucible is a bowl like item that is used in distilling or separating metals for the purpose of refining.

Portal – a hole created by generating a large amount of energy, either naturally or mechanically, that Peregrines use to time travel.

Mungo Park – He was an actual living person who did explore Africa and the Niger River for the African Association in 1796-1803. This part of the story and some of the information given about him is and are factual events.

Nikola Tesla – He was an actual living person who did invent the Tesla coils.

Garganthera – (Gar gan THERA) a fictional place made up for the
        storyline.
Barriers Edge – an opaque shield that separates dimensions, also a
        fictional thing made up for the storyline.
Bermuda Triangle - most of us are familiar with the strange tales that
        come out of the Triangle. I just elaborated and explained why.
Reader's Island – a fictional place created for the story.
Hausa Language – used in Africa around the Niger area for trade
        purposes, and was a blend of several different languages.
Jager – pronounced (Y**A** ger)

Some of the storms that are listed in the book series are factual storms
that took place throughout history. Some places in the book are actual
places and researchable. Some places are fictional and are made up for
the benefit of the storyline.

This book series is a work of fiction. Although it is based upon some
Biblical truths, all characters are fictional and in no way represent any
living or deceased persons. Any similarity is purely coincidental.

Peregrination Series Book 1: Earth

But if we hope for what we do not
yet have, we wait for it patiently.

Romans 8:25

Chapter 1

April 17th, 1906, San Francisco, California.
7 pm. Harbor-Docks

Seth Jager quickly strode past the Harbor master's office after a long day on the tugboat. He straddled his motorbike, pumped the pedal to start it, and headed home, anticipation about the evening ahead making knots in his stomach. The scent of the ocean and docks filled his nostrils, settling his nerves just a bit. The crisp morning air ruffled his hair and cooled his skin for the short ride home. Home wasn't much, but his quaint little apartment was all he had needed up to this point in his life. He had lucked into finding the quiet, single-dwelling when he first sailed into town. Sitting at a table at Shelley's Diner with a cup of coffee and a listing of local places for rent, a waitress had mentioned to him that a recently widowed woman was seeking a renter for space above her garage.

Mrs. Lampke was an older woman of about sixty who needed the income since the abrupt death of her husband, who had no life insurance. He had used the rental space as an old workshop, and Mrs. Lampke needed to transform it into a livable space. She couldn't do the work herself and had no living relatives in the area. All Seth had to do was help her turn it into an apartment and she would discount his rent for however many months was agreeable. He had slept on a cot in the garage apartment for the few weeks it took to transform the rooms, while Mrs. Lampke' happily fed him breakfast each morning and dinner each night until the work had been finished and the apartment had its own working kitchen. Stella Lampke' was still fiercely independent for her age, and a very likeable woman. She had a quick wit and playful sense of humor. She reminded him of his dearly departed grand-mother who had raised him.

Seth remembered when he was just four years of age. His father abandoned him and his mother. She took to drinking to dull the pain of rejection and heartache over being left alone with a toddler and no source of income. It had killed her only a few years later. She had been drunk one night when walking home from work where she served drinks for tips at the local bar. She apparently staggered into traffic and was hit by a motor car. It was a hit and run and she had been killed instantly.

Seth's heart lurched in his chest at the thought of his mother. She hadn't even cared enough to stay alive and continue living for him. He had learned early on in life that there weren't too many people you could really depend on.

His grandmother had been the exception. However, she had died from Angina eight years after his mother, leaving him completely alone in the world without a single relative to take him in. If there were any distant cousins, he had never met any of them. It was then that he decided to take a job on a schooner headed anywhere before child services found him and forced him into foster care. He knew a few kids from school who told him about being shuffled from home to home, and how some of the care givers were cruel and used them like slave labor. He was fourteen years old at the time and was already wise to the ways of the world.

He was big for his age and people always mistook him for being older which helped him immensely in a lot of areas.

Growing up with little else to depend on, Seth learned how to handle himself well and was a hard worker. Since he followed directions, and kept his mouth shut Captain Matt Walker of the sailing vessel the *Mattie May,* took a liking to him and basically treated him like his own son; in a standoffish sort of way. Matt taught him everything he knew about sailing, navigating, and business, and Seth quickly became an able sea captain at an early age.

He had traveled the world for most of his teen and young adult years from one seaport city to the next, never staying anywhere for long. Three years ago, their schooner had put into San Francisco harbor for supplies and a weeklong furlough. That's when he had seen her, Caroline Palmer. He was never one to believe in love at first sight, but with Caroline, he was definitely very interested. The first time he laid eyes on her he couldn't get her out of his mind for an entire week. That was when he decided to give up life at sea and take a local job as a tug-boat captain at Stanley Tug Services. It was decent money, and he still got to spend his days on the water. He spent the next six months wooing Caroline Palmer until she finally agreed to a date with him. He quickly learned that she was a cautious woman and a devout Christian. He had never met anyone like her. She was caring, kind, thoughtful, and selfless, just to name a few of her admirable qualities. The only other person he had ever known that was a Christian had been his grandmother. Grams had tried to teach him what she could, but he had been young, stubborn, and angry, and didn't like being told what to do or believe. Especially about a God that would allow the things that happened to him at such a young age.

Seth bounded up the steps that ran up the side of the garage and entered his apartment, tossing his keys onto his dresser. He opened the top drawer and slipped his hand into it, feeling for the small, smooth, jewelry box. A slight smile crossed his lips as he caressed the velvety box with his thumb. In all his twenty-seven years, he had never felt this way about a woman, or anyone for that matter.

As Seth sat contemplating his decision, he glanced around his small, two-room studio type apartment. He sighed, smiling at the memories of good times he had while living here. He would miss this place, but he knew he would have to make some changes soon and look into purchasing a home in the Mission Bay area; a nice home with a yard. One close enough to the bay and harbor where work would be close to home. San Francisco Bay was no place to raise a family, and he often worried about Caroline walking by herself at night. Men outnumbered women seventy to one, and life for a single woman here could be treacherous. Most of them ended up in prostitution with no other options for supporting themselves.

Caroline, much like Seth, had no real family here. She and her father had moved here years ago, and he had passed away shortly after from a heart attack. Luckily, Caroline and her father lived in a boarding house run by an elderly gentleman and his wife, Mr. and Mrs. Barnes. They took Caroline in as their own and looked after her. Mr. Barnes was a retired police officer and a tough man at that. Most people knew him and his reputation, and that alone protected Caroline for the most part.

Seth showered, dressed, grabbed the box, and headed out the door to Luigi's Fine Italian Restaurant, where he had reservations for eight p.m. Caroline said she would hail a cab and meet him there since she had a late shift at the library that evening and didn't want Seth to have to drive across town to pick her up. Seth agreed to the arrangement since his nerves were on edge, and it gave him a little more time to prepare for their evening. He had never been more nervous and excited at the same time. His grandmother would be proud of the man he had become, and the woman he had chosen to spend the rest of his life with. He had never been a religious person but decided to offer up a quick prayer to God, if He were real, in hopes that Caroline's answer to his question was in his favor.

Seth reached the restaurant at five minutes to eight and procured their table. Luigi's was a bit quieter tonight being that it was a Tuesday. He was grateful for the quieter atmosphere this evening. It would make the proposal easier and more romantic he hoped.

Seth sat looking over the décor of the restaurant, sipping on the glass of wine the waiter returned with. Luigi's was a classic Italian restaurant, rival to any that existed in Italy. Seth had been to several while traveling the seas, and Luigi's was definitely authentic. Even down to the décor. Large open beams graced the ceiling, with electrical lighting hanging from them. The lamps were made of scrolled iron with grape vines, also made of iron, winding around the exteriors. The wooden chairs were upholstered with brown leather, and the tables were tiled in hues of earth tones. Several men walked the restaurant serenading the guests with guitars and mandolins dressed in Italian garb.

Luigi's was his and Caroline's favorite restaurant, and where they had their first date almost two years ago. She had wanted to make sure they truly knew each other before jumping into a relationship, deciding to take it slowly and see how things worked out. It had been a long, hard, two years. Caroline's faith did not allow for sex outside of marriage, and because of his feelings for her he withheld his advances even though at times it was extremely hard. He had messed up after just a few dates early in their relationship when his emotions had gotten the better of him and had almost lost her for good. He managed to convince her to give him another chance after months of pursuing her yet again. Since then, he always made sure to carefully plan their dates where they had plenty to keep them occupied and were never alone for long.

Seth sat and watched the few people in the restaurant while he waited for Caroline to arrive. There was a relatively young-looking couple a few tables over that had a little girl who appeared to be around the age of two. She had big brown eyes, and curly brown pigtails hanging from both sides of her head. She was smiling and giggling at something her father said to her. They all seemed very happy. As Seth watched, he wondered what his and Caroline's children would look like should they have any. He also worried about the kind of father he would make, not having had much of a father figure himself. Matt Walker had been a kind man and had done a nice job of basically raising him on board a ship, even taking him in when in port, but Seth had longed for that special bond between father and son that some of the men aboard ship had spoken of when regaling his younger self with stories from their childhoods.

Seth shook himself out of his thoughts just in time to see Caroline come in the door. His breath caught in his throat when she entered the establishment. He often found himself holding his breath when he would glance at her. She was unknowingly beautiful and always impeccably dressed. She always wore a more simplistic style of clothing, with straight lines and few, if any, ruffles. She wore pants often, which got her a few *questionable* looks from most of the high society women, but she always stated that comfort and practicality were best.

Caroline had long strawberry-blonde hair that had just the right amount of curl and wave to it. She usually kept it pulled back into a bun or loose ponytail of sorts. Her eyes were the color of the sea after a storm, deep greenish-blue pools that seemed to bounce light from every direction. She was tall and thin but not skinny, and her movements were naturally graceful and effortless. She was brilliant and extremely knowledgeable about almost everything, he supposed from working in the library since she was old enough to do so since her father had been head librarian before he passed, a position she had eventually been asked to step into, assuming his role at the library.

Seth shook himself from his thoughts. When making plans with her, he hadn't mentioned to her that tonight would be special, only that they were meeting for dinner. He wanted to truly surprise her with his proposal. He waved at her and stood to receive her.

"Hello Beautiful." His deep, baritone voice welcomed as he bent down to kiss her cheek and pull her chair out for her to sit.

"Seth, you always know just how to embarrass me," she replied with a quick smile, and a twinkle in her eye as a slight pink color flushed her cheeks.

"You know me. I call it as I see it."

Caroline smiled, her pulse quickening at Seth's slight, crooked grin that accentuated the dimple he had in his right cheek.

"Yes, you are brutally honest. It's just one of the many things that I love about you." She grinned, gazing into Seth's deep brown eyes from across the small, round table.

"Ah, but you do love me." He winked and grinned from ear to ear.

Caroline's smile and giggle made Seth's stomach do a flip flop. The approaching waiter overhearing the light-hearted banter smiled at them both and took Caroline's drink order. The waiter quickly returned with her lemonade and took their meal orders.

When their food arrived, they chatted about how their day went while they ate their meal. While dining, the restaurant began to fill with more patrons. Those either too tired to cook or too hung over to remember how. He was guessing the latter since most were stumbling around and getting rather loud and obnoxious. Seth decided to wait until after dinner and take Caroline for a stroll along the seawall. That would be the best place to propose. It just wasn't quite right to do it here in the restaurant with so many people watching them. It was a private matter between the two of them, and he wanted her all to himself when he asked her.

They soon departed the restaurant and climbed onto his bike for the short ride to the docks. Caroline loved riding his motorbike as much as he did. Seth loved the feel of her arms wrapped around his waist as she rested against his back. Seth enjoyed the ride, anticipation making him feel so alive, the night air made slightly cooler by the force of wind blowing around them. He truly enjoyed his bike, even if rain at times made it inconvenient. However, if things went the way he wanted, he would also have to look into buying a motorcar as well as a house. Seth parked his bike and took Caroline's hand as he led her down to the water's edge. The night air by the water was breezy and warm. The waves from the bay slapped rhythmically against the walls and boats docked there as the full moon shone brightly through the small, wispy, clouds that graced the night sky. It was the perfect night. There were a few other like-minded people out tonight, but they pretty much had the seawall to themselves.

The city had done a nice job over the last several years in turning the docks and seawall barrier into a place where its citizens could enjoy strolls by the water. Sparsely placed lamp posts illuminated some of the darker areas, while wooden and iron benches tucked beneath large oaks graced the outer edges of the wooden boardwalk.

Ok, here goes everything, he thought, as they walked arm in arm with Caroline resting her head on his bicep.

Seth took a lungful of the salty sea air and exhaled slowly, trying to steady his nerves.

"Caroline," he said a bit shakily, clearing his throat as they continued to walk.

"Yes?" she breathed, sighing contentedly, unaware of his nervousness.

"I've never really told you the real reason I moved here to San Francisco Bay."

She lifted her head to look at him as they continued to slowly walk along the wharf.

"It was because of you."

She stopped at that, and he nudged her to keep walking, placing his large hand atop her smaller one, keeping her hand neatly tucked under his arm. She already knew the story of his childhood and how he came to be a sea captain. Now he had to explain why he chose to stay here of all places.

"The day we stepped off the boat to furlough here for a week, my shipmates and I were walking into Shelley's Diner for lunch, and I just about ran you clean over. You were bending down to tie your shoelace on the sidewalk outside, and I didn't see you for ogling the cities sights and sounds. One of my mates grabbed me just in time." He smiled slightly, remembering the day as if it were yesterday. Caroline smiled at him in return.

"All I could do was stare at you. I had no words. You were the most beautiful thing I had ever seen. You stood up, brushed off your skirt, looked up at me with those soulful eyes, and smiled that bright, beautiful, smile of yours; then turned and walked up the street. I watched you go for a while to see if I could tell where you were going, and to my good fortune, you turned and walked into the library."

"Why haven't you ever told me this before?"

"Well, I didn't want to scare you off. I was afraid you'd think I was a stalker or some deranged psychopath." Seth chuckled.

Caroline smiled and giggled at his words as he continued.

"For the next few days as we toured the Bay area, all I could think about was you. So, I went to the library to see if I could find you and there you were, standing behind the counter. I asked a gentleman who worked there if you were married or attached and he told me no. That was all it took. I spent the rest of the week getting my affairs in order and explaining to the only father figure I had ever known that I was leaving the Schooner, the *Mattie May*, and staying in San Francisco."

The look on Caroline's face was one of quiet disbelief. She started to speak but Seth quickly stopped her, brushing his thumb against her lips as his hand rested against the soft skin of her cheek. They had stopped walking and were facing each other.

"Caroline Palmer, I have never loved anyone as much as I love you. Never in my life did I think I could feel this way. I waited for a few months to ask you out. Just watching and studying you. Not in a creepy way," -he smiled and winked at her- "but I wanted to know a little about you first. I know I messed up a time or two in the beginning there, and it killed me that I almost lost you. I can't stand to be without you in every part of my life any longer." As he pulled the box out of his pocket he slowly descended to one knee and gazed up at Caroline's shocked, tear-stained face.

"So, what do you say, Beautiful, will you marry me and make my life complete?"

"Oh...my...goodness...Seth. Yes, yes I'll marry you!" Caroline stammered through tears and smiles.

Seth leapt to his feet, grabbed Caroline, and spun her in circles, both of them giggling and laughing like school children. Seth kissed her with all that was in him, not wanting to let her go for fear it might all be a dream. They slowly released one another and decided to find a justice of the peace to get married that same night since neither he nor Caroline had any family to explain their decision to. They would explain to Barneses tomorrow morning. Mr. Barnes already knew Seth was asking Caroline to marry him. Seth had done things the right way and had asked her guardian Mr. Barnes for his permission first.

Seth awoke at 4:45 a.m., which was normal time for him to wake up for work. Even though he had taken time off this week in hopes that Caroline would say yes, his internal clock wouldn't let him sleep longer. Seth lay there staring down into the face of his beautiful wife. He couldn't believe he could feel this way about anyone. He also couldn't believe his good fortune. She said yes! He smiled to himself in the dark as he stroked a stray, wavy, lock of hair away from her sleeping face. He decided to acknowledge that maybe there was a God, and perhaps He had something to do with Seth's luck after all. Just in case, he offered up a quick thank you to the man upstairs.

Caroline, sensing him stirring, awoke and looked up into the face of her husband. She smiled a big goofy smile of contentment, kissed him full on the lips, and asked sleepily, "What time is it?"

Seth stretched and looked at the clock. "Almost 5:00 a.m. What do you say we get dressed, and head down to the diner for our first breakfast as Mr. and Mrs. Jager? We can share the good news with Charlie and the rest of the gang over there. Then we'll swing by your old place, get your things, and explain to the Barnes family."

"Sounds great, I'm starving!" Caroline stretched and jumped up to get dressed while Seth did the same. At 5:03 a.m., they left Seth's small garage apartment for the short ride to Shelley's Diner. Seth was happier than he had ever been in his life. He replayed the previous night's events over again in his head, all of them. He smiled to himself as Caroline climbed onto the back of his bike and wrapped her arms around him. The newlyweds sped off down the winding coastal road totally oblivious that in just a few moments, their lives would change forever.

On the morning of Wednesday, April 18th, at 5:12 a.m., just a few minutes away, the earth underneath San Francisco Bay would open.

Chapter 2

Seth steered his motorbike along the winding roads unable to contain the smile spread across his face, excited for his and Caroline's future together. The morning air was cool and tinged with the smell of the salty ocean breeze. Although it was still dark outside due to the early hour, Seth's future couldn't seem brighter. It was the perfect day to start his and Caroline's new life together as Mr. and Mrs. Seth Jager.

Just as he turned the bend in the road the earth began shaking violently. Seth, through the headlight of his bike, could see rocks and boulders falling and bouncing along the road all around them. Trees began sliding and disappearing down the slope of the hillside into the ocean as he swerved to try and avoid pieces of earth falling in their path. Seth could barely hear Caroline yelling in the background as the rumbling grew louder and the chaos escalated. Suddenly his bike was airborne, and he and Caroline had been torn apart by the force of the motion. He sensed himself falling, but it was too dark to see anything. Offering up a quick plea to God to protect them both, the last thing Seth heard was Caroline screaming his name as he screamed hers.

SETH!!

Seth flinched at the piercing scream, his body twitching restlessly, "Caroline?" he whispered.

"Shh... just lie back and rest my boy; you've been through quite a lot."

Seth could hear someone's muffled voice flitting through his subconscious, but he couldn't open his eyes. He didn't recognize whoever it was.

"Caroline...whe...where's...C...Caroli...?"

"Shush now, don't worry about that now young fella'. Just rest, you're going to need all the strength you can muster once you've fully awakened."

Seth still couldn't make out what the person was saying. It sounded as if he were underwater. He tried opening his eyes once more. All he could make out was a shadowy figure standing over him. Whoever it was, Seth was completely at his or her mercy. If there was a God in heaven, Seth prayed He would hear him. He offered up a quick prayer for Caroline first and then himself. May God have mercy on them both. Seth then drifted back into unconsciousness.

Simon Lane sighed. "This is going to be enough of a shock as it is without all the side effects. PS can really take its toll on a first timer. Poor lad, I don't know who this Caroline is, but I seriously doubt he'll be happy to learn that he'll likely never see her again. Come along Jason, let's let him sleep it off. No tellin' how long it'll take this one to wake. He's a pretty big fella'. Sometimes that's a bonus and sometimes not."

"Why do you think a new Peregrine would appear at the same place I exited? Has that ever happened before?" Jason asked.

"Not during my time. This is a first. I'll have to do some research in the Dragoman Archives and see if it says anything about it there. Maybe it's just a coincidence. Just don't mention it to him until I have time to research it, all right?"

"Sure thing, Simon. Now how about some dinner?" Jason smirked, slapping Simon on the shoulder. "I'm starving. This last trip was long and hard." Jason turned and looked at the sleeping giant, unconscious on the small bed. "I have a feeling when this guy wakes up, it's going to be an interesting explanation. Especially considering where he landed on his first time. I don't envy you your job on this one Simon."

"Yes. Neither do I," Simon concurred.

The two men left the room leaving their patient to rest. Simon was an old hand at this. A new Peregrine was never a surprise, and he had dealt with this sort of thing often. The part he hated the most came just after they came out of Peregrination Sickness and having to tell them that they would never see their loved ones again, and that their life would be forever changed.

SETH!!

Seth startled awake, hoarsely calling Caroline's name, with little to no sound at all escaping his lips. His mouth felt like it was full of cotton as he tried again, barely whispering Caroline's name; still no answer. Seth tried opening his eyes, not sure what was happening and unable to focus on where he was. He squinted against the dull light that penetrated...what? Where exactly was he? He sat up, trying to focus again, his eyes blurrily adjusting. Totally expecting to find himself buried under a heap of rocks and trees, he was thoroughly confused as his eyes began to focus on what appeared to be a room. He swung his legs over the edge of the small, twin-size bed that he was laying on, causing his head to spin and pound. He quickly shut his eyes again, deeply, and slowly controlling his breath, trying to relax, laying his head in his hands. His thinking was fuzzy due to the massive headache, and he assumed that he must be dreaming and just needed to wake up.

As he sat there quietly, he thought he heard someone speaking but couldn't make out what was being said. They weren't in the same room, but they were close. It sounded like the voice of a man. Maybe someone had found him and Caroline after the wreck. The wreck...did that really happen? Where was Caroline? Seth shook his head a bit, shrugged the ache from his shoulders, and rubbed his neck, tried standing. His knees shook as he squinted into the dim light filtering into the room through a small window, the sunlight dancing around a small curtain blowing in the breeze of the opening. He dared not look out the window for fear the sunlight may cause his head to pound even harder if that were possible. The light cast shadows on the sparse furnishings of the room. A small table and chair sat in one corner near the bed. A bowl of water, and a small towel draped over the side sat on top. The other side of the room had a small chest with three drawers. The empty walls were in sore need of paint or papering.

Seth slowly stepped forward to make sure his balance would support his weight. Finding that his legs were still good beneath him he slowly moved the rest of his body, assessing whether there seemed to be any type of injuries. The only thing that seemed to be wrong with him was this headache and some dizziness. He looked himself over and could not find even one scratch. How is that possible? The whole wreck must have been a dream, but that didn't explain where he is, or where Caroline was.

Looking for some answers, Seth strode across the tiny space to the small, closed, door. As he opened it and stepped through, the voice he had heard speaking suddenly stopped. Seth squinted into the light and scanned the room, his vision stopping on an elderly gentleman looking at him from around the corner of a wall.

"Well, you've come out of it then. You seem to be handling the headache relatively well. Any other aches or pains we need to know about then?" the man asked Seth as he slowly made his way over to where Seth stood.

Seth tried to speak but his voice, still a bit hoarse, just rasped out a partial, unrecognizable answer. He simply shook his head no, hoping this headache would soon pass and his voice would return. He stepped further into the room which looked like some kind of office. Papers were strewn over every available surface. Maps, and what appeared to be news clippings, were pinned to the walls. There were some navigational tools which Seth quickly recognized, and some other rather foreign-looking objects that he did not.

Seth turned to look at the man who began speaking again, taking in his appearance. He was about mid-fifties with short, slightly unkempt salt-and-pepper hair with a few unique white streaks, a short, trimmed beard and mustache connected to sideburns that ran to his hairline just in front of his ears. He wore round, silver, wire rimmed spectacles, was about six-feet-tall, and weighed about one hundred and eighty pounds give or take. His style of clothing was a bit odd. His Shirt was untucked, long sleeved with vertical stripes, which woere cuffed at the forearms. He wore a brown unbuttoned vest which appeared to be light-weight, and very short pants, military green in color that hit him just above the knee. It looked as though he wore a type of sandal on his feet.

"Ah, I see your voice is a bit off kilter still as well. No worries, that sometimes happens with your first time, the headache too. It'll return to normal soon enough. Here, have a glass of lemonade. That ought to fix you up."

He poured Seth a glass from a pitcher setting on a table in the center of the room and handed him the cool glass, still watching him closely as if studying him.

"My name is Simon. Simon Zedekia Lane to be precise," He gave a brief, tight-lipped, grin.

Now that Seth's head was clearing a bit, he recognized an Irish accent as Simon spoke. Being at sea almost ten years, traveling from port to port, you learned to pick up on these things. He could usually pick up even the slightest hint of an accent and tell where someone was from. He had even learned a bit of the language from several foreign countries. He wouldn't call himself fluent, but he could hold somewhat of a conversation. One had to learn fast as a seaman. You had better know what you were agreeing to when talking to the local water rats when on a furlough, or you may end up somewhere you never wanted to be.

Seth took a cautious sip of the lemonade, making sure that's what it was. That was another thing he had learned; you couldn't trust just anybody. The cool, tangy liquid worked wonders on his dry throat. He thirstily drank some more and decided to try speaking. His voice still cracked a little on the first attempt, so he cleared his throat and tried again.

"I'm Seth. Seth Jager," he managed to squeak out.

"Would that be Jager with a J, or Y?" asked Simon.

"Uhmm...a J." Seth, puzzled at the question, watched Simon move about the room as if looking for something.

"Look, where am I exactly, and have you seen my wife Caroline? We were separated during what I think may have been a landslide. Or maybe I'm still having a really strange dream?"

At the mention of a wife Simons movements about the room ceased. His back had been to Seth at the time, and he noticed the older man's shoulders slump forward just briefly before he straightened and turned to look at him.

"She isn't here I'm afraid. There's a few things I need to explain to you and I really believe you should sit down before we start. It can be overwhelming to say the least."

Still not in any condition for sudden movements or arguments, Seth did as Simon asked. The man seemed genuine enough, and Seth was obliged to cooperate, for now. Besides, he was desperate to find out anything about Caroline.

Simon pulled up a chair across from Seth and looked at him. His expression was troubled, and he seemed to be searching for words.

"Seth, I'm afraid your wife, for all reasons and explanation of how you're here, is most probably dead or badly injured."

Seth's breath caught in his throat. What was this man saying? Seth could only look at him with disbelief and doubt. Surely not; not his Caroline. How could he know that if he didn't even know who or where she was? He did say probably didn't he? Seth's head pounded harder from the stress of what Simon was saying.

"Look, I don't know who you are or where I am, but I've got to get out of here. Obviously, you found me and took care of me so...thank you. But I've got to find Caroline, especially if she could be injured as you said, and I can't do it sitting here."

Seth's nerves were shot, his head pounding even harder as blood rushed to his head from his racing heart. His stumbled as he quickly stood, taking long strides across the room toward a door. Seth grabbed the knob swinging the door open and stepped outside into the bright sunlight, stopping abruptly. Was what he was seeing real? Where in the world was he? Or was he still *in* the world? More importantly, how did he get here and when? Seth turned around to look at Simon, a look of complete confusion crossing Seth's features.

"Where *am* I?" Seth shockingly asked, half-turning to take in the view behind him once more. He must be going mad! That could be the only explanation.

Simon answered, unmoving. "I told you my boy, there is a lot to explain. Would you care to rejoin me here inside for a thorough, yet somewhat lengthy, explanation?"

In Him *we were also chosen,* having been
predestined according to the plan
of Him *who works out everything in*
conformity with the purpose of His will.

Ephesians 1:11

Chapter 3

Sumatra, Indonesia, Barisan Mountain chain,
Mount Kerinci-April 29th, 1936

Alec Chevalier, Peregrine and Frenchman, crouched behind
the large urn just outside the temple doors. It was still early
enough for the darkness to give him enough cover to not be
easily seen, but the native warriors were keen hunters, and
he took great care to not draw attention to himself. He only
hoped Odessa would do the same. Odessa Megalos was a
fierce warrior herself, trained by a whole temple of Japanese
Samurai Warriors for the majority of her early Peregrine
years. But he still didn't like the position they were in. Two
against a village were pretty steep odds. Even if he never
missed a shot, he wasn't sure he would have enough bullets
to get them out safely. Besides, a massive slaughter of the
natives was not what they had in mind. All he and Odessa
needed to do was get inside the temple, retrieve the scroll,
and get up the mountain in time. They only had a few hours
remaining before the portal would close, and they would be
stuck here for who knows how long.

Alec looked back over his shoulder to see Odessa
scaling the sides of the temple wall up to a small window
just a few feet below the roofline. Fortunately, this

particular temple was smallish in size. Only about ten-feet-high and surrounded by jungle on three sides giving them plenty of cover. These people had few relics and artifacts to preserve and protect, so little space was needed. Most things were lost to volcanic eruptions and lava streams. Few things were of great importance as these people often ran for their lives during such times as severe eruptions. But they had one particular item that was of great value to the Dragoman. The very reason he and Odessa were here. He watched as she slipped through the window inside the temple, listening for any disturbances inside or outside as he made his way to the window, grasping the rope Odessa had thrown down for him.

As Alec pulled himself through the small opening, he could make out shapes in the room, illuminated by the moonlight streaming into the other windows that encircled the top of the wall. There wasn't much here. A few large statues guarded the doors, a few smaller ones sat atop a ritual table, some decorative urns depicting the history of the people here sat near the doors. About a dozen unlit torches stuck out about five foot up the wall, sitting in holes in both longer sides of the building. A tribal chieftain's chair and a medium sized chest sat against the back wall, the chest undoubtedly housing the very item they needed. Odessa carefully, and quietly, slinked her way back toward the chest as Alec slowly lowered himself to the ground. He followed her path to the back of the room, and they looked at each other with cautious anticipation as she slowly lifted the lid of the unlocked box. He took out the small flashlight he carried with him in his pack to illuminate the contents of the chest. There were smaller artifacts, a few pieces of jewelry, tribal robes, a headpiece worn by the chief during ceremonies, and a tribal staff. In the bottom of the chest, underneath it all, were five scrolled parchments. Taking them in hand they began quickly but carefully unrolling them to find the one they needed.

"Ah, here it is," Odessa breathed, handing it to Alec to tuck away.

"All-right, let's get out of here before our luck runs out," he whispered in his French accent, rolling up the scroll to tuck it away as he gestured to the window in which they came.

"You know it isn't luck Alec," she admonished quietly with a shake of her head, standing defiantly with her hands on her hips as the traces of a small grin split her lips.

"Yes, yes, I know. Can we go please? We can discuss this later." He made his way to the window and the hooked rope he had switched around upon entering the same way earlier.

Alec climbed the rope to the window, squeezed through, and as quietly as possible dropped to the ground outside. Odessa behind him, unhooked the rope as to leave no traces that anyone had been there and dropped it to Alec. She dropped to the ground without a sound, and off they went, into the dark jungle and up into the Barisan Mountains with just over an hour and a half to spare to make it to the peak of Kerinci.

Alec and Odessa, being as quiet as possible while still near the village, moved as quickly as they could through the dense jungle floor, keeping an eye out for wild animals as well as natives. Both of which were equally treacherous. As they moved further from the village the sun began to peak over the mountain ridge and illuminate the jungle with pale green light, reflecting off the surface of the lush green canopy that loomed far above their heads. Alec removed the scroll from his pack as he and Odessa glanced at the contents more closely.

"How do you know this is the right scroll? I can't make heads or tails of what it says." He spun the article around looking at it in confusion.

"Simon told me what to look for. He gave me the symbols used for *Scroll of Rubric.* Besides, I also listen for urgings from God. He speaks to me when he needs to. This is after all His missions that we go on for the sake of all mankind. You would understand more if you were a true child of His." Odessa continued walking ahead without looking at Alec or continuing the conversation. They did not have time to get into a heated discussion again about his lack of belief. Even though his Peregrine status was only possible through the grace of God, Alec Chevalier was as hard-headed as they came.

As Alec glanced at the parchment in his hands, he looked up to see a native warrior of the tribe they just 'borrowed' the scroll from returning to the village from a hunt, a boar draped across his shoulders. The man looked at the scroll in Alec's hands and began yelling in his native tongue. Odessa pulled her Katana from its sheath and stood staring at the man, wordlessly warning him to keep his distance. Keeping his hands on the boar, food being a great necessity to his people, he took off running toward his village. Alec and Odessa looked at each other, returned the scroll and katana to their places, and began running as fast as possible up the mountainside. They knew the man would return with many more warriors. They only had maybe another forty-five minutes or so to reach the top before the portal closed. Walking, they would have made it in time. Running, they would get there too soon and would need to lead the natives on a wild goose chase or find a place near the top to hide until jump time. By the time the hunter returned to the village and gathered warriors for the return, they should have a good hour head start and may not run into much trouble. Not willing to chance it, they paced themselves for the next twenty-five to thirty-minute trek through the jungle. Hopefully, the noise they were making would scare off any wild animals that were in the area.

As they breathlessly reached the mountain's peak, they stopped briefly to catch their breath and determine where the best place for portal entry would be. As they stood breathing in great lungfuls of oxygen rich air, though thin from the elevation, they surveyed the area.

"There, on the west side of the mountain peak," Alec said, pointing to an area clear of vegetation. "We need to make our way around to there."

As they began to move, the oversaturated black clouds floating above them opened up and rain began to pelt them. Visibility was affected some with the downpour, making their movements a bit slower than they would like. It had taken them longer to make their way up the mountain side than they had expected. So running into the hunter had been a fortunate event after all. It had made them travel quicker, aiding them to the top in time for jumping. Just as the rain began letting up some, Alec heard the shouts and tribal calls of the native men chasing after them.

Alec raced along the mountain ridge glancing back over his shoulder ever so often to make sure Odessa was still behind him.

"Hurry Dee, the natives are closing in on us. They are very fast if I do say so myself!"

"You just mind yourself, Alec, I can take care of myself!" She also raced the ridge slightly behind him, glancing over her shoulder as the yelling seemed to increase.

Alec laughed out loud at Odessa's remark, fully expecting her to reply in such a manner, being careful not to slip on the muddy spots left by the hard, tropical, rain that had started fifteen minutes earlier.

The screams and yells of Native warriors could be heard closing the distance between them. Alec, starting to get nervous, suddenly felt the earth beginning to shake beneath his feet. The natives, having great respect for Mount Kerinci due to constant volcanic activity, would not follow them any higher into the mountains center, especially now that they too had felt the quake; the mountain being known for near constant ash and unpredictable eruptions. Unpredictable by man's standards in this period of time anyway. Alec could hear their fearful shouts growing weaker as they had surely turned in terror and headed back down the mountain. Sighing in relief from not having to dodge arrows and flying spears, Alec smiled and slowed his speed. If it weren't for the Dragoman and their unique abilities, they would be waiting around for portals to open instead of seeking them out.

As the two reached the edge of the volcano's opening, Alec noticed a mudslide directly in front of them. It would give them a greater chance of making it to the portal in time. *Fortune had smiled on them once again,* Alec thought with a smile. He gave a whoop and yelled to Odessa over the noise of the rumbling earth.

"Hurry Dee, we haven't much time left!"

He pointed to an area just fifteen feet ahead of them. Reaching the muddy, earthen slide that would take them deep into the volcano, he jumped feet first into the mud as it abruptly washed him down into the volcano's center. Odessa, eyeing the muddy, earthen, slide, rolled her eyes and groaned, following him. As the two of them were whisked along down into the heart of the volcano, magnetic energy electrified the air around them, creating a bright flash of light which Alec and Odessa disappeared into as Mount Kerinci erupted, shaking the earth with explosive power as volcanic ash spewed from the center into the sky above it.

Chapter 4

First Dimension, Garganthera borderlands

Alec and Odessa stepped out of the Portal into the rain and lightning of the massive thunderstorm taking place on the mountainous borderlands of Garganthera. Making their way through the storm they sought some shelter to wait it out, abruptly finding a cave and ducking inside, making a quick scan of their environment. They had to always be alert in the first dimension where demons took on human form and were skillful at hiding.

It wasn't long before the storm ended, and they could resume their journey. Feeling safe enough to keep moving, Alec and Odessa quietly walked outside the cave into the filtered light of the forest around them, not speaking until they could see well enough what lay around them. It only took a few minutes for them to find access to a gateway to the fourth-dimension plane where Simon's place sat.

Demons could also roam here if they happened upon a gateway, which was unlikely but possible. They were also easily spotted in the fourth dimension being characteristically noisy when on the hunt, and plus, their true forms were revealed once they crossed Barrier's Edge. Not only that, but Peregrines and Dragoman were the only people who ever walked the fourth dimension. No one else could cross or even see the barrier.

Keeping a cautious eye and a trained ear alert, Alec spoke as they traipsed along the damp forest path on the journey to Simon's home.

"Let's get this scroll to Simon, shall we, and get a nice hot meal and shower."

"I don't know about you, but I need to find a stream or river to wash some of this mud off me now. It's starting to harden and is driving me crazy." Odessa's lips curled unpleasantly as she brushed and plucked hardening mud from her skin and hair.

"We will be at Simon's in about an hour if you want to wait and shower there?"

"Uhh...no. I'm not waiting an hour. Besides, I'll still need to shower when we get there. No soap here, you know," she smirked.

"All right, there should be a creek or stream just around the bend up here. Besides, we need to eat something anyway. We haven't eaten since yesterday and we still have an hour's journey. I could do with a little break and rest myself after the last hours jog across the Sumatran mountainside." Alec stretched his long, slender, yet muscular arms, and arched his back against the sky.

Alec and Odessa hiked another fifteen minutes through the woods until they came upon a small creek bed just big enough to wade into hip deep. They removed their leather belts, shoes, and weapons. Removing the bulkiest parts of their clothing without fully undressing, they stowed their gear under a bush beside the water's edge as they carefully took in their environment. They were always on alert no matter where they were or what they were doing. They could never be too careful. Awareness of their surroundings, especially when their weapons were removed, had saved their lives more times than once. There were precious few places in their travels where they could completely let down their guard for a few hours and they weren't there yet. Simon's place on the rim of the fourth dimension at Barrier's Edge of Garganthera was just such a place. The security measures that he had taken and the hidden rooms he had created were genius. No one could find his place unless they knew what they were looking for. Only a few of the most trusted Peregrines who knew Simon knew of his place. He was one of the best Readers that had ever lived.

As Odessa soaked a bit longer, Alec made a small fire and prepped some of the dry soup packs with some distilled creek water. He also pulled out some jerky they had lifted off the villagers in Sumatra. He assumed it was boar but wasn't really sure what he was eating. Sometimes during peregrination, you had to do what you could to survive. Other times, things were just there or provided with no explanation as to why or how. Odessa, of course, could always give a convincing explanation or answer. He just didn't quite buy into all the hype about God. He believed enough he supposed, he was traversing the world through miraculous ways and circumstances trying to help save the future of mankind. But he still wasn't clear what they were fighting against. He knew there was something bigger to come in the future, but he didn't know what. Besides the demons they currently battled at times, those seen and unseen, he really didn't get it much past that. Odessa had tried to explain it, but they always ended up butting heads and arguing so they both tried to avoid the subject as much as possible.

Alec watched Odessa washing her dark skin in the stream's clear waters. She was a beautiful woman, extremely powerful as well. She could hold her own against most men. In her born time period -before her peregrination- a woman was a slave to her husband, or any man really. Ancient Greece was a time ruled strictly by men, and women had no rights at all, not even in deciding who they married. They were not even inheritors of their deceased husband's property. Women were viewed as only good for certain tasks and nothing more, especially a woman of mixed race, like Odessa.

Peregrination suited Odessa just fine. She was happy to be free to live and think for herself, even if her God seemed to control her every move. To her that was different. She was called by her Creator to a greater good. To Dee, being called by God in such a manner was a great honor. One she would die for.

After they dried off a bit by the fire and had eaten enough to give them energy and quiet their growling stomachs, they packed on their gear and weapons and set out for Simon's place, hoping to reach it by noon. Even though they time jump from place to place and era to era, the time of day from leaving to arriving always seemed to stay the same. Perhaps it was a provision from God himself so as not to throw off their internal clocks too much.

As they made their way through the forest, they traveled in silence, each lost in their own thoughts. Fortunately, this small trip from arrival point to destination point was uneventful so far. Hopefully, it would stay that way for the next fifteen minutes that it took them to get to Simon's. They were tired and hungry for real food and needed sleep. Neither Alec nor Odessa had slept in the last thirty-six hours, their mission for the scroll pressing down on them.

Alec patted the spot on his satchel where the small piece of parchment lay inside. Simon had said it was of utmost importance and they could not fail this mission. This was the only item to contain certain information imperative to the future. The amount of information the

Readers knew, or as some liked to call them Dragoman, often amazed Alec. Their minds could hold vast amounts of knowledge. Not just book knowledge either. One Reader he had met in Ireland by the name of Ryan Halloran was a technology whiz. He was young and knew way more than Alec could ever fathom, and Alec was not an uneducated man. Of course, Ryan lived in the year 2015 where technological advances were unbelievable from what Alec had seen.

Alec's father, being wealthy aristocracy -family money from the early fifteenth century through the early nineteenth century- had made sure that Alec received the best education money could buy. That was how he had become such an excellent marksman with both gun and bow. His father had also been an excellent marksman as well. They used to travel in certain circles to competitions across the country. His father had never lost a competition and had expected the same dedication and expertise from Alec. Alec had a decent relationship with his father and mother. He had not seen them since his original Peregrination in 1866. Now time had no bearing for him. He knew that in some timeline somewhere, his parents were alive, and others, long gone, or not even born yet. He held no hope of ever seeing them again.

He was content with his life now though, especially since he and Odessa had become paired together for peregrinations. He glanced over at her, watching her briefly as she too was lost in her own thoughts. He had never told her, but he was in love with her. He didn't want that to become a distraction to either of them. They had missions and bigger problems to deal with. Now was not the time for such a confession. He was happy just to be near her daily.

"Alec…"

Alec shook himself out of his thoughts and looked at Odessa.

"We're here." Odessa grinned slightly. "Deep in thought eh?"

Alec looked up to find himself standing just outside Simon's place. *So much for no distractions* he thought. He hadn't even realized they'd arrived.

"Great, let's get this scroll to Simon and enjoy a little break." He smiled at Odessa as they rounded the corner of the house toward the front door. They both suddenly stopped and looked at the giant of a man standing in front of Simon's door staring out at Barrier's Edge. They must have startled the man because he jumped and staggered back against the house, holding his head in his hands.

"You all right man?" Alec said as he stepped forward to try and help the stranger right himself.

Seth held up a hand to stop the man from approaching while holding his head with the other. He didn't know how many more surprises he could take today and really wanted some answers.

"Ah, just in time I see." Simon's voice interrupted the silent exchange between the two men. "I was just going to explain a few things to our new friend here."

Seth stood, found his legs again, and they all stepped inside the house. Simon pointed Seth toward a chair and told him to have a seat. Seth willingly obliged since his head didn't want to relent.

"Alec Chevalier, Odessa Megalos, meet Seth Jager." Simon offered the introduction, knowing everyone else was too surprised or shaken for good manners at the moment. Seth stood to shake the hands of the two people he had just encountered outside.

"Are you a new Peregrine?" Odessa asked Seth.

"A new...what?" Seth asked confused as he sat back down, both he and Odessa looking at Simon for answers.

"I haven't gotten around to any kind of explanation just yet, so he has no idea what you're talking about." Simon looked at Odessa, eyebrows raised.

She gave him a knowing look. "Oh. okay then." She turned, placing her satchel on the hook by the door as Alec did the same.

"Simon, do Alec and I really need to hang around for this? We're really exhausted, hungry, and dirty."

"No, I suppose not. I can handle the majority of it, and if, well, *when* he has questions, you two can answer those later." Simon grinned. "You two go get cleaned up. Lunch is ready in the kitchen. I made a large pot of stew. Jason is here somewhere as well. He's the one who found Seth here. They both came through the same portal," Simon said, watching their reaction.

Both Alec and Odessa stopped and looked back and forth between Seth and Simon, curiosity etching their features.

Seth looked at Simon, but not before he noticed the odd reaction of the other two strangers who had just entered this new world of his. He made a mental note and filed it away in his memory for later questioning. He did not know that someone else had found him. He had thought that Simon was the only one here.

"Oh yes, what about the mission? Did you acquire the scroll?" Simon asked, glancing back and forth between Odessa and Alec.

"Oh! Yeah...yes!" Alec answered. "The scroll is in my satchel." He crossed the room again to dig in one of the bags hanging on the hook by the door. Pulling out a small parchment and handing it to Simon, the two newcomers retreated from the room. Seth watched them as they looked back at him once more, then at each other, then they disappeared through another of the room's doors.

Simon turned to Seth once again, ready to tell him all he could about what had happened to him.

"Well, my boy, I have quite a lot to fill you in on. Would you care for something a little stiffer to drink than lemonade before I regale you of impossible tales and quite possibly, painful possibilities?" Simon asked with a somewhat sympathetic expression on his face.

"No, no thanks." Seth carefully watched his host, still nursing a headache. "I just want to know what all this is about, and the sooner the better."

He reveals deep and hidden things: He knows
what lies in darkness, and light dwells with Him.

Daniel 2:22

Chapter 5

Simon's Safe House

Simon looked at the man sitting across from him and began.

"What I am going to tell you will, no doubt, be hard to comprehend, let alone believe. But you've already seen Barrier's Edge for yourself and what lies beyond, so the rest shouldn't be too unbelievable. First off, the place where you now sit, my home, lies in a fourth-dimension plane. The opaque, bluish, electrical-looking shield that you see just at the edge of the yard is what we call Barrier's Edge. It runs from the ground all the way to the heavens and borders every known and even some unknown civilizations. Those of us here in the fourth dimension can see everything on the other side, which is in the first or other dimension, but no one there knows this dimension exists. We can all travel through the barrier at certain points, doing so carefully as to not attract attention to ourselves. We must travel into lands in other dimensions to locate certain artifacts that are required to complete our main mission, which is to save the future of mankind. You time traveled here via a storm or natural catastrophe that occurred during your time-period which was the year 1906. Just the fact that you're here and did not perish in the earthquake means that God has chosen you for a greater purpose. You are one of the chosen to peregrinate the universe and help the others to save humankind."

Seth listened as intently as possible until Simon mentioned an earthquake and God.

"Wait just a minute here. You're telling me that I was in an earthquake and survived because God chose me for some...what, Quest? What about Caroline? Where does that leave her?"

"Seth, I've never seen God choose more than one Peregrine from the same time period. And with the extent of damage that the San Francisco earthquake of 1906 caused, I just can't say for sure what happened to Caroline. I'm sorry, my boy, but I fear the worst."

Seth abruptly stood, almost falling over from the spinning in his head either from the intense headache or from what Simon was saying. He paced the room, wobbling from side to side, his equilibrium still off as he spoke.

"Am I to believe that a God that I'm not even sure I believe in chose me over Caroline, a woman who most certainly believes, to be some sort of soldier to do his bidding? Well, isn't that just about how my life goes! Here I was, offering up little prayers and thanks to God for Caroline accepting my proposal. We had just started our lives together, and now God has decided to snatch the only thing that has *ever* made me happy away from me! Just like that?" Seth fumed, anger and disbelief fueling his temper as he paced the room, head still throbbing, the pain increasing again from his rising blood pressure due to the information Simon was feeding him.

"I know it's a lot to take in. I don't know why God chooses whom He does. There are several other unbelievers who are being used of God the same way. You may not believe in Him, but apparently, He believes in you. God can use anything to work for His good. Evil deeds, believers as well as unbelievers, pain, suffering, and yes, storms. He uses all things for the good of His works. You may not understand it now Seth, but in time you will."

Seth stopped pacing and stared at Simon for a moment, trying to take it all in.

"What if I choose not to do what God wants me to do? What then? Can I return to my time-period as you call it? Can Caroline and I choose to just live out our lives as we see fit?"

"I'm afraid not Seth. Your path has been determined for you before you were conceived. God created you for just such a purpose as this. I know this is going to sound cliché, and maybe even a bit harsh, but be grateful for the time that you had with Caroline. Hopefully if you have any other family, they are all well and safe, but there is no way of knowing."

Seth fell back into the chair he had been sitting in before and, running his hands through his hair and down across his face, looked at Simon and said, defeated, "I have no other family. Caroline is everything in the world to me and she was only mine for a full…seven hours maybe. We'd only been married for seven hours before the quake." Seth looked at Simon, pain evident upon his features. He leaned forward and placed his head in his hands with nothing more to say. He didn't want to know anymore right now. He needed some time to mull over everything that Simon had just told him, especially the news about him and Caroline. Seth couldn't, no, he wouldn't believe that she was dead. He had to keep hoping that she had survived the earthquake. Maybe she had been thrown to safety. If God chose him to do His bidding, then maybe He had listened to Seth when he had asked for God to take care of Caroline.

He did remember that much, the feeble offerings of a desperate man falling into oblivion.

"I'll give you some time to process what I've told you, and to grieve your loss. I truly am sorry Seth, but you're not alone in this. There are many others who have been through similar trials. Three of them are here in other rooms of the house. When you're ready to talk, come find one of us. I'll be in the kitchen tending to supper."

Simon patted Seth on the shoulder as he left the room. Seth didn't move or speak for what felt like an eternity. He just sat in the chair, head in his hands, elbows resting on his knees to support the heaviness of his head and his heart. Tears stung his eyes as they rolled down his cheeks. Seth sobbed like he never had before. He had always taken loss fairly well, trained at an early age, but this was his Caroline. His sweet, beautiful, caring, faithful-to-her-God, Caroline. He couldn't bear the thought of her lying hurt somewhere and he was unable to help her. Worse still, he would never see her again, even if she were all right or survived. No! He had to believe she had made it. That thought alone would keep him sane. Seth determined in his heart that no matter what Simon or anyone else said, he would try to find a way back to Caroline. No matter where or when God sent him, Seth would never stop looking. If he time jumped here, wherever here was, then certainly he could time jump back to where he had started, if for nothing else but to know what happened to her. Seth wiped the tears from his eyes and cheeks, took a few deep steadying breaths to gather his composure, and decided to make a plan. He sat thinking about what he could do to rectify his situation. After several minutes of deep thought, he rose to his feet in search of Simon, determination now driving the very heart of him.

"All right God, you want me, you got me!" Seth said through gritted teeth. Angry at a God that, he had to admit, apparently does exist, at least according to what Simon told him about being chosen. Seth would do his part, whatever it was, if it meant possibly finding a way back to Caroline.

Not knowing which door Simon had taken when he left the room, Seth just chose one. He knew the bedroom where he exited earlier and the outside exit. There were only two others, so he chose the one he had seen Alec and Odessa leave through before.

The door opened up onto a rather large hallway. The other rooms he had been in before were rather standard in size. Nothing in either room would have made him think that the rest of the home would look like this. This hallway seemed to open up into tall ceilings about fifteen feet high, with archways made of stone on either side, just shy of the roof line. The right side of the hall opened into a larger room with doors on the far side. The floors were covered with large planks of wood sealed to give a matte finish. The room was furnished with large settees and chairs, a few tables, large, round, decorative, area rugs, and a large stone and iron fireplace that stood in the center against what he assumed was a back, outside, wall. There were animals mounted on the walls, large suits of armor standing against the room's four corners, and a very eclectic collection of different items from places all over the globe; some of which he recognized and placed from his years traveling the seas. There were also large bookcases brimming with leather bound books against several walls running from floor to ceiling, small ladders with rail systems attached to a shelf on the front of each to reach the books at the top. Seth kept walking slowly taking in his environment. It almost reminded him of the inside of a castle he had had the opportunity of visiting when making port working aboard the *Mattie May* years ago when they'd had cargo from Japan to deliver to some wealthy Lord in Scotland. It had been a long jaunt across the sea, but the pay had been worth the journey. When arriving at the Seaport in Glasgow Scotland, one of the man's servants had been waiting for them to unload. The wealthy lord sent word that he wanted the crew of the *Mattie May* to carry the precious cargo to the castle themselves. Perhaps he had been an untrusting sort of fellow and wanted as few hands touching his merchandise as possible. Captain Matt complied with the man's wishes and some of the crew took the cargo up. Seth being the captains favorite, of course got to tag along. He hadn't been but maybe sixteen at the time, but he remembered the inside quite well, what he got to see of it anyway. The walls and floors of the castle much like these, had been made of weathered stones probably laid centuries before by indentured servants or poor commonwealth folks.

As Seth walked the hallway, he listened for sounds coming from anywhere. He knew there were at least four other people around here somewhere. Just as he passed an open archway on the left side of the hall, he spotted the man named Alec. Seth stepped inside what was obviously a kitchen as Alec looked up from where he was sitting and nodded a hello, his mouth full of his latest bite of food. Alec motioned him over to the large wooden table and patted a spot beside where he sat, gesturing for Seth to sit while he chewed and swallowed to be able to speak.

"I see you've found your way around a bit," Alec said with a grin. "Are you hungry, man? When was the last time you ate anything?"

"Actually, I am a bit hungry. To be honest I have no idea when I last ate. As far as I remember it would have been last night about eight p.m. To be truthful, I have no idea what time it is now. I'm looking for Simon, I still have a lot of questions, and he said he would be here in the kitchen."

"Well, let's fix you up with some of Simon's venison stew, and maybe I can answer some of your questions for you until Simon turns up." Alec stood to serve Seth some lunch, saying, "Simon was here, but said he needed some provisions for dinner and headed out. He shouldn't be gone too long. As far as what time it is, it's just after noon. Time really isn't something we pay too much attention to anymore," he said, scooping stew into a bowl for Seth.

Alec returned to the table with a bowl in hand and placed it in front of Seth, along with a glass. As Alec sat back down, he took a pitcher from the table's center and poured Seth some water. Seth nodded, and offering Alec his thanks, took a large piece off the loaf of bread Alec offered him. The two men ate in silence as Seth, finally realizing how famished he was, ate quickly, breaking off pieces of bread to sop up all the gravy remaining in his bowl. As they finished up their meal, they pushed their bowls away from them and resumed their conversation from earlier.

"So, if I have this right, I'm called a Peregrine?" Seth said to Alec, who shook his head in confirmation. "Doesn't peregrination mean 'to travel'?"

"Yes, my new friend, it does. Specifically, to travel over or through something," Alec explained in his heavy French accent. "See, we travel by way of storms. Through the storm, you see? And we travel over vast periods of time. In old Latin text, Peregrinatio means, to travel for love of God, hence the name! Your first time was unexpected, and you had no control over it. But now, we will train you to know how to find approaching storms for traveling. And you will receive missions from Simon."

Seth looked quizzically at Alec, "So...what, you just walk into any kind of storm?"

"Sort of. The storm has to be a particular strength, um...you know, generate enough energy to create a portal."

"Hey fellas', what are y'all discussing?" Odessa asked, entering the kitchen.

Seth turned to see a freshly bathed Odessa enter the room and head straight for the stove.

"Just telling our new friend here about peregrinating," Alec replied.

"I am starving!" Odessa groaned, leaning over to take a big sniff of the simmering pot on the stove. "Mmm...this smells amazing," She scooped several ladles full into a bowl and headed over to the table to join them. "This is the first real home cooked meal we've had in almost a week."

Seth watched her sit and reach for the bread. Alec had gotten up and returned with a glass for her. Seth watched the exchange between the two as Odessa looked up at Alec and kissed the air toward him. "Thank you darlin'," she said exaggeratedly, smiling at him.

Alec air kissed her back, grinning. "You are very welcome my friend."

Seth wasn't sure what their relationship was, but he was about to find out.

"So, are you two a couple then?"

"No, no, no, my new friend," Alec answered shaking his head and hands back and forth in reply. "Dee and I are traveling partners. We have faced many dangers, trials, and temptations together over the last...what?" He looked to Odessa for confirmation. "Nine years now?"

She agreed, shaking her head as she took another bite of food as Alec continued.

"We have a very special kinship. I would die for her, and she for me. But our lifestyle leaves no room for such pleasures as loving relations. We can't afford the distractions," he said, returning to his seat at the table.

"What do you mean by dangers and dying for each other? What other than traveling by storms is so dangerous about this mission stuff that God has called us all to?" Seth watched Alec's face for any signs of untruth.

"We have many enemies Seth. There are dangers from just finding what we search for. Illness, climate, the local natives that may not be too friendly, but the worst enemy we face is the demons that roam the earth. They can easily hide in the first dimension, but here in the fourth they are very visible. They do not travel beyond Barrier's Edge on this side too often for that very reason, but a few rather stupid or brave ones chance a crossing on occasion. We must always be alert no matter where we are. But here-" Alec emphasized his words by raising his arms and gesturing to all that was around him. "-here we are safe and can relax, rest, bathe, eat, visit, refuel, resupply our weapons, catch up with old friends, and make new ones." He grinned, gesturing at Seth. "There are very few Dragoman that exist with the kind of power and resources that Simon has. His home is safe and secure. We come here, and he tells us where we are to go, and who or what we are to find next. It is like our very own spy headquarters, no?" he said, looking at Odessa.

"Oui," Odessa replied, grinning at Alec. She turned to Seth to give her point of view on the subject.

"Our job is to follow God's leading Seth. Our Creator has called us to save man from himself. I come from a time when men were very evil, but storms were few. With time jumping, I have seen many wonders. Things I never thought possible. But I have also witnessed man's greed and hatred for one another. It has blinded them to their own ruination. As men become more evil storms become more frequent and more powerful, for whatever reason. Right now, we travel to find items or people for the Dragoman. But I know there is something greater coming. I'm just unsure what it is."

"So, what you're saying," Seth pondered, "is that God is guiding us to things and people who can possibly fix or stop the ruin of man? And, during this search we also have to fight demons and whatever else just to stay alive to do this work?" He watched as they both shook their heads yes. "And the two of you are all right with this?"

"Yeah, yes absolutely!" they both answered emphatically, smiling at the incredulous look on Seth's face.

"And we are not the only ones. There are more like us," Odessa finished.

"Well then, when does training start?" Seth asked, a half-smile crinkling the dimple in his cheek. Although his smile was ingenuine and his words laced with a bit of sarcasm, they didn't seem to notice.

"In the morning my emphatic friend," Alec replied. "Tonight, we rest, visit, eat, and just live. Surely you will meet Jason later. He probably went with Simon to market in Garganthera. The third-dimension city you observed through the barrier," Alec stated, noting the questioning look crossing Seth's features at the mentioned name.

The trio left the kitchen, and Alec and Odessa gave Seth a quick tour of Simon's home, showing him the restroom, and a bedroom he could use while there. It wasn't the same room as before.

This one is much nicer and suited to royalty, Seth thought. He stretched out upon the large king-sized bed with its post legs reaching almost to the ceiling where it tied into a roof-like structure that covered the whole bed. As he lay there, he thought about everything he had learned so far. He wasn't sure he truly understood this whole world and concept of following God's leading to travel the world through storms and battle demons. His headache seemed to be returning from trying to make sense of it all and he was growing tired. The events of the last twenty-four hours, if that is how long it had been, were taking their toll on both his mind and body. He drifted off to sleep vowing to Caroline that he would find her, remembering the last few precious hours they had spent together as husband and wife. Those memories would have to hold him through until he could be with Caroline again.

For I know the plans that I have for you
declares the Lord, plans for welfare and
not for calamity, to give you a future and a hope.

Jeremiah 29:11

Chapter 6

SETH!

"Caroline!" Seth awoke startled, yelling her name. He was sweating profusely, and his body was shaking from the dream, the earthquake running through his memory and all the possibilities the unknown held for him. He sat up looking at his surroundings and suddenly remembered where he was. *Well,* he thought, *it wasn't a dream. This was really happening.* What in the world God wanted with him; he didn't know. He scooted to the edge of the bed and crossed the room to the door. Seth walked out into the large living area to find Alec and Odessa sitting and chatting with another man whom he hadn't met yet. He assumed he was the one called Jason. As he exited his room, they all looked at him.

"Seth, my friend, you must have fallen asleep. It is almost dinner time. Come, meet Jason Marshal. Jason this is Seth Jager." Alec looked back and forth between the two men.

"Hey," Seth said, shaking Jason's hand. "I understand you were the one to find me. Thank you for taking care of me." Seth stood looking down at the man in front of him. Jason appeared to be about six-feet-tall, stocky build, sand-colored hair with green eyes.

"No problem. Nothing anyone of us wouldn't have done," Jason replied with a small grin.

"How did you know I was even alive?"

"Well, dead people don't peregrinate. Only live ones," Jason said, watching Seth's reaction. "Besides, before my first peregrination I was somewhat of a doctor."

"I see." Seth seemed to ponder his remarks. "What kind of doctor?"

"A veterinarian," Jason answered as he returned to his seat. "I had a large animal practice in Montana. I spent the first four years after high school in the marines to help pay for Veterinary school. I had my practice for a few years before Montana was hit by a Tornado and I woke up here. Just like you."

Seth suddenly remembered what Simon had said earlier about others with similar stories to tell.

Simon appeared just under the archway to the room and announced that supper would be ready in about twenty minutes. Feeling the need for a bath, Seth inquired of his newly found friends where he might be able to clean up. Jason volunteered to show him where to find a change of clothing that would fit him, explaining that Simon had purchased some appropriate attire for him in Garganthera earlier when they went to market. Seth mentioned the tour given him earlier, so Jason just had to explain to Seth how the shower worked since Seth had never seen anything other than a tub, and then left him to it.

Seth, feeling refreshed after thoroughly enjoying the new invention called a shower, reappeared in the kitchen where everyone else was either helping prepare the food or setting the table for dinner. As he watched these people interact, he marveled at them having only known one another since this whole peregrination thing. He would have never guessed that at one time they had all been strangers.

The camaraderie they all shared was obvious. They seemed like they were genuinely joyful people. One would think the scene before him to be one of a normal family gathering around the dinner table. The closest thing he remembered to a scene like this was with his grandmother when it had been just the two of them.

"Can I do anything to help?" Seth's booming deep voice broke through the room.

"Seth, lad! No, no; nothing left to do. Have a seat at the table wherever you like. We are about to have some supper." Simon smiled as he peered at Seth over the top of his glasses.

Seth walked around the table to one of the large chairs. Feeling a bit out of place and unsure what to do, he simply sat and watched the rest of them buzz about finishing the last of the requirements before they could eat. After everyone found a place to sit, Simon asked them to bow their heads for grace. Seth was used to this with Caroline, so it was no surprise to find that this group of God soldiers would do the same.

After their meal of chicken pot pie with green salad and apple pie for dessert, they cleaned up the kitchen together, made a pot of coffee, and retired back into the living room to discuss the next day's schedule and answer more questions that Seth surely still had. Seth was still amazed at some of the more modern inventions that Simon had in his home that made life quite a bit easier. It was all very interesting to see.

Everyone, cup of coffee in hand, found a place to sit around the large coffee table in the living area. Simon had pulled a large leather book from one of the shelves in the room and sat upon a large armchair placing the book on a side table.

"Now, Seth, over the next several months there will be things that you'll still be learning about, but a lot of it has to be covered in the field. Only experience can lend teaching and explanation to most of it. But I'm sure you still have questions, and we'll do our best to answer them for you." Simon sipped from his coffee cup.

Seth sat and thought for a moment before replying. "Well First, can you tell me how long I was out for? I'm not even sure what day it is."

"You were unconscious for about two days. Your body experienced what we call PS or Peregrine Sickness. It happens to all first-time travelers. Some last longer than others depending on size, health, and other factors."

"Two days? That explains the hunger at lunch earlier today. Is two days normal, and what exactly is Peregrine Sickness?" Seth questioned.

Simon took another sip from his mug then answered.

"Well, your body is thrown into a new dimension or time period, jumping through electrified portals via violent storms that rank 4.0 or above on the scale system. Your body's initial reaction can take a while to adjust. That's why you awoke with a headache and other symptoms. As far as normal, you came out of it pretty quickly compared to most."

"I think I get the basics of what's happening. I just want to know more about the things I saw outside earlier today. Is my mind playing tricks on me or does the barrier distort things? Because the size of the people, buildings, and animals I saw on the other side were absolutely huge. I've met some big men in my travels, especially in other countries. But I've never seen the likes of these people," Seth asked, puzzled by the memory.

"What you saw was truly genuine. No distortion or tricks of the mind. That is the country of Garganthera. It is home to a race of giants called the Nephilim. The Bible speaks of the Nephilim as being men of renown; huge, strong, men, the offspring of fallen angels that mated with human women."

"So, you're telling me that Angels slept with human woman creating another race of people?" Seth asked, unsure of what he was hearing. "Why? I mean, what was the point? Couldn't they breed amongst themselves?"

"In this way, Satan tried to infect the lineage of King David to stop Jesus from being born. Angels were not made for procreation. They are the most trusted servants of God. They are not human but are spiritual beings. The fallen angels would have had to inhabit the bodies of men to procreate."

"You mean like possession?"

"Yes, exactly so. The Bible also tells us that even the demons know the prophecy of the Christ child born of a virgin that God would send to save mankind. Tell me, Seth, have you ever heard the story of King David?"

Seth shook his head no, and Simon continued.

"He was born a shepherd boy, and at a very young age defeated Goliath who also happened to be a giant. There are many speculations as to why David gathered five stones instead of one, but I believe he knew he may have to battle more than one giant. See, Goliath wasn't one lone giant of a man. He had four brothers or relations, hence the reason for the five stones. He used one stone and a slingshot, striking Goliath with it in the forehead, killing him. He knew Goliath's relatives may become a problem and readied himself for battle against them all should the need arise."

"Wow, that's some story," Seth offered.

"Not just a story, Seth. History! All truth, and some of them can be proven through archaeology. But we still live our lives through faith because Satan uses man's wishes and wickedness to dispel God's truths, no matter how much proof there is."

Seth sat for a moment and pondered what Simon told him, thinking about his next question.

"How do you travel beyond the barrier without being spotted in a city of giants? It's pretty obvious you'd definitely stand out?"

"We aren't the only people our size here. Not all giants are huge like some of the ones you saw, just as men in our world are not all the same size. To us, you are considered to be somewhat of a giant. You're a very large man, Seth, by any standard. Most men are not equal to you. In Jason's born era, there are more large men than in your own, some of them reaching nine feet tall. Still, at that time these men were not the typical average male. Jason is about the height of most men in the year 2017."

"Do you mean two thousand and seventeen? Jason is from the year 2017? What about Alec and Odessa? What years are you from?"

Alec answered first. "I am from the mid-1800s. My first Peregrination was the year 1866."

"I am from the Byzantine Era, around 1285 AD," Odessa replied.

Seth stared in amazement. "What time period are we in now? Here, at this present time?"

"This is the year 1115 BC. My Safe house was placed here during this time period simply because I like Garganthera. It helps me keep things in perspective," Simon said with a smile.

"BC? Really? I don't understand how this is possible. I mean, in reality, none of us has even been born yet!" Seth exclaimed.

"True," Simon stated, "but, we know the God of the universe. The creator of all things including the heavens and space! If He decides we are going to time travel, then we time travel," Simon shrugged his shoulders and took another sip of coffee.

"So how do we age?" Seth asked curiously.

"The same as everyone else. You age at the same rate you would if you were still in your time period. Each day here is a day there. You...we- " Simon responded gesturing to the rest of the group, " -just live out our days in different time periods."

Seth looked at Odessa, "How long have you been doing this?"

"Fifteen years," Odessa answered.

Seth's eyebrows rose in surprise as his mouth dropped slightly open. "What about you Alec?"

"Slightly less, about ten years." Alec answered.

"Jason?" Seth nodded questioningly.

"About eight years," he said with a smirk, shrugging his shoulders. Crossing his arms across his chest, and using his head, he gestured toward Simon. "Simon here has been at this longer than anyone that I know of. I think this makes...what, thirty years Simon?"

"Yes, give or take a few." Simon ginned. "But there are many more who have lived and died before us carrying on this way of life for centuries," he said, patting the large, thick, leather-bound book he had placed on the table beside his chair earlier. "We are only this generation."

Seth's countenance seemed to drop at Simon's answer. *Thirty Years! Would he have to do this for thirty years before returning to Caroline?* Realizing everyone was watching him, he spoke. "That's a long time to be living the kind of lifestyle you've described. I just gave up a life of traveling on the sea after ten years of it. I was ready to settle down. I had just really gotten used to living on land for the last three years when I ended up here," he admitted with a heavy heart.

"But, if this is where I'm destined to be, as you say, then there isn't much else I can do about it is there," Seth stated glumly. He sighed and looked up. "Alec mentioned that we start training in the morning. What will that entail?"

"Yes," Jason answered. "We will gauge your abilities first off. We will train hard and fast over the next few days, so try to get a good night's rest. You seem to be in good shape just judging by appearances. But this lifestyle isn't just about strength it has to do with endurance as well."

Jason stood to his feet and stretched. "I don't know about the rest of you, but I think I'm ready to turn in. These restful days are about as hard on me as the traveling and training," he grinned.

Everyone else also agreed with Jason. Standing and saying their goodnights, they headed to their separate rooms. All except for Simon who agreed to take care of everyone's coffee cups. Simon watched Seth enter his room and shut the door. He offered up a prayer to God that He would ease Seth's troubled spirit and give him focus for the dangers that lie ahead. He prayed God would protect them all from what he believed lay in their near future. He believed Seth to be the last of 'The Twelve' chosen to do serious battle in the end times. He just needed to see if he bore the mark. He would give him time to settle into his new life before throwing that bit of information at him. He had enough to swallow as it stood right now. He drained the last bit of coffee from his cup, picked up the leather-bound book he placed beside his chair earlier, and began looking through the archival notes made by earlier Dragoman, studying, and looking for any information that he could on the events that brought Seth to them, and any explanation for the way he had appeared. Seth and Jason's fates must be intertwined somehow with them appearing together at a portal opening yet jumping from completely different storms, and completely separate time periods. Simon needed to do some serious digging and pray that God would lead him to an understanding of what he needed to do to guide them all in the right direction. Simon felt that the battle to end all battles would happen soon. How soon, he didn't know, but he doubted it would take another thirty years for him to witness it. He would send word to the other Dragoman within the next few days, and soon after, make a peregrination to meet with them to discuss these most recent events. As soon as Seth was trained, he would pair him with Jason and set them on a mission. Then he would prepare for his own journey.

As Simon leafed through the pages of the Dragoman Archives in his hands for the next several hours, he hoped for some clue or information that would help him understand the recent strange event. If he couldn't find anything, perhaps the others may have an answer. Maybe the answer was as simple as Seth being the last. Perhaps that was the explanation? But unless there were others somewhere that they didn't know about yet, Seth was only the eleventh marked Peregrine- if Seth had a mark, that is. Simon would have to keep his eyes open when around Seth. He didn't want to reveal everything just yet, but he did need to know if Seth was marked as one of the final Twelve.

He makes my feet like the feet of a deer;
He causes me to stand on the heights.
He trains my hands for battle;
my arms can bend a bow of bronze.

2 Samuel 22:34-35

Chapter 7

The morning sun was already brightly shining, and the few sparse clouds lining the sky offered little protection from the sun's rays beating down on them as their training commenced. Seth, Jason, Alec, and Odessa were hiking the ridge of the cliff that ran a bit of distance along Barrier's Edge. Seth occasionally glancing at and watching some of the happenings he could make out taking place in Garganthera. People milled about as in any other city, performing daily tasks required for living. He noted what Simon mentioned to him the night before about people being different sizes there. He was right, unless some of the people he was seeing were actually just very large babies or children.

As they walked the ridge they moved higher up, and visibility of the city became increasingly harder to see. Seth decided to concentrate on where they were going, curiosity growing within him. It was a good thing he wasn't afraid of heights. They were already pretty high up and still weren't at their destination. Wherever it was they were going it was quite a climb to get there.

They had all risen early just before sunrise, had a hearty breakfast, packed some water, jerky, and fresh fruit, and headed out. Jason explained they had to hike a bit before training could start, so Seth assumed they were going to some sort of training area.

They all spoke very little to conserve their energy and breathing since the hike into the mountain's interior required more than just walking. They had to scale part of the cliff side upward over rocks and boulders, using their hands and a good deal of body strength. Seth noticed Odessa seamed to handle all this more effortlessly than the rest of them. Her movements were precise, and easy as though she were just leaping over a log or climbing a ladder. She had barely even broken a sweat while the three of them were already perspiring.

Jason announced that they only had a few more minutes to go before they reached the training grounds. Seth felt like he had been walking for hours, but in truth, it had only been about forty-five minutes. They passed through a large opening in the side of the cliff and Seth could barely make out the layout inside the darkness of the cave. Filtered light trickled inside from other end where another opening appeared. The smell of damp, musty air filled his nostrils as they passed through the cave's interior. Water trickled between the rocks somewhere within. As they passed through the cave opening on the far side into the open air of daylight, Seth's eye's adjusted to the sudden burst of daylight. He noted they were in a small clearing approximately equal to ten acres and surrounded by woods on the other three sides. There were some targets for shooting set up on the far side of the field, along with what appeared to be stuffed grain sacks on sticks about average height that stood opposite of the targets. There was an obstacle course of sorts that had ladders going to high platforms with ropes extending out from it leading down to a wall, some of the ropes were at ground level and others stretched out to lower platforms. There were other ropes extending from the bottoms of the platforms to others of the same height with higher ropes on either side. He figured they were used for balancing and walking across. There were barrels, walls, wire fencing woven within itself going in every direction and strung just about a foot above ground, covering about a twenty-foot area. There were large boulders or stones about six foot in height and width which stuck out of the ground. Also visible were large wooden walls that extended straight upward about fifteen to twenty feet, with ropes that hung down, and pegs of sorts, attached at different levels going all the way to the top. He had never seen anything like this place before.

"All-right, let's take a bit of a break to catch our breath and hydrate some before we get started," Jason announced.

They all pulled their water bladder or canteen out of their packs and either leaned against the rock-facing or sat on boulders or pieces of logs lying on the ground.

Seth looked around some more at the scene before him as he took a few more drinks of the cool liquid. He glanced at the sky at the top of the clearing and noticed something that looked like the barrier glistening just at the tree line covering the entire area.

"What's that?" Seth asked no one in particular, motioning to the sky above them.

"That would be an enchantment spell that Simon placed over the area so we could train without fear of being heard or seen by any demons that may have strayed this far inland from Garganthera," Jason answered, stowing his canteen back into his pack.

Seth glanced sideways at Jason. "You mean like magic?"

"Yes, exactly like magic," Jason smirked. "Magic is real, at least here in the fourth dimension. I'm not sure if Simon is able to use his gifts in the other dimensions. It isn't something that I've ever seen him have to do."

"So, you've seen him use magic then?"

"Yes, but only when necessary. Odessa has known Simon longer than any of us and had seen plenty. She's even met most of the other Dragoman over the last fifteen years."

Seth looked at Odessa and she grinned, shaking her head in agreement as she swallowed another mouthful of water.

"So, there are other Dragoman as well as other Peregrines?" Seth questioned her.

"Yes, many more," she said, looking at him.

"Are they all 'gifted' as you called it the same way Simon is?" Seth stood to stretch a bit and stow his water.

"Not in the same way. Alec and I met a guy on one of our peregrinations at one of the outlying charging stations that's a genius when it comes to electronics, anything to do with power really. But he had no magic, not that we could see anyway. But we were also in the first dimension at the time. We are all gifted differently. Even we Peregrines have different strengths and abilities to aid in our missions. God calls many different people to do His work."

Seth pondered what she said for a few minutes then, turning to the group with a questioning stance, asked, "All right, what do I do first?"

Jason stood and looked at Seth.

"First we need to assess your strengths and weaknesses. I have a feeling just from the sheer size of you that you're exceptionally strong."

Seth gave a little nod in agreement.

"We also need to know how fast you are, how quick you can think on your feet, how your reflexes are, and what your stamina is like. This can be a hard life at times, and you need to be prepared to handle whatever it throws at you. Alec here is a sharpshooter; he never misses a target. He's good with both a rifle and a bow. Odessa is a samurai warrior trained by an entire army of Samurai. Interesting story she has there. Remind her to tell you about it later. Me, I'm a marine trained in strategical maneuvers. I'm pretty strong myself and can shoot pretty accurately, though nowhere near Alec's abilities." Jason motioned toward Alec.

"Have you had any kind of combat training Seth?"

Seth shook his head no, adding, "Not really combat training, but as a young lad on board a ship full of men, I saw my share of fights. I had to defend myself a time or two as well. We used to have boxing competitions on board ship. The men would get bored and need to blow off steam so they would wager against one another. I participated in a few matches when I was about nineteen, but soon, no one would go up against me and my short-lived boxing career soon ended. There was always heavy lifting of cargo and the like, and plenty of hard work to keep me busy, so strength was something that most of the men had acquired. That is if they made it any length of time aboard ship. I can navigate any chart known to man and navigate by the stars as well. I can read some Latin and can speak a bit of several foreign languages. Other than that, I'm afraid that sums me up."

"That's not a bad list of qualifications. Some new Peregrines have come with no discernible skills at all, but somehow God provides, just like He did for Odessa," Jason continued. "She and I can train you in hand-to-hand combat, more than just boxing techniques. She has martial arts training as well, and I have a mixed martial arts background." Noticing Seth's questioning glance at his remark Jason explained. "MME is a type of fighting style from the late twenty-first century. It combines kickboxing, wrestling, and fighting styles such as karate and judo. Alec will train you in shooting both gun, and bow-and-arrow. You never know what you might need. Try to learn what you can, and what you don't pick up, well, God knows your strengths more than we or even you do."

They spent the next five to six hours training Seth in the skill sets that they had discussed. Seth was leery of a fighting a woman. But soon learned that Odessa was not an easy target, making him apply himself much harder when going up against her.

Turns out, he was a decent shot with a rifle and picked it up quickly. The bow, however, would take more practice. Hand to hand combat, other than boxing skills, would take a bit longer for Seth to figure out. He had never thought a person could move the way Jason and Odessa did as they sparred. Even in his travels to China and Japan, he had never seen movements like this before. They also spent an hour or so going through the obstacle course, jumping, climbing, crawling, running, and balancing their way through the intense maze of objects.

Seth was exhausted and glad when they decided to call it a day. Jason seemed satisfied with the progress Seth had made so far. They would return to training over the next several days to continue, but for now they headed back to Simon's for a late lunch. Jason mentioned that they had other things to discuss and work on as well for the rest of the evening, like getting their next mission assignments from Simon.

After returning to the house, they each took turns using the two available showers, then met up in the kitchen for chicken sandwiches, garden salads, and iced tea. When they finished eating and cleaning up the kitchen, they met Simon in the front room of the house where Seth first saw all the maps, navigational equipment, and other *unique* items that he knew nothing about.

"Well, here you all are!" Simon said. "I had been wondering if you were all going to come back soon. I figured hunger would win out eventually and you'd be forced back." He looked at them over his spectacles with a wide grin.

"We have a lot to cover in a short time to get Seth lined out. We plan on taking the next few days and using them for more training. Probably pack lunch tomorrow so we won't have to break so early," Jason stated, settling upon a high stool, crossing his arms and his ankles.

"I may venture up with all of you tomorrow." Simon replied. "So, tell me, how did training go?" He looked at all of them with a questioning brow.

Alec answered first, explaining that Seth had good balance and was a good shot. Jason talked about him being good with his hands, but MME style would take some training, and the fact that his old school mentality about fighting a woman might get him killed. They all grinned and giggled at that one since they had all faced the same turmoil themselves when first training.

"Well then, let's get to the business at hand, shall we?" Simon said, walking to the extensive map collection he had pinned to one of the walls in the room.

"Your next assignment will be to retrieve an important artifact called the *Goddelikheid Crucible,* otherwise known as the *Divinity Crucible.* Seth, you will partner with Jason. You two will retrieve this item and return it here to me. It is located in the jungles of North Africa. The last time I heard of its existence was around the years 1796-1803. It was found on an expedition by Mungo Park. He was a Scottish explorer sent to explore the Niger River by the African Association in 1795. He didn't realize the significance of his find, probably discarding it as a bowl used by a tribe at some point in history. Not too many people know of its existence or importance, so it shouldn't be hard to obtain the artifact." Simon glanced between Jason and Seth as he retrieved a large leather-bound book from one of the shelves. Simon opened the book in search of a photograph of the crucible so Seth and Jason knew what to look for.

"Ah, here it is," Simon said emphatically, pointing to a bowl-shaped item as he explained further.

"Mungo left the crucible behind but at least he took a photograph before he did, purely accidental of course. It was grouped in with other artifacts too large to carry. He made a detailed map of the exact location and how to get there in hopes of returning one day to remove them, but he never made it back."

"Why didn't he ever return?" Seth asked quizzically.

"He did return to Africa, and the Niger River on another expedition, but his boat was attacked by a native tribe and he drowned." Simon watched Seth's expression change to one of surprise.

"So, this is obviously one of the dangers you were telling me about that comes with the job."

"Yes, but the locals are easier to deal with than the demons that will likely be following or tracking you." Simon moved to a table in the center of the room to lay down the book and make a sketch of the picture for them to take with them.

"How do demons track us, and why would they be interested in this crucible object anyway?" Seth moved to stand by the table next to Simon to watch him.

Jason looked at Seth. "It isn't the crucible they want. They want to stop us. You've drawn attention to yourself just by being chosen by God. Now, anytime you're walking in the first dimension, you're free game. Demons tempt and torment everyone on the face of the earth. But the harder you work for God the more of a target you become, especially since we are trying to stop Satan from destroying the earth and mankind."

"Well then why aren't they seeking us out here?"

Jason crossed the room toward Seth and Simon. "God shields us here in the fourth dimension. They don't walk on this side of the barrier very often. We still have to watch and listen when we're here. A few have been known to cross the barrier. Usually following a Peregrine or Dragoman that wasn't careful when passing through a gateway. Or it just got lucky and found a gateway." He shrugged.

Simon handed the drawing of the crucible to Jason and he tucked it inside his pocket to stow in his travel bag later.

Simon then addressed Alec and Odessa. "The two of you will need to retrieve the Staff of Moses."

Odessa perked up. "The one he used in the plagues and when he parted the Red Sea? Well, the one he was holding when *God* parted the red sea?" She asked excitedly, correcting her mistake.

"The very one!" Simon exclaimed.

"Awesome!" she squealed as the guys chuckled at her excitement.

Alec questioned, "So where do we go for that?"

"Jerusalem, in the year 587 BC, precisely around the end of June."

"Hopefully, the contents of the Ark of the Covenant will still be intact and not hidden away at that time. If you get there and the Ark is empty, we will have to try an earlier date. Solomon's Temple was destroyed by Nebuchadnezzar in the summer, roughly August of 587 BC. So, to insure the staff is saved we must get to it first. My Meteorological books and Dragoman Archives reveal a thunderstorm that took place in Jerusalem around such a time. You will have to be extra careful because everyone will be on edge at this time with the threat of war and siege being imminent."

"Wait," Simon held up his hands in dismay shaking his head at his own near mistake. "I can't believe I almost made this mistake! Blast this fool head of mine! Odessa, I am sorry, but I cannot send you to Jerusalem at such a time. A woman would never be allowed into the places you must go. You and Alec will have to trade missions with Seth and Jason."

"Well that just stinks!" she said in disappointment, crossing her arms across her chest and pushing her bottom lip out in pouting form at Simon. "But I understand." She turned to Seth and Jason. "I truly envy the two of you for what you will get to see and witness. To look upon the actual Ark of the Covenant and to hold the Staff of Moses!" She pined in almost anguish and awe as she looked at them.

"It is all right *Mon Amie.* We will have a grand African adventure!" Alec assured her emphatically.

Odessa couldn't contain the giggle at Alec's declaration. He always knew how to make her feel better.

Jason handed Alec the drawing with instructions, and the map on where to locate the crucible, then turned to Simon to await instructions.

Simon looked at Alec and Odessa. "There is a Haboob that you will enter through in about three days, so we will need to prepare you for travel soon. Jason, you, Seth, and I need to look through the wardrobe room and see if there is any appropriate attire for that period that will fit. Especially you Seth, I hope I can find something to fit you."

He slapped Seth on the shoulder and continued instructing them on the layout of the temple, the laws and customs concerning entry into the temple, and where exactly they should find the Ark. Simon gave them all a bit of homework. They each had to study a bit of the language for the period, just the basics for simple conversations. After prepping them on their missions, they went in search of clothing to suit the regions and periods in which they were to visit to try and blend in as much as possible.

Seth marveled at the two massive, intricately carved oak doors. Trees, leaves, and forest creatures adorned each. They passed through them, entering a large room just off the living area. The walls were all built of large stones and had large stone archways that were built into the walls all the way around the room's perimeter. Long, heavy, velvety maroon curtains lay against the wall inside the archways, mirroring the look of windows. Seth was overwhelmed by the amount of clothing and items from all over the world that the room held. Anything you could possibly imagine needing had to be available. On the far side was a large wall of weapons stacked and hung. It appeared that Simon had acquired quite a collection over his thirty years.

Seth picked up a long sword with a large handle that seemed to fit his hand perfectly. He smiled as he pulled it from its sheath and swished the blade through the air; the blade and tang balanced to perfection.

"Simon, may I keep this?" He apparently was going to need a weapon anyhow.

"Absolutely. Anything you need, my boy, is yours for the taking."

They continued their search and were successful in securing clothing suitable enough to fit Seth and, realizing that the evening had come upon them quickly, decided to have some dinner. Afterward, everyone retired to their individual rooms for a bit of homework.

Seth spent the better part of the night studying the layout of the temple and the map of Jerusalem. The language part came pretty easy for him as well as the map study. He never dreamed that all the years spent at sea, and the things he learned, would ever benefit him in this way. It seemed as though God *had* been preparing him all his life for just such a time as this, as Simon had mentioned earlier.

Seth soon drifted off to sleep, waking suddenly a short time later, sweat beading on his forehead as he replayed Caroline screaming his name, over and over in his head. It had become a nightly occurrence and he doubted it would ever stop. He slept little the last few times he tried, and what sleep he did manage was restless, wrought with dreams of Caroline and what he lost.

He threw the covers off, slung his feet over the edge of the bed and grabbed a t-shirt. The cool stone of the floor made him shiver a bit as he walked into the kitchen for a cup of coffee, only to find he wasn't the only one awake. Jason was sitting at the table with a glass of water. He looked up at Seth as he entered the kitchen.

"You couldn't sleep either huh?"

"No. I don't believe I've slept decently since I woke up here. You want some coffee?" Seth asked Jason, who nodded a yes as Seth crossed the room and started a pot, remembering what he learned yesterday evening about how to work the newfangled device.

"What's your reason for restless nights?" Jason inquired of Seth as he watched him move about the kitchen in search of coffee cups, sugar, and cream.

Seth sighed. "I have a reoccurring nightmare. Every time I close my eyes, I hear Caroline screaming my name, like when we were separated by the earthquake." He turned to face Jason and leaned his long frame against the counter waiting for the coffee to finish brewing.

"What about you?"

"Well, those dreams stopped long ago, but they were replaced recently by nightmares of the last battle I was in." Jason ran a hand down his face, stretched his arms and back, and repositioned himself in his chair before he began. "I lost my last travel partner in a demon attack about a month back."

Seth looked at Jason with understanding, realization setting in that he wasn't the only person dealing with loss here in this strange existence. The coffee finished and he handed Jason a filled cup, then placed the sugar and cream on the table.

Seth took a seat. "I'm sorry to hear that. What happened?"

"Her name was Phoebe. We were on a mission in Germany looking for one of Simon's artifacts when she was injured. It wasn't a particularly bad injury, but bad enough to slow us down, and inhibit her ability to fight well. She had lost quite a bit of blood and needed to rest. I was tired as well from carrying my weight and hers for several miles when we came upon a stand of trees and bushes. We had been going for days with little to no rest. We sat down for a little while and she fell asleep, so I let her sleep. We weren't but a few hours walk from the charging station and weren't in any hurry so to speak. I guess I drifted off too because something startled me and I woke up to her struggling to fight off three demons by herself. I woke just in time to see them kill her. I was so angry at them and myself that I really don't remember what happened. All I know is when things settled down, they were dead and so was Phoebe. The guilt eats at me for not making sure the perimeter was secure. All my training as a marine and the years that I've spent doing this should have ruled out something like that happening." Jason finished speaking and took a drink from the steaming cup in his hands.

"I'm sorry man. That sounds rough. Fighting normal men is tough enough. I can't imagine what battling a demon is like."

"You'll more than likely soon find out."

The two men sat in silence for a while drinking their coffee, each deep in thought over their own internal demons plaguing their every moment, both awake and asleep. They made small talk as they each drank a second cup. The rest of the house began stirring, ready to start another day.

But you are a chosen people, a royal priesthood,
a holy nation, God's special possession, that you
may declare the praises of Him who called you
out of the darkness into His wonderful light.

1Peter 2:9

Chapter 8

The group reached the practice field early wanting to get started and make the most of their day. They had a hearty breakfast and packed snacks and lunch, planning to stay as late as the day would allow them. Simon glanced around at the scene with appreciation and then back at the group of Peregrines in his midst.

"It's been awhile since I've been up here. You all have made some great improvements. I'm thoroughly impressed!"

Jason stated, "You have to stay up with the times as much as possible. Especially since you never know where you'll be sent next." He grinned as he moved to the battlefield's center where they sparred.

"All right, Seth, let's see what you remember?" He wielded his sword and took a ready stance.

Seth grinned and replied, "Just remember, I'm still new to all this." He walked out to meet Jason, pulling the sword he had found in Simon's wardrobe room from its sheath and brandishing the weapon, mimicking Jason's stance. "I've never held a sword or any weapon before this so, be gentle." A teasing smile split his lips and amusement danced across his features. Even though he was being sincerely honest, he also knew what he was capable of strength wise.

Jason returned Seth's grin at his remark, knowing full well that the large man would be an able opponent. For not only was Seth strong, but Jason had witnessed his speed and agility the day before. Once he figured out how to move wielding a weapon, he would be a force to be reckoned with in a battle.

Odessa, Alec, and Simon stood to the side watching, curious to see how Seth handled himself. The two men started toward each other swinging, the clang of metal striking metal filling the air as they moved around the sparring field. Jason quickly got the better of Seth, his sword stopping just shy of Seth's throat. Seth swallowed hard, his eyebrows shooting up in surprise.

"You've got to protect yourself with each move or it may be your last. Strength is only worth so much. If you leave yourself vulnerable, it could mean your life," Jason instructed, showing Seth what he meant and how to prevent it from happening again.

Seth nodded as they began again, handling the sword better. This time he was able to keep Jason's advances at bay, but he knew he needed more work on making his opponent take the defense.

The two of them spent the better part of the next few hours sparring with weapons, while Alec and Odessa took to the obstacle course to keep up their endurance training.

Simon sat watching the people before him, amazed at the physical prowess of all of them. Especially Odessa, she could probably out do any of the men, her speed and movements as graceful as though she were simply dancing. He was truly proud of, and grateful for, the Peregrines that God had chosen to send his way for him to mentor. They were all people of tremendous character. Even Alec and Seth, although they were not believers, Simon knew they would still fight with integrity for the mission. Simon prayed regularly for all of them, and also that God would win Alec and Seth over to His side for eternity, the alternate being an unpleasant thought. Simon would continually pray that somehow God would break through those tough exteriors. Why else would He have chosen them if not for an eternity in His presence?

As they broke for a drink of water and a high protein snack to refuel their bodies for continued training, they sat under the tree canopy for shade from the intense heat of the sun. Seth and Jason's shirts were completely soaked, so they removed their T-shirts to wring out the sweat and allow them to dry a bit. As Seth pulled the shirt over his head, he turned to place it on a nearby rock in the sunlight exposing his back to the group. Simon noticed exactly what he hoped he would see. Directly in the center of Seth's shoulder blades sat a tattoo of a lion's head. It covered the majority of the center of his back, and the lion's mane ran in all directions. Some of it trailing over his shoulders to the front of his chest, and down across the top of his shoulders to the top of his biceps. The Lions face was one of peace and quiet strength. The neck part of the mane ran down to the small of Seth's back stopping just below his waistline. It was an impressive size, especially considering what a large man Seth was, yet very skillfully and tastefully done.

"That's some tattoo!" Simon commented as Seth turned back to the group and the shade.

"Yeah, a stupid mistake made by a drunken kid about nine years ago." Seth took a long drink of water not offering anything more and noticed everyone watching him, questions written across their expressions. Apparently his short answer did not appease anyone so, he took another drink, grinned slightly, and began with more of an explanation.

"Our schooner was furloughed in a coastal port in Morocco, at a smaller town on the outskirts of Casablanca. I can't remember the name exactly. Me and a few of the other younger crew decided to go exploring, drinking, you know, all the stupid stuff teenage boys get into, especially in a place like Morocco," he said with a lopsided grin.

"We got too drunk and ended up at a little shop just on the outskirts of the town where we were. There was a young woman there with her father, I assume, that told me I was destined for something great and that I needed a tattoo to mark my destiny. Being drunk, young, and full of ego about some great destiny, I listened. Next thing I remember, I woke up with this lion tattoo taking up the majority of my back and then some." Seth shrugged and grinned, a defeated smile playing across his face. "That was the last time I let drink get the better of me."

"I've never had a tattoo, but I do have a rather oddly shaped birthmark on the outside of my lower calf muscle here on my right leg. What do you think it looks like?" Alec asked the group, looking from person to person as everyone contemplated their answer.

"I would say a round squiggly group of...something," Jason answered, making a puzzled face as he analyzed the mark.

"I would say it resembles a small bunch of flowers. But I have seen it many times and have had plenty of time to come up with my own opinions on what it might be," Odessa stated.

"Well, since we're comparing and sharing special spots, I was kicked by a horse once when I was examining the animal. I gave it a shot and it laid a back hoof directly into the front of my hip. I had to have about twenty stitches, leaving a major scar just below my waistline. The mark resembles a cup or goblet of sorts," Jason shrugged, finishing his sentence.

Odessa stood turning her back to the group and pulled the cap sleeve of her shirt up to reveal a scar.

"This is my... 'Special mark'." On the shoulder of her left arm was an image of a gate or doorway with a sword lying at the base, the edges pointing downward and upward as though the gate rested upon its blade. "I was branded as a young girl. This is my master's mark," she said, a bit of anger apparent in her voice.

"Branded? I've heard of slavery but what kind of animal brands another human being as property?" Seth asked, agitation lacing his words.

Simon answered him, "In Odessa's time, women were property. They had no rights at all, and the men of their family could do with them as they saw fit, even going so far as to brand them so no one else could claim them. There are many instances throughout history where people were considered property. Even in the Old Testament after a battle or war, people were taken to serve the victors. They worked as servants or slaves." Simon continued.

"What you must realize here though, is all of your marks do represent something no matter where or how you obtained them. God has marked you for a very special reason. I believe The Twelve will fight in a great battle. You see, your marks each represent one of the Twelve tribes of Israel. Odessa's mark is the symbol for Simeon. Alec's is for Reuben, Jason's is for Asher, and yours Seth, is for the tribe of Judah. You are what, I believe, to be the last Peregrine chosen."

"I thought you said there were twelve? There is only four here," Seth questioned Simon.

"There are other Peregrines that train under other Dragoman that have tribal marks. We are, however, missing one, the tribe of Zebulon. I researched how you came to us in the Dragoman Archives and it stated that the last of the Peregrines chosen would bear the mark of Judah. That would be you, Seth, but I only know of ten others. If you are the last, then there is one missing Peregrine out there who has already been chosen that I have yet to discover," Simon explained as each person sat listening and thinking about what exactly Simon meant by his revelations of their marks and the meanings.

"I will be leaving on my own Peregrination soon to meet with the Dragoman Counsel, after I see you all off on your missions of course. Perhaps one of the others already knows of this Peregrine and just hasn't gotten around to revealing their existence yet.

"What about this great battle you mentioned?" Alec questioned Simon.

"I'm not exactly sure about the details of that just yet Alec. That will take further study, research, and prayer. I'm sure it won't be for quite a while yet so don't trouble yourself over the details," Simon said, hoping to dispel any more questions about that bit of information. He really didn't know much more about it yet himself and secretly chided himself on revealing too much too soon. They had enough to think about and deal with concerning their present upcoming missions. They needn't think too much further past that.

Seth thought about what Simon said, about the great battle being 'a-while' off. He may be adjusting well to his new life, but he still harbored hope of returning to Caroline. Somehow, when all of this was finished, he would hopefully have found a way to return. Until then, he would keep his eyes and ears open and ask as many questions as he could without drawing suspicion to himself.

"All right boys, and girl," Jason said with a smile aimed at Odessa, "Back to work! We still have the whole afternoon to train. We need to work on battle sparring."

Jason turned to Seth. "We need to train you to handle more than one opponent. In an all-out Demon war, you could have more than you care to count attack you at once. All three of us will help you in strategizing moves and using your senses to help you handle that sort of situation."

The four of them returned to the sparring field to explain and show Seth some moves before they started up again; explaining to him how to use his hearing and peripheral vision to help him in battle, emphasizing the importance of being able to think on his feet, especially during battle. Seth, being agile anyhow, picked it up rather quickly, and they spent the remainder of the morning, and afternoon, sparring while Simon went off in search of wild mushrooms to prepare with dinner.

They broke for a late lunch when they saw Simon return from his trek into the surrounding woods, after which they ran the obstacle course for another hour or two and then spent the rest of the evening at the shooting range.

By the time they returned to the safe house, the moon had already waxed full and high in the sky, and the night creatures were stirring about in the underbrush of the woods. Crickets and frogs chirped and belted out their respective songs as the group entered the house in search of showers and a nice clean change of clothing. Simon headed straight for the kitchen to begin supper, placing an already cooked roast with vegetables in the oven to warm, adding the mushrooms he had picked earlier. He then went into his office to compose messages to be sent to the other Dragoman concerning the meeting he wished to call. He wrote out the invites to each one and placed them into the canisters to be sent out over the grid.

Taking an empty basket from one of the shelves on the wall, he placed the canisters inside and walked through the door into the mapping room in the front area of the house, and out the front door. He was surprised to see a freshly showered Seth leaning against a tree in the front yard staring out over Garganthera.

"Interesting sight isn't it? I know it's hard to believe all this is real even though you're witnessing it with your own eyes," Simon asked a surprised Seth who seemed to be shaken out of his reverie. "Sorry, I didn't mean to startle you."

"No problem," Seth answered, straightening to walk with Simon toward the Barrier. "Just lost in thought I guess. In answer to your question...yeah, it is pretty amazing. I still feel like I'm in some sort of dream or something." Seth grinned slightly.

"It will take some time for it all to sink in. Besides, it has only been a few days since you awoke and we threw all of this at you," Simon said, switching the slightly heavy basket to another arm.

"So, what are you up to? What's with all those cylinders if you don't mind my asking?" Seth said, curious about the contents of Simon's basket.

"No, not at all. I am relaying messages to the other Dragoman. Sending out invites for a council meeting."

"How do you send those things? Does some large, trained bird swoop down out of the night sky and carry them off to their destination?" Seth stated with a raise of his eyebrows.

Simon laughed at Seth description, "No, no, my boy, although I'll have to file that away for future reference if the grid system should ever fail," Simon said teasingly, pulling one of the canisters from the basket and handing it to Seth.

"These canisters are hollow inside and can carry small items or letters wherever you wish along the barrier's outside surface."

Seth turned the metal canister over in his hands as he studied it. It was cylindrical in shape, and approximately a foot long, and maybe six inches in diameter. One side was flat, about two inches across, and both ends were round-nosed-bullet shaped. "How do you place messages inside?" Seth queried.

"Like so." Simon took the canister from Seth's hands, pushed a hidden button on the end of the canister, and a curved door opened up in the center of the tube running almost the length of it. Simon pushed the door closed and placed the cylinder back into the basket.

"Come, I'll show you how the grid works should you ever need use of it, although we Dragoman are the only ones who ever do use it."

The two men approached the edge of the barrier, and Simon took out a canister the shade of black onyx and whispered a name against the outside of it. He then laid the flat side of the canister against the glistening electric surface of the barrier. As he let go, the canister took off across the barrier creating sparks and a trail of electricity behind and around it as it slid at breakneck speed across the surface.

"First of all, I don't understand how it stays on the surface. Why doesn't it fall through if we can walk through, and how does it know where to go, and how do you know who each one is for?" Seth asked.

Simon smiled at all of Seth's questions, "Firstly, they are attracted to the surface and an unseen grid like pattern that lies beneath the barrier. Second, the canisters are spelled, meaning they work by magic. Each one is a bit different in color which helps me to tell them apart. I made them specifically for each Dragoman that I wish to contact. That way, I don't have to open each container to find out which is whose," Simon said with a grin as he tapped his temple with his forefinger.

"As far as where it goes, you must whisper the full given name of the person you wish to receive the message. However, be very careful to annunciate properly so it goes where it should, and that no one hears you, or you could inadvertently betray a comrade. There are betrayers who work with us. No one here mind you, but they do exist."

"Do you mean first, middle, and last birth name? What if you don't know it?"

"Then you had better learn it. It could go to anyone without proper instruction."

"Couldn't that happen anyway? I mean people have similar or identical names all over the world."

"No. Even though sometimes, people have the same name it is unlikely they have the same given full name. Plus, the grid only delivers to the fourth dimension. No one in the other dimensions can receive it. So, that greatly decreases the chance of accidental delivery."

"When that canister flies across the surface that way with all the energy encircling it, doesn't something appear in the other dimension?"

"Yes, but they only see it as lightning jumping from cloud to cloud without storm presence or ground connection. I believe most call it heat-lightning," Simon stated as he took another metal, colored canister, whispered a name, and laid it on the grid to be whisked away in another direction.

Seth watched as Simon released a total of five canisters, each flying in a different direction across the barrier much like the navigational lines that plot the earth's surface, but a bit more random.

Finishing the task at hand, Simon and Seth turned toward the house.

"Tomorrow we will see Alec and Odessa off on their mission, and after, you, Jason, and I will venture into

Garganthera and show you how to find gateways when needed, and also how *not* to draw attention to yourself. Besides, you seem very curious as to what all lies on the other side of that wall, as well you should be," Simon said with a chuckle, slapping Seth on the shoulder.

"That I am Simon. That I am." Seth grinned at the older man as they entered the house and headed to the kitchen for supper, finding the rest of the group already there.

For by Him all things were created, both in the
Heavens and on earth, visible and invisible, whether
thrones or dominions or rulers or authorities
all have been created through Him and for Him.

Colossians 1:16

Chapter 9

The next day everyone awoke early to see Alec and Odessa off on their mission. Simon spent the better part of the morning going over the particulars with them, after which they all set out on a fifteen-minute jaunt to the charging station Simon had well hidden in the heavily wooded forest behind his home.

As they walked beneath the thick tree canopy and the dense brush and undergrowth, small animals scattered and ran for a more secure hiding place. Rabbits, deer, mice, a fox or two, and few birds that were startled out of their quiet existence. Seth wondered at the strangeness of it. To exist in another dimension that bore so many similarities to what he had always known, yet also, so completely different. Like Garganthera, it was truly extraordinary to see, even though he still felt like he was dreaming at times. *How many other places or worlds did he have yet to discover?* He always did like traveling. He only stopped for Caroline and she had been enough to make him happy. He would have been completely contented to stay in one place forever with her.

Seth shook himself out of his reverie to ask another question.

"Simon are there more dimensions past the fourth one?"

"Not to my knowledge, Seth. But one never knows what God may reveal, or when," he said, glancing back at Seth over his shoulder.

"I just wonder what all else is out there. Seeing just the little that I have, it makes me curious to know what else might exist. I've never heard of Garganthera in history before. Did I just miss something?"

"No, it may possibly exist in the same dimension, but it also exists on a different plane of time. Like a whole other planet of sorts. There are things you will witness, Seth, that may make you question your own sanity. Just remember who created it all and that you work for him. Eh?" Simon replied with a reassuring nod at Seth.

"We're here," Jason announced to the group, probably just for Seth's benefit.

Seth, looking around, saw nothing but a large moss-covered rock-face surrounded by trees and bushes. Simon lifted up the walking stick Seth noticed him carrying before to the training grounds, and tapped the rock in a triangular shape, mumbling something as he did. Suddenly, the front of the rock disappeared to reveal a stone staircase that appeared to circle deep down into the ground. Simon led the way as they all descended down into the earth's depths. When the last person passed through, the rock covering reappeared, hiding them away from the world. Seth's jaw hung open at the phenomenon. *Would ever stop being amazed by this new world?*

Simon took his staff and touched a torch hanging on the wall, and all of the torches lining the walls down around the spiral staircase lit with fire, one after the other, illuminating their path. They continued walking downward until they came upon a large, open room. Inside were wires, viewing-screens, a lot of other electrical-type equipment, and two, large, coiled, objects standing in the center of the opening. Seth decided to give the questioning a break and just watch and observe. If he didn't understand something, then he would ask.

Jason tapped Seth on the arm and motioned for him to follow the rest of them to a large metal cage, while Simon walked to a metal box covered with switches, levers, and wires. He flipped a few different switches, pushed a few buttons and the room illuminated from all directions.

The hair of Seth's arms stood up as the coils loudly vibrated with electrical current. Bolts of electricity vibrated between the two coils, sizzling, and bouncing off the floor and nearby walls. Seth's body buzzed with the power of it all.

Simon then stepped over to a type of screen, inputting the location and time of Alec and Odessa's destination. He walked over to where they were all standing, and turning a knob in a circular motion, increased the coil's power. He looked at the two travelers and asked, "Ready?" They nodded yes, then covered their faces with masks and their heads with hoods to protect themselves from the large sandstorm blowing wildly on the other side. A bright light appeared between the two coils quickly increasing in size, resembling a wavy, undulating, oval doorway. Seth could actually see through to the other side, the large sandstorm rolling through the landscape as Alec and Odessa gave them a wave farewell and took off running through the opening. As soon as they were gone, the doorway closed, and Simon shut down the coils.

"That is incredible!" Seth exclaimed.

"Isn't it? This is a Tesla Coil, named after Nikola Tesla, the man who invented it. It's a very delicate machine to operate. One wrong move and we're all...history," Simon said with a slight chuckle, amused by his own wit, then continued.

"I simply input where you need to go on the computer, generate enough energy to create a hole in the space time continuum, and voila! You have a gateway to anywhere in the world. That is, of course, if there is a storm with an open portal for you to walk out of on the other side."

"I thought we traveled by storm only?" Seth asked.

This time Jason answered as Simon busied himself turning things off.

"We can't always rely on the weather. Older Peregrines had to wait around until a storm large enough and with enough power blew through. With all the technology now available, the Dragoman found a way to create these charging stations. But they aren't always available. Charging stations are only in a few specific spots where there is a Dragoman who can operate it. Simon here, like most Dragoman, knows when and where all past storms occurred. So, when we're on a mission, we know how, and where to go, to get back. If we miss the storm to return, then we have to wait until one strong enough comes through before we can peregrinate. But traveling that way doesn't ensure where you'll end up. You really have to pay close attention to what the Dragoman tell you or you can really get frustrated and, well, straight up lost."

"How do we know if a storm is large enough?" Seth questioned as the men ascended the stairs to the exit.

"They have to read 4.0 or above on the scale. That may sound hard to understand, but once you've been through a few intense storms, you'll learn how to read if they're strong enough to make a peregrination. Besides, if God wants you to travel, He'll open a gateway. Only Peregrines and Dragoman can see the portals, so there's no worry about others questioning things." Jason finished speaking as they all stepped cautiously into the forest outside the rock's entrance.

Simon stated, "What say we grab some lunch and then we can go to Garganthera so Seth here can have a look around." The two men agreed and they all quietly made their way back to Simon's place.

After eating and changing into some more appropriate clothing for their journey, they headed out the door and walked the opposite direction from the training fields along Barrier's Edge. Able to see the edge of Garganthera through the shield, Simon could navigate a safe entry place for them.

Simon explained as they walked. "Honestly, we could enter anywhere we wish along the barrier, but if we were seen, it could have catastrophic consequences. People seeing you just appear out of thin air has a tendency to cause an all-out witch hunt. So, we search for a hidden alleyway or backdoor to a storage shed or the like. Like here, do you see Seth? The barrier has areas that allow for safer passage into other realms, displaying a distinctive yellowish color."

Simon soon stopped in front of a dilapidated building whose back door bordered the shield. The shield at this particular point had a yellowish tint to it approximately twenty feet across and twenty feet high. He opened his hand, palm facing out and made a pushing motion. The barrier moved forward toward the building until the door to the building was in the fourth dimension. Simon reached out and opened the door, stepping through to the other side into the abandoned building. Jason and Seth followed, closing the door behind them.

Seth was in awe once more, deciding to make a mental note to ask later if he had to learn to move the barrier as Simon had.

They walked through the building, peeking through the broken windows to see if there were anyone around that might see them exit the building. There was a side door that exited into a narrow alleyway. Pulling the hoods up on their robes to hide their faces and to keep from drawing attention to themselves, they slowly opened the door and stepped out into the city of Garganthera. Seth wondered if the robes might draw attention, but it seemed that at least half of the people he could see wore robes. Possibly due to the damp humid air that seemed to circulate here. The temperature was a bit on the hot side, and the cotton robes did provide some protection from the hot sun blaring down on them. The temperature here was quite different compared to the other side of Barrier's Edge. He didn't really even notice the temperature there except when they were at the training fields, and most of the sweating they did there was from sheer exertion. If he was recalling correctly, Simon's place seemed to have almost perfect weather.

Now that Seth got a clear inside view of Garganthera he was even more amazed than before. He tried to be careful and not seem too over-whelmed by what he saw. He didn't want people staring and wondering about him.

Seth spun as he walked, taking in the different sized buildings made of stone, brick, and mortar with very little wood adorning them, mainly being used more as accent pieces in doorways and windows. They were absolutely huge in size, width, depth, and height, with very little walking room in between, at least for the larger people. The streets were cobblestoned in an array of light sandy colors. There were large lamps that used oil and fire to light the streets after dark, and shops of every kind lined both sides of the street with what appeared to be dwellings that lay above each. Some parts of the town seemed to house larger shops while other areas housed smaller ones. The place was laid out more like an ancient stone village, tucked neatly beside, over, and around the mountainside on one end and stretched out beside a great ocean bordering the other.

Simon was right about the different sizes of people here, although most were astoundingly tall with shoulders just as broad. Some even had extra fingers and toes, such as one man in particular who also had a second row of teeth that Seth noticed when the giant laughed, sending a booming sound that rattled and bounced between some of the smaller buildings nearby.

Simon stopped every so often to converse with a few people in the market, bargaining and buying some supplies they needed back at the safe house, while Seth marveled at the scenery, and Jason, ever watchful, kept an eye open for trouble of any kind.

Winding their way through the streets, they came to the town edge where the countryside with sparsely placed farms lay over sprawling vast fields. Large animals to match the size of the people here were used to plow fields and haul crops to the market. Turning to take in the scenes before him, he also noticed a large bay with docks to tie off boats; the likes of which he had never seen! The ships were made in a more Viking style design and were absolutely huge. The *Mattie May* could have been placed inside these at least six times over, and she was a large vessel for her time. The fishermen were hauling in small whales and very large sharks as their daily normal catch, along with nets full of smaller fish that surely supplied the more *vertically-challenged* citizens of Garganthera or were eaten as sardines by the others.

Continuing their walk through the streets once again, they came upon a smaller place called *Willie's Pub* that seemed to cater to the smaller folks, although most there were still bigger than even Seth. They ventured inside for a bit of a drink to quench their parched throats. Seth hadn't realized it, but they had been walking and observing for several hours.

"Well, my boy, what do you think?" Simon asked Seth as they ordered three ales and took a corner table to sit and enjoy the cool beverages.

"This place is unbelievable. The size of those ships, and the catches they were bringing in, I just can't believe it's all real." Seth took a thirsty drink from the massive cup in his hands.

"Yes, a place like this can be overwhelming at first, but there are other places even more spectacular than this. I'm sure in all his years of travels Jason has even seen things I have yet to see. You Peregrines get around a bit more than we Dragoman do."

"I highly doubt that Simon," Jason interjected. "After all, you've been at this peregrination thing thirty years to my eight remember?" he said with a slight grin and a raised eyebrow, drinking some ale from the overly large mug. A one size fits all type container, probably designed to avoid the expense of stocking different sized mugs.

"Now, let's finish up our drinks here and head back. We need to get you two prepared and lined up for your journey tomorrow. We need to find where and when your returning storm will be, and make sure you know how to complete your mission. Getting into the temple will not be easy. Especially since only certain people are allowed into The Holy of Holies," Simon finished saying, sipping some of the cool liquid from his mug.

"Jason, do you have a plan for that? You are the specialist here," Seth asked.

"Well, I think I've got it figured out. With the history of the temple and its workings laid out in the Bible, it shouldn't be too hard to formulate a plan. Besides, I did some web searching last night and discovered that there were most likely underground tunnels leading into the temple." Jason downed the rest of the liquid in his mug and leaned back in his chair, arms crossed against his barrel chest awaiting the other men to finish. "The only thing we really have to worry about is being seen entering the Holy of Holies. It is after all sacred, and only certain men were allowed in. Not only that, but if you weren't sanctified by God, He would strike you dead. I figure since this is God's mission, we shouldn't have any trouble with that." Jason smiled at the look on Seth's face when he mentioned God striking men dead for entering unsanctified. "Besides, I plan on praying very hard that God will just move all obstacles out of the way for this one."

"You really think it could be that simple? That God will just...open a way?" Seth asked unbelieving, filing away to question Jason later about what web searching was.

"Seth, if you could only have seen even just a few of the things that I have and how God just works things out on some of these missions, you'd understand what I'm saying."

Jason spoke with such animation and feeling that Seth wondered if he would ever understand.

"You'll see Seth. You think what you see here is miraculous? This is just the tip of the iceberg. You are about to be taken on the journey of a lifetime. Especially since you'll be awake for it this time."

Seth listened intently as Jason spoke about God and his previous missions and watched the expressions that flit across his features. If the inflection in Jason's voice wasn't enough to convince him, then the complete look of reverence and awe that washed over his face as he spoke should have been. Seth wasn't sure what to expect, but he decided that he had better be ready for anything.

"Well, all right then," Seth said, draining the last of his mug. "Let's go be amazed."

The men stood and exited *Willie's Pub* heading back to Simon's the same way they had entered Garganthera. Seth was growing apprehensive just because of the unknown factor. He had to admit, it was all very interesting, excitement growing in the pit of his stomach. All this adventure and new worlds was amazing, no doubt. But he'd never forget Caroline, no matter where he went or what he saw. She was what was important to him, and he would use anything and everything he saw, heard, and learned to try and get back to her.

They spent the better part of the evening preparing for the next day's journey, packing essential tools, easy prep meals, water, and an appropriate change of clothing for the time period. They also went over the plan to enter the temple and practiced general conversations with each other in the local native tongue should the need for conversation arise. After dinner, they retired to the map room with their coffee, and looked for storms by which to enter and exit the time period. Locating the place and time that they needed to arrive, they made sure to leave themselves a few days between storms to accomplish the mission at hand, just in case they failed the first attempt at retrieving the artifact.

Deciding they had best head to bed, Simon led them in prayer for a restful night's sleep and safe travels the following morning, with Seth wondering all the while if he or Jason would get that restful sleep. They said their goodnights, each heading off to their own rooms.

Seth was a bit wound up from the day's events and anticipation for what was to come the next morning. He decided to do a bit of reading before bed, hoping it would relax him enough to fall asleep. He scanned the room for a book when his eyes landed on a Bible that Simon had lying on a writing desk by the window. Seth picked up the book, running a hand along the smooth cover and lay down on the bed. After getting comfortable, he looked toward the ceiling and began a conversation with God.

"I suppose since I am working for you, I should at least get to know what all this is about." He opened the book — feeling the thinness and what seemed like frailty of the pages— and began reading at Genesis. He read the better part of Genesis chapters 1 and 2 when the day's events overcame his tired body and he drifted off the sleep.

*My prayer is not that You take them out of the
world but that You protect them from the evil one.
They are not of the world, even as I am not of it.*

John 17:15-16

Chapter 10

Sleep had not been Seth's friend the night before, nor had it been Jason's. It seemed they were confined to just a few hours precious rest each night. The two men met bright and early in the kitchen as had become the custom. Jason already had the coffee made and was also placing some biscuits in the oven to bake when Seth appeared. Seth headed for the refrigerator and took out butter, jelly, and creamer placing it on the table. The men sat and talked about the mission ahead as they waited on Simon to wake for breakfast. They didn't have to wait too long before he made an appearance claiming the coffee and biscuits wafting through the house enticed him from his dreams.

The three men sat and conversed over breakfast well into the late morning hours, making sure that all possible scenarios were covered. Being satisfied with the mission plans, Jason and Seth returned to their rooms to change into appropriate period clothing and grab their packs and weapons. They would head to the charging station within the hour and be off on their peregrination by noon.

Once inside the cave of the hidden charging station, Jason went over with Seth what he would experience with time travel.

"You won't get PS like before, but you may still experience some light headedness when you first exit. Even though peregrination is quick, things do speed by when inside the portal. The jump lasts about a total of ten seconds, but when you first travel it can seem like forever, especially if you experience any dizziness. When you come out on the other side you are inside a storm, normally in the middle or on the backside of it, so you do experience some of the impact. The ten seconds allows you to judge the best possible exit area so try to stay alert. I'll lead us out on this one so you can see what I mean."

Simon turned on the coils and the noise inside the room escalated as the portal began to open.

"You ready man?" Jason yelled over the hum of the Tesla coils to the apprehensive looking Seth.

"Do I have a choice?" Seth asked pointedly, looking at Jason.

"Not really," he answered with a wide toothy grin, shaking his head, and slapping Seth in the chest with the back of his hand. "Let's go!" He motioned Seth forward with a wave of his hand and head.

"God speed boys!" Simon yelled over the noise as the opening to the portal between the coils reached full capacity. Seth could feel the electricity in the air, the hair on his arms and legs tingled and reached straight out toward the static mingling around them. He and Jason donned their robes and hoods and adjusted their gear to make sure nothing would fall off. *I must be going crazy,* Seth thought. *To run into an electrical field such as this was completely mental, deadly to be sure.* If he had not seen Alec and Odessa do just this very thing yesterday, he may not have believed it possible. The trust he had to give all of his new-found friends was unreal to say the least. These people actually held his life in their hands several times over already just in the four days he had known them. Even still, he felt closer to Jason and Simon than he had ever felt with any other man, including Matt Walker. Matt had been a good man but wasn't much one for talking. He taught Seth and was as kind as a sea captain aboard a ship of unruly men could be. But that was as far as his kindness had gone. Even though he had taken Seth in during his younger years at sea, he had still been only his Captain. These men had become closer than any family he had ever known except for his grandmother and Caroline.

Seth took a deep steadying breath, gave Jason a nod, and off they went. With Jason leading, they both ran straight into the center of the electrified air and into the portal. Once inside, still moving quickly ever forward toward the other end, Seth could see different colors of light whizzing by along both sides of the portal's interior. He could also make out shapes like blurry buildings or objects flying by. The scenes, ever changing, appeared to be other places or time periods. Could there be periods between where they left and where they were headed? He made a mental note to question Jason or Simon about this later as well.

Communication inside the portal was all but impossible. The noise inside the portal was as loud as the electrified charging station they just left through. Visual communication was all they had. Seth focused on keeping an eye on Jason and the exit and not being distracted by the pieces of civilizations whizzing past.

All of a sudden, they were outside the portal and inside an intense haboob, sand grating across their exposed arms like hornet stings, strong wind gusts blowing their robes nearly sideways. Seth could barely see Jason's outline against the darkness, although technically, it was approximately noon here as well. The storm was so intense and the sand so thick it was like dusk. Jason turned to look at Seth and motioned him toward a small building just to the right of them. He couldn't make out what the sign on the overhang read. Jason disappeared through a door and Seth followed, hoping that whatever was on the other side, he was ready to encounter.

Seth stepped through the doorway into a small narrow hallway that opened into a larger room lined with tables, chairs, and a counter. It appeared that they were inside a diner of sorts. There was also a counter with a stairwell that ascended to another level just to the right of the diner, possibly housing rooms to let. That would explain the board full of very large keys hanging just above the counter.

They brushed at the sand clinging to their clothing and hair before entering the establishment's main area. Jason walked to the counter for the diner side and inquired after two hot meals and the possibility of renting a room. Seth watched and listened as Jason spoke to the barman who looked at Seth with a bit of nervousness. Could it just be his size that intimidated the man? Seth was used to that reaction and he hoped that was all it was. Jason finished his conversation and they retired to a corner table in a darker part of the establishment to await their meals.

"Well, how do you feel, any dizziness?" Jason inquired after Seth.

"No, none at all. It felt like being at sea during a rough storm. I'm quite accustomed to that," Seth replied, taking in his surroundings while slipping his pack over his head and off his shoulder, laying it next to his feet on the floor. His strap lay across his bent knee just under the table's edge. Jason followed suit, keeping his pack close to his feet due to little street urchins that were cunning at snatching anything unattended for long.

"We'll wait the storm out here and eat our lunch. Probably go ahead and grab a room as well. I believe we are fairly close to our *objective* here," Jason said, careful to not mention the temple since their food had been delivered by a young woman at that particular moment.

Seth stared down at his plate. "Fish huh?"

His plate had two large baked fish, with heads and skins intact, two fist size rolls of bread, and a grits-like consistency side item.

"What, you don't like fish?" Jason asked, a smile forming on his lips at the look on Seth's face.

"I've just had my fill of it all those years at sea." Seth grinned at Jason and ate his meal regardless. The meal at least was very tasty and filling, and by the time they finished eating the sandstorm had all but ceased completely and the sun was shining brightly outside the windows located just below the ceiling's edge. They pulled on their packs, deciding to wait on securing a room, and headed out the door to investigate the area and see what course of action would be best to achieve their goal.

Stepping out into the sunlit street, the men headed in the direction of the temple, unaware of the shadowy figure lurking in the alleyway just around the building's corner.

Watching the men, the cloaked figure walked up the street behind them, blending in with the people milling about the street's marketplace.

Jason abruptly stopped, causing Seth to almost run into him. Jason turned to look into the crowd of people behind him, searching the faces.

"What are you looking for?" Seth questioned, following Jason's gaze.

"I feel like we're being watched," Jason replied as he turned and continued in the direction they were going.

"How do you know with all these people around here? Any number could just be looking at us," Seth stated.

"God gives me a feeling, an intuition of sorts. Usually when I get this feeling, I'm right. And it's usually demonic.

It's a provision we are given, a gift, to help aid us and keep us safe. Yours will likely kick in soon as well. This being your first real mission and journey you have more distractions," Jason replied, keeping a watchful eye on the people around them as they moved about the city's dusty cobblestoned streets.

Weaving their way through the tightly packed buildings, they stepped out into a larger area at the edge of the city. Roads packed with people led out toward a large, gated, courtyard, the top and roof of buildings just visible over the tops of the wall that wrapped around the entire outer courtyard.

It only took about a ten-minute walk to reach the wall. Walking through a large double-door gate into the outer courtyard, Seth could see the outside walls of the inner courtyard. He knew that's what it was from the scaled drawings given to them by Simon to study the temple layout for the mission. The architecture was truly amazing. Stone and marble graced the building and columns that supported the roofs stone overhang. The marble columns rested upon a large stoop at the top of a staircase leading into the inner area of the temple. At the bottom of the steps, approximately twenty feet or so away, stood another raised stone area with steps and a flat angled slope leading up to the top. Animals were walked up the slope and sacrificed upon an altar at the top of the platform.

Seth was amazed at the size of the area and temple, and the amount of people roaming the open courtyard. Animals being led by ropes, pulled in on carts and in cages, all being led to slaughter. Seth couldn't understand why these people would take the time, energy, and money to do this. Why was this so important a task to these people?

Jason noticed the questioning look on Seth's face as he looked around and watched the people go about their business.

"Aren't you glad we don't have to take such extreme measures anymore?" Jason stated more than asked.

"What do you mean?" Seth said, his gaze never leaving the scene playing out before him.

"Animal sacrifices," Jason clarified, getting Seth's attention. "We don't have to do this," he said, motioning around them at the happenings.

"Why are they sacrificing these animals?"

"To atone for their sins. See, we are in the year 587 BC. Jesus hasn't been born yet. These people have to atone for their sins through sacrifices because Jesus hasn't become that sacrifice yet," Jason said as they walked around the yard viewing the activities and taking in the workings of the temple and all the entrances and exits.

"I believe we'll have to finish this conversation later. I have a feeling it is a bit too deep for light banter in the middle of a mission," Seth's grinned.

Jason and Seth, trying not to draw attention to themselves, roamed the courtyard making mental notes of the amount of people working in and around the temple. They took up a space out of view, and over the next few hours each watched certain places and people to try and gauge their next course of action. They had the layout already, but the plans they had were only speculative based upon the details of the Bible. Many men over the years had come to their own conclusions on the exact layout of Solomon's Temple, so a few pieces of paper compared to the real thing could be quite different. And since the temple had been, or would be, completely destroyed by Nebuchadnezzar in less than a year, there was never any way to know what it truly had looked like until now.

Trying to appear like they belonged as much as all the other travelers and admirers who were there to see the colossal undertaking by Solomon three hundred years before, they entered the inner courtyard. It was drawing close to nightfall, so they watched when the last person would be allowed into the temple courtyard. Walking the inside of the temple cloisters and open yards Seth couldn't help but be mesmerized by the ornate beauty of the carvings on the doors and walls. Palm trees, cherubim, and flowers adorned almost every available space in intricate detail. To say it was beautiful was a massive understatement. As they walked, they came upon the Holy Place where the tables of bread and the Altar of Incense were placed. Also located within this area were the Chamber of Secrets—the room set aside for anonymous giving for the needy, and the Chamber of Utensils—a room for needed supplies for use in the temple. There were rooms and doors located everywhere, and they piqued Seth's curiosity. As they continued through the room to the back end, they came upon two doors that were covered in gold and as intricately carved as everything else. It had to be the Holy of Holies—the very place where God had dwelt amongst His people.

Seth let out a low whistle as he gazed upon the doors, grabbing Jason's attention.

"Pretty impressive place huh?" Jason offered, understanding the awe that Seth was feeling. This was also his first journey to the temple. If Seth was impressed, imagine how much more it meant to a believer to be standing in Solomon's Temple, soon to walk into the Holy of Holies and place his hands on the Ark of the Covenant, to obtain the Staff of Moses. Jason felt overwhelmed, feeling his knees buckle slightly at the thought. He completely understood Odessa's chagrin at giving up this mission. He would never be able to do the feeling justice in relaying what it was like should she ask, and he was sure she would.

It was growing ever darker and the priests and porters began ushering people toward the doors and the gates to exit the outer court. Jason and Seth watched as they too were ushered out, unsure as to whether this was the normal practice or if it was due to the possibility of war with Nebuchadnezzar that had everyone being more cautious. Fortunately, their presence hadn't seemed to draw any unwanted attention so they knew how close they could get to the Holy of Holies without question. Literally to the doors leading into the throne room of God. Getting through those doors would be the ultimate challenge.

Before exiting the outer courtyard and out the temple wall gate, Jason inquired of one of the porters the time that the gates opened in the morning for worship and re-entry into the temple. The porter told them that entry to worship was at dawn, then they turned and headed back to the inn where they had lunch to procure a room for the night.

As they walked the city streets in the moonlight and lit windowpanes, Jason got the feeling again that they were being followed. There was no use searching the crowds since darkness made visibility almost impossible past the barely lit streets. He would just have to be vigilant and on guard at all times until the mission was over. He would discuss security measures with Seth once inside their room.

They entered the inn once again, rented a room, and ordered their dinner to be sent to their room at the earliest availability. They climbed the steep narrow staircase to the third level of the building, and entered a small room with two beds, a small table separating them, and a wash basin with water placed on top of the table. There was a window in the center of the room just above the bedside table that, should the need arise, they should be able to exit through. They closed the door and secured the lock as they both brushed at the dust on their clothing, removing their packs and robes and tossing them on the beds. They then washed their hands and faces in the water basin, after which Jason peered out the window, glancing down toward the street to see what lay below before sitting upon the bed. Seth took up residence on the opposite one. Jason had just removed the building plans for the temple when a knock came at the door. He quickly tossed the plans back into his pack as Seth stood, inquiring of who was at the door and cautiously opened it to a young servant boy delivering dinner. He received the food and gave the boy a tip for bringing it to their room. The boy, seemingly overjoyed by the gesture, thanked him emphatically and quickly left, smiling at the money in his hand as he went. Seth smiled to himself as he watched the boy skip away and run down the stairwell. Closing the door and securing the lock, he turned and resumed his place upon the bed, taking his dinner plate in hand. They quickly ate their meals and spent the next few hours looking over the temple plans and the printout of the hidden passageways believed to lie underneath the temple. They discussed how and when to attempt to retrieve the staff, and some possible scenarios to help with whomever had taken an interest in them earlier.

Tired from the busyness of the day and the leap through time, the men turned in early, hoping to maybe get one good night's sleep. Seth, not accustomed to the noise of the busy diner and inn just two floors below, had a hard time getting to sleep. He wearily pulled himself out of bed after an hour or two of tossing around to glance out of the room's one window. As he pulled open the shutter and looked out into the night, he took in a slow deep breath of the cool night air, and closing his eyes, spoke Caroline's name into the light breeze passing by, imagining her standing there with him. When he opened his eyes, he looked down at the busy street and saw a figure standing just across from the room. They apparently couldn't see him standing in the window for the darkness of the room because they didn't move, possibly due to the lack of moonlight occasionally peeking through the broken clouds floating across the night sky. They just stood there, stock still, watching, waiting. *For what?* Seth tried focusing on the figure again to better make out a description for later use if needed. It appeared to be a woman, that he was sure of. As he leaned forward and stepped to the side to get a better angle, the woman stepped out into the light of the street. Seth's breath caught in his throat. It wasn't possible! Was he dreaming?

"Caroline!" Seth leaned out the window and yelled her name. The woman glanced up at him and turned to walk up the street.

Jason stirred from his sleep as he heard Seth calling someone's name. Seth, tripping over things in the darkness of the room was scrambling to get dressed to catch up with Caroline.

"Seth what are you doing?" Jason asked hurriedly, trying to calm Seth down.

"I just saw Caroline. She was standing in the street below looking up at the window," he said, sitting on the bed and pulling on his shoes.

"Seth it wasn't Caroline, how could it be? I mean, think about where we are, man?" Jason answered calmly yet sternly.

"We're here, why couldn't she be? Besides, I know who I saw Jason! I don't understand it myself, but I know I saw her." Seth stood, ready to bolt out the door.

"Seth, stop!" Jason stood placing his hands on each of Seth's shoulders as his eyes adjusted to the dim moonlight filtering in through the open window.

"I'm telling you it couldn't be her. Did she hear you call her name?"

"Yes, I... I think so. Why?" Seth asked exasperated.

"Because if it was Caroline, and she saw and heard you, don't you think she would have answered?"

"I don't know, Jason, but I've got to find out," Seth ran out the door.

"Seth!" Jason called to a disappearing, unresponsive Seth. He let out a sigh, pulled on his clothes, and grabbed his and Seth's weapons, running out the door after Seth as quickly as possible, the feeling of being watched earlier in the day returning to his mind.

Seth bounded down the narrow stairwell, through the dining area, and out the door, turning the corner of the building where their room overlooked the street. *She was gone. But where?* He had to think, to remember which way she went. He stopped to slow his train of thought.

"Seth!" he heard Jason yell.

"Over here," Remembering which way she had walked, he took off in that direction just as Jason caught a glimpse of him headed down the alleyway.

"I have a very bad feeling about this," Jason said out loud to himself as he took off running after Seth.

But mark this, there will be
terrible times in the last days.

2 Timothy 3:1

Chapter 11

*Barriers Edge, Garganthera, Simon Lane's
charging station, Fourth Dimension*

Simon set the Tesla coils to automatically shut down after he entered the jump site for his journey to meet with the other Dragoman. He much preferred traveling over land through the barrier's gateways, but that would take too much time, time he didn't have. So, storm travel it was. He had packed his own travel supplies before their trek to the charging station for Seth and Jason knowing he wouldn't be returning home today. Now that Jason and Seth were off on their own adventure, hopefully safely so, he needed to be off on his own.

Inputting his destination coordinates to Casablanca, Morocco, in the year 1950, and setting the timer for shutdown, he grabbed his pack and staff, and jumped into the charged air through the portal, and out the other side of a major thunderstorm taking place. His first stop would be to pick up Safra Driscoll and transport her to the fourth-dimension plane for the meeting. Safra was neither Dragoman nor Peregrine, and so therefore had no way of receiving grid-mail or traveling by storm alone. She was an old, trusted friend and colleague who had been helping them all on their missions for the glory of God. She had become a believer at a very young age, and following in the footsteps of her father, continued to help as much as she could.

Safra's faith and devotion to God amazed Simon. He literally saw miracles everyday through magic and Peregrinations so believing was easier for him. She lived in the first dimension in a very poor, and treacherous part of town where miracles or even regular kindness was mostly void. But that did not stop her faith or devotion to God. The heavenly Father had given Safra a great gift, the gift of sight beyond that of any other human. She could see many things in her realm as well as many other realms. Many a Peregrine and Dragoman had been found and saved because of Safra's gifts. Simon hoped that she could find one more such missing person.

The torrential rain made it near impossible to see where he was going, and he hoped that it would soon end. The most intense point of a storm; which was what was needed to peregrinate; was usually directly in the center. Meaning that depending on how long it lasted, he still had halfway to go through it. He could barely make out a little doorway off to one side of the street and decided to duck inside to wait out the storm. Once he was inside and had closed the door, he heard the familiar jingle of the unique bells and realized where he was. He was actually in Safra's shopfront. What were the odds of that happening? Was it coincidental him walking out so close to his destination, or did God plan it that way? Turning to greet his old friend, he realized that no one else was there. *Where was Safra?* It wasn't like her to leave her shop unattended in the middle of the afternoon. Maybe she had gone to her living quarters to wait out the storm knowing full well business would be nonexistent until it was over. Simon, having been here many times, knew which way to go. Heading through the maze of supplies and items she sold, he made his way to the back of the shop, calling Safra's name along with his own so as not to frighten or startle her.

"Safra, it's Simon. Are you here?"

Simon stopped walking, suddenly sensing something out of place. He took his walking staff in his right hand and, grabbing the top end which was carved to fit his hand perfectly; he slowly pulled the sword from the center of the staff revealing a thin, sharp, blade, much like that of a fencing sword. Wielding the weapon in his left hand, and his staff in his right like a club, he carefully continued down the narrow hall toward Safra's home in the back. As he reached the curtained doorway, using his staff as an extended arm, he pushed back the curtain and slowly stepped into the candlelit room. Safra was lying on the floor unconscious, blood trickling down the side of her face, her shop torn apart. Herbs, mortars, pestles, and books strewn across the floor and surfaces. Simon carefully looked around to make sure no one else was still in the room. Satisfied they were alone, he bent down to check Safra's vital signs. She was alive but still unconscious. It looked as though she had been hit with something on the head just above her left temple at the hairline. Safra was a tiny woman, making it easy for Simon to lift her into his arms, dead weight and all, and place her on the couch just around the corner. After depositing her on the settee, he returned to the front of the shop locking the door and turning the sign around to closed. He then headed back to the living area, walking over to the sink in the kitchen he grabbed a bowl of water and a clean washcloth. He passed a rack of healing herbs and spices Safra often used in her business and grabbed what he might need to patch Safra up. He pulled up a chair beside the couch and began tending to the older woman's wounds. *Who could have done this to her?* She was up in years but Safra was no fool and not easily misled. Could this have been the work of demons? Did they know about Safra? She was a skilled warrior if need be, but in this time period she was all of sixty-nine years old, and certainly no match for demonic forces.

Simon had her wounds cleaned and bandaged by the time she awoke from unconsciousness.

"Safra, it's me, Simon," he offered, just in case she didn't recognize him right off due to any unforeseen injuries.

Safra smiled at Simon despite her wounds.

"Hello old friend," she said, slightly wincing at the pain caused by the injuries.

"How do you feel?" Simon questioned, watching her pupils for dilation and any signs of a concussion.

"Other than a massive headache and a few aches and pains, I feel just dandy," Safra replied, trying to sit up.

"Now Safra, you of all people know better than to rush an injury," he stated, trying to stop her assent.

"Yes, I know," she said with a bit of frustration lacing her voice. "That is why I know I am capable of sitting up at least." She pulled herself up to a sitting position.

Simon smiled at her persistence and helped her to sit up.

"What happened here, Safra? Do you remember?"

"Well, I was just fixing to close the shop due to the impending thunderstorm, when a group of young people came through the door. I informed them that I was closing early today when they circled around me forcing me here into the back. Knowing I have an herbalist shop, they were looking for opium. They were angry when I told them I had nothing like that here and they attacked me. I did get in a few good shots before they knocked me out though." She finished her story with a giggle and a smile, causing her to wince in pain at the movement.

"Well then, there's that anyway." Simon smiled at his old friend, relieved that it had not been a demonic attack. However, this would not due. Simon would do his best to find the people responsible for this. Safra was a well-known healer and beloved member of this community. When her neighbors caught wind of this happening, they would surely help find, and take care of, whoever did this to an honored elder. It may not be the best part of town, but those that lived here tended to watch out for each other.

"Are you sure you're all right then?"

"Yes Simon, I'm fine."

"Regardless, we'll take a day or so to let you rest a bit before traveling. Besides, that will give me time to find who did this and make sure it never happens again. I did allow some traveling time for mishaps, so it won't make us late for the council meeting," Simon said, standing.

"Now that I've seen to you, I'll get busy cleaning this mess up. Afterward, we'll take to the streets and ask some questions. If you're up to it?"

Simon busied himself cleaning the mess made by the thieves, as Safra cooked them a light dinner, insisting she was well enough to handle the task. When he finished and they had eaten dinner, it was nearly six p.m. and the storm had settled down hours earlier. The two of them took to the streets, enquiring of Safra's neighbors about any other such happenings lately and who was involved. Everyone they spoke with ensured Safra that they would keep an eye out for the people she described, vowing to come to her aid if necessary. Simon discovered there were five teenaged kids that attacked Safra that day and that they were from a gang that decided to take up residence in the surrounding area a few months back. They had grown brazen and had started attacking the older shop owners in the area, Safra being the fifth one attacked in the last two weeks.

The events of the day and the walk after dinner had taken its toll on Safra, so she excused herself to turn in early due to fatigue and a returning headache. This gave Simon the opportunity to take to the streets himself without worrying her. After seeing her safely to bed, he made sure her home was secure, placing a protection spell over her doorways and windows. No one would be getting in there tonight. He didn't use magic much in the first dimension for fear of being caught, but he would chance it for Safra's safety. Simon, with his staff in hand and his pack thrown across his chest and shoulders, pulled the hood up on his robe and ventured into the Moroccan streets in search of the offenders. He wasn't sure yet what he would do if he found them, but hopefully it would eventually come to him. He offered up a prayer for guidance and safety, and walked through the crowded streets, carefully searching, watching, and listening, enquiring of the neighborhood vendors of the gang's where-abouts.

He had been walking the streets for about an hour when he noticed a commotion at another shop just a few blocks up on a darker side street. As Simon watched, he realized it must be the same five teens that had terrorized Safra and the others over the last few weeks. What to do about it though was the question? Simon thought about the time period and part of the world where he was currently. He recalled a legend dealing with Moroccan culture that parents used to terrify their children into obedience. It was about a woman named Aisha Kandisha who lured mostly men, but women as well, to their death. She was said to be extremely beautiful, even though she had the legs of a camel. Once she had the men in her grasp, she turned into an old hag and tore her victims to shreds. Legend had it that she never spoke, but he would have to say something to get his point across.

Simon ducked into a dark alleyway on the side of the shop they were terrorizing so as not to be seen and, using his magic, cast a spell transforming his outward appearance to an image of Aisha Kandisha he had seen years before. Then, he stepped out of the alleyway; glad for the cover of night; and stepped into the shop. Simon quickly took note of the situation. The shopkeeper lay unconscious by the counter as the teens ripped through his shop with abandon. The shop's door chimes caught the attention of the teens, stopping them in their tracks. Their faces went almost white with fear as he spoke in a threatening voice, pointing at them.

"You have defiled this land and your people! You shall all turn from your wicked ways, or I, Aisha Kandisha, shall hunt you down for the rest of your days until you all are destroyed!"

He barely finished his speech before they all ran away in terror, vowing to never return and to change their evil doings, tripping over themselves and everything they had thrown to the shop floor as they went.

Once clear, Simon bent forward in booming laughter, slapping his knee as he recalled the terror on their faces. Superstition was a powerful thing, especially in the earlier years when education wasn't as prevalent and didn't reach the lower classes of people. Not to mention, Aisha Kandisha was a powerful Moroccan legend, even in the current years.

Simon transformed himself back to normal and went to check on the shopkeeper. He was alive, but he wasn't sure how badly he had been injured. He stepped out onto the sidewalk in front of the shop in search of help for the man. Several of his neighbors were coming toward the shop. They had been watching the commotion from their own locked doors and windows in fear. Once they saw the teens leave, they ventured out to help. Simon explained only that he had tried to help and had managed to scare the teens off but that the shopkeeper was injured. He excused himself, knowing they would tend to the injured man, and returned to Safra's.

He doubted the people here would have any more trouble from that group of kids again. And, sure they would tell their story to anyone who would listen, doubted anyone else would brave terrorizing this particular area for quite some time.

The next morning, Simon told Safra of the happenings the night before. She listened intently, giggling at the images playing out in her head.

"I do believe you and your neighbors will be free from bullying for some time, Safra. How are you feeling this morning?"

"I am feeling much better Simon, thank you," she said with a smile. "Now, how about we get ready for our journey?"

"If you're sure you're feeling up to the trip?" he asked her, concern evident in his voice and expression.

"Yes, yes, I'm fine. Stop worrying over me," she said, smiling at her old friend's concern.

"All right then, let's get packed up and head out to catch that thunderstorm that'll be brewing tomorrow in Marrakech." Simon stood to start getting supplies gathered and packed. Safra joined him and the two spent the next several hours moving about her shop, packing whatever spices, herbs, and supplies she carried when making a journey and readying her place to be closed down, unsure of when she would be returning.

They departed Safra's about ten a.m. and decided to grab a bite to eat at a local diner so as to not have to spend time cleaning up. After brunch, they headed to Casa Voyageurs station to catch the noon train to Marrakech.

Simon always liked to leave himself time in between travel points to allow for any hiccups or disruptions like what happened at Safra's. They would arrive in plenty of time before the storm hit tomorrow morning.

Simon and Safra boarded the train, securing a private car to discuss trip plans and the Dragoman meeting. They stowed their bags on the overhead racks and settled into their seats across from each other. The train pulled out of the station just before noon for the nearly three-hour ride to Marrakech, giving them ample time to talk and catch up. About an hour into the trip, Simon had an overwhelming feeling that they were not alone. He could sense a demonic force very near and held his finger to his lips to alert Safra who instantly fell quiet, watching and listening. Simon stood and grasped the handle of the compartment door. He pulled his sword from the sheath of his staff, and brandishing it with his left hand, quickly slid the door open stepping out into the train's hallway. There was no one in the hall. Simon turned back to the compartment room and noticed something flapping in the wind outside the top edge of the window. It appeared to be the edge of a duster coat or robe. Was someone on top of the train just above their compartment? Simon stepped back into their room quietly pointing at the roof to Safra. She stood and walked to the door behind Simon, pulling it shut. Simon softly whispered a revealing spell, waving his unoccupied hand toward the roof of the car. The roof of the train vanished, appearing like a glass, two-way, oval mirror to reveal a man perched above them. He seemed poised to break through the window at any moment to surprise Simon and Safra and overtake them. Simon quickly spoke again, and the mirror vanished to reveal an actual hole in the roof, enabling him to take the demon by surprise, stabbing him as he tried to enter the car through the now gaping hole. The demon fell backward off the side of the still speeding train. Simon stood for a moment waiting to see if anyone else would appear through the roof's hole. He stepped on top of the seats in the compartment, and carefully peered over the open edge of the roof to make sure there were no more of them, but it appeared he had been alone. Simon stowed his sword in its sheath, then spoke another spell to reseal the hole in the top of the train.

"Well, that worked awfully well didn't it?" he said, surprise and relief both evident in his voice.

"We can't hope for better than that for an altercation with a demon now can we? I wonder what that was about?" Simon spoke looking at Safra with raised eyebrows. "I can't imagine why they are hunting us right now or why they wish to stop us. It makes me wonder if the attack on you back at your place was coincidental or linked with this somehow? We're going to have to be extra careful and on guard the rest of the trip." He grabbed their packs from the overhead stow, placing his on his back and handing Safra hers.

Safra replied, "Perhaps it is about the lost Peregrine? Maybe the demons know of their existence and wish to stop me from revealing them. If the lost is found, then the hunt for the pieces of armor begins. Lucifer would stop at nothing to prevent the final battle from taking place, would he not?"

"I do believe you're right, Safra. I just pray you can locate whoever it is before the demons do." Paranoia evident in his voice.

He and Safra decided to walk the train for a while, hoping the crowds of people in the open cars would ward off any future attacks. Hopefully, there was no one else following them.

And now these three remain: faith, hope,
and love. But the greatest of these is love.

1 Corinthians 13:13

Chapter 12

Northern Africa, Mali, 1795

Alec and Odessa, pacing themselves through the storm headed for the nearest shelter they could find to escape the dust of the haboob. Ducking into a dilapidated shed on the outskirts of whatever small town they had landed in, they waited out the storm until it died down enough to be able to see where they were going and breathe actual air into their lungs.

Sand blew through the many cracks in the boarded walls and in and around the still barely hanging door. The building offered little protection, but it was better than being outside in the intense wind and blistering sand. They rested against the most solid wall they could find, squatting against the floor and pulling their robes around their bodies and over their heads for more protection. They were only huddled in the building for about fifteen minutes when the storm slowed enough to allow for decent traveling.

Shaking the excess sand from their hair and robes, they exited the building and looked for a town sign to find out where they had ended up. They knew they were in Mali, but unsure of exactly where the storm had carried them.

Odessa asked an older man that was walking past them, "Excuse me, but can you tell me how far Timbuktu is from here?"

"Just about a half an hour's walk south and you'll get there."

"And how far is it to the Niger River and a town where we can acquire a boat?"

"Just past Timbuktu about ten miles south."

They thanked him and headed in the direction they needed to go. It was a hot, dry, dusty, walk but at least the haboob had completely stopped now. They were glad for the cotton robes they wore to keep the blaring hot sun off their backs and heads, and for the water bladders that hung at their sides. They would have to make sure they stocked up on plenty of drinking water for the remainder of their journey once they got to Timbuktu.

One of the great things about having access to time-travel is the amazing, detailed maps from every decade and century, and the mileage that was available to them. They knew almost to the minute how long the river journey should take them, as long as they didn't encounter any problems along the way. African travel, especially some of the unexplored areas, was treacherous during this time period. But Simon wanted to make sure the *Goddelikheid Crucible* was still there. If they got to it just after Mungo Park's photo was taken they should definitely find it, and all the hard work of clearing a path through the dense jungle and cave entrance would have been done for them. They would just have to rely on God to get them through safely.

Alec and Odessa both had brought guns, both hand and rifle on this journey. The guns weren't necessarily time appropriate, but they looked the part. They just had a few modifications with modern technology to aid them in the success of their trip. They had also each packed a stun gun. It would slow any attackers without lasting damage. Neither Alec nor Odessa wanted to kill anyone, but if the decision was between them and another, the other person would die. They would try wounding before killing if at all possible. Hopefully, it would not come to that, but Mungo Park and many other explorers before and after him, had died doing the very thing they were about to do.

Finally reaching Timbuktu, they stopped in at an eating establishment to find some food and drink to quench their parched throats. They would eat, rest up a bit, and fill up on supplies, but only what they could carry on their persons. They would then discuss whether to travel the majority of the trip by river, or to walk it. The river would be faster, but walking may be safer. They had the approximate location where Mungo was attacked, but they needn't travel that far southeast. The cave where he had located the crucible was further upstream. His second journey had been to explore the remainder of the Niger, it had not been an excavation trip. So perhaps that meant they could avoid the tribe that had attack Mungo and his traveling party.

If Simon's calculations were correct, they would find the crucible in an unmarked cave whose opening would likely be easily accessible now after Park's discovery. He may have hidden the opening somehow, but it should still be easily enterable. Alec and Odessa sat looking over the map of the river and where they should find the cave.

"X marks the spot," Alec whispered, not wanting to attract any unwanted attentions.

"So it does," Odessa said smiling, thoroughly enjoying the ice-cold beverage in her hand. Using a handkerchief from her pack, she wiped the cool condensation from the glass to use across her face and the back of her neck.

"It is getting late already. Perhaps we should get a room until we are guaranteed more daylight. It would be suicide to attempt this tonight, journeying into the dark, dangerous, unpredictable, jungle," Alec said playfully, noticing the discomfort she was experiencing with all the sand that was stuck to their skin.

Odessa smiled at him from behind the drink in her hand. "I agree. It would be suicide to go out there tonight. Plus, that will give us more time to plot our course and resupply. Besides, you know full well I could do with a bath. I also know that you are probably as miserable as I am with all this sand still stuck in unmentionable places." She grinned, finishing her glass, and stood to go in search of a room to be let and a bath to be had.

Alec, following Odessa's lead, stood and donned his pack. They walked out of the establishment and southward down the street, taking in the activity of the major trading post for many people in this area of Africa —salt, gold, and slaves being amongst the more popular trades. It was centrally located between the western part of the river and the southeastern part, not to mention the mining areas of Nigeria to the far north. Timbuktu saw a lot of tourism and its population was near one hundred thousand at this particular time in history.

Odessa and Alec avoided the slave trading stages set up in the city. She didn't need any unpleasant reminders from her past creeping into her subconscious. She needed to stay focused while on their mission. She had been at this peregrination thing a long time now but being this close to slave trade tended to quickly make her recall the past evils done to her. Plus, if she saw anyone being mistreated he was afraid she would have to take matters into her own hands, and that could get both her *and* him killed.

Alec watched the streets cautiously as men dealing with the slave trade roamed everywhere. He and Dee were well covered by their robes, not much being visible, but Dee was an extremely beautiful woman and didn't realize the attention she unknowingly drew to herself. He would have to watch and make sure no one seemed to take a particular interest in her. She could handle herself well to be sure, but a woman with her skills that looked like she did would draw even more attention and quite possibly a higher price, making her very valuable. She would die first, as would he, to protect her.

"Alec, look there!" Odessa's excited words drew him out of his thoughts and his careful inspection of their immediate surroundings. He looked in the direction that she was pointing and saw what had captured her attention. There was a small herd of elephants roaming the streets.

That's not something you see every day, he thought.

Odessa loved animals. She had a great respect for all living things, and a tenderness for anything hurting. She had a tough exterior, but once you got past that to her heart she was a softy. Elephants were one of her favorite animals and this particular herd was used as pack and transport animals.

"Let's go see what they would charge to take us to a river town tomorrow?" Odessa said, stepping past him to head in the direction of the elephants. Alec followed her over to the merchant and made a deal with him for his services for bright and early the next day. All the while, Odessa was enjoying herself, petting and playing with the large, gentle, beasts. After securing transportation for the fifteen-mile journey, they went in search of a hotel to rent a room. They always rented one room to make sure people, especially men, believed them to be a couple. Not only did it protect her more on these peregrinations to the past, but one room;

with two beds of course; also aided them in private discussions and quick getaways if necessary. As partners with time-sensitive missions, they couldn't afford to be separated for long or they could miss their next jump site. There were no charging stations in this time period, and they would never leave each other behind.

They rented a room on the second floor overlooking the busy city streets. The room had beautiful, large, French-style doors that opened onto a public balcony, adorned with metal scrolled handrails that wrapped around the whole second floor of the hotel, allowing guests to mingle and walk the length of the hotel above the street on all four sides. On both ends of the hotel, there was a set of metal steps leading down to the street below.

The room was decorated in an African theme, with animal prints, pictures, and statuettes throughout. They did not, however, have a private bath. Each floor of the hotel had two public bathrooms located on separate ends of the hallway.

They settled into their room, then went in search of available bathrooms to clean the dust and dirt from their bodies. Once clean, they dressed casually and went down to the first floor to inquire of a place close to the hotel to have dinner. They didn't often find time on missions to simply sit and enjoy a peaceful, relaxing meal, but this trip seemed to afford them this one small pleasure. They did pack a nicer set of period appropriate clothing on each journey for just such an occasion, or in case role playing was needed. Alec looked at Odessa who was dressed in a turquoise-blue, buttoned, long sleeved, cotton, blouse, and a nice pair of off-white, straight-legged slacks. She never wore dresses just in case she needed to defend herself. They also always packed a weapon somewhere on their persons. They exited the hotel and walked the clatter-board walkways that ran along the sides of the buildings separating the dusty roads from the tourist's shoes. The restaurant wasn't a far walk, and the two slowly strolled up the street arm in arm. They were as comfortable together as any two people could be. If things were different, Alec wondered if they would be able to make it as a couple.

They enjoyed the rest of their evening, just sitting and talking about nothing in particular and dancing to a few songs to the sounds of the restaurant's band. After dinner, they returned to their hotel, entered their room, and walked out onto the balcony to enjoy the sunset as it went down over the roof tops of the city.

Odessa sighed, as the sun disappeared. "We better turn in early, we have a long day ahead."

"True, but this is really nice." Alec grinned at her and she returned his grin.

"Yes. One day we will have many days like this."

"Let's hope."

"It's called faith, Alec. Have faith that God will do as He promised."

She smiled and turned to go inside, taking the first turn at changing into her bedclothes behind the dressing screen located in the corner of the room. They discussed some of the plans for the next morning and climbed into their separate beds.

"Goodnight, Dee." Again, biting his tongue to stop himself from revealing his feelings.

"Goodnight, Alec."

It was nights like this that sometimes drove Alec crazy. To have an evening like they had, to hold Dee in his arms while dancing, and to be this close to her was enough to drive him crazy. He almost always had to implement an immense amount of self-control just to keep from telling her how he felt, pretty much on a daily basis. Tonight, it had been especially hard not to tell her or act on how he felt. He looked up at the ceiling thinking about the life they led because of a God he wasn't sure he was ready to believe in yet. Then again, if it wasn't for this life, he never would have met Odessa in the first place. He needed to get some rest and decided to give the thinking a break for now. It took hours of tossing and turning, but eventually Alec drifted off to sleep.

The next morning, Alec felt a little on edge, sleep had been restless. They left the hotel to meet with their guide, mounted the elephants, and began the trip south. Riding the elephants was slow going, but it was still faster than walking. Not to mention it was a rare treat to be able to do something like this. Most of their peregrinations were spent walking or running to or through their destinations. Either in haste to make it somewhere, or to stay alive from whatever was chasing them.

Alec smiled to himself as his thoughts took him on many a journey he and Dee had experienced together over the years. He looked over at her, watching the pure joy on her face as she sat swaying side to side with each step of the huge animal. The weather so far that morning was mild and pleasant. However, the sun had not been up long and was still low in the sky. By the time they reached the river, it would be close to ten a.m.. It was strange to think how much slower travel was in this period compared to the future; being able to speed across miles in just minutes.

The trip was a pleasant one so far and Alec hoped it would remain so. Most peregrinations had some element of danger to them, causing him to wonder when and where it would rear its ugly head. As they moved closer to the river and Africa's interior, the desert landscape slowly changed to jungle, and danger became more apparent with disease, pests, animals, and natives all playing a possible part in what their futures held.

They reached the river shortly before noon, and as Alec went in search of a boat to rent, Odessa paid the guide the remainder of what they owed and hauled the supplies to the river's edge near the boats. Alec soon returned, pointing to one of the boats tied to a small dock extending out over the water about ten feet. The boat was plenty big enough for the two of them, but small enough to easily navigate with paddles. They stepped into the boat, stowed their packs and supplies under the seats and ends of the boat, and headed upstream.

The caves location was about a twelve-hour boat ride, and then another half-hour trek by foot into the jungle. They would make camp, then at first light make the thirty-minute walk into the jungle by daylight. All in all, they should have the crucible, be back at their end destination on the river, and settled into a small encampment area by nightfall on the second night of river travel.

As they paddled the river they didn't speak. They watched for signs of danger and listened to the sounds of the jungle. The sun grew ever higher in the sky, heating up the day as they traveled the long river. They saw quite a few animals as they traversed the slowly moving currents of the Niger. They watched as a giant python swam by their boat, its long, thick body twice the length of it. Monkeys swung from branch to branch in the tree-tops high overhead along the riverbank, and a few antelope and smaller creatures dipped their heads to brave a drink from the water's edge, cautious of crocodiles and hippos. Their destination drew ever closer as they looked for a place to pull the boat up to the shoreline. They found a spot underneath some tree roots that sprawled out into the water from the higher bank's edge, giving them the ideal spot to hide the boat, just in case someone else might come by and spot it.

They grabbed their packs and supplies, leaving nothing behind; always ready for any scenario, and entered the thick underbrush of the jungle to make camp for the night, making sure to stay as hidden as possible —no fires and no noise. They didn't want to draw attention to themselves with the native headhunters. They woke early the next morning and, making as little noise as possible, headed deeper into the jungle. The thick net of bugs, mostly mosquitoes, buzzed around them making them grateful for the repellent they carried —just one of the little perks from the future they could fit into their packs.

It didn't take them long to find the cave with the artifacts documented in the photograph by Park's group. Once they were inside, they removed the convenient flashlights they carried and inspected the caves interior.

"Look, Alec, there it is." Odessa walked over to where the item lay, Alec following behind.

"Yes. It doesn't seem like much does it?" Alec picked up the large bowl-shaped item, inspecting it.

"No, but then God uses all manner of things. The Bible talks about how He uses the least."

Alec ignored her mention of God. Their conversations always seem to steer in that direction. He secured the item inside Odessa's pack, wrapping it carefully in a thick cloth to protect it from breakage. They replaced their flashlights, secured their packs, and headed back toward the boat, which they found still secure where they left it. They stowed Odessa's pack underneath the seat for safe keeping, climbed inside, pushed off from the bank, and headed downstream this time, retracing their path. They traveled the river uneventfully for the majority of the day until they got close to their end encampment. As they turned the bend in the river they were suddenly under attack. Spears whizzed by the boat with some piercing the boat's exterior shell. Alec and Odessa quickly removed the revolvers they carried in holsters at the small of their backs and fired a few shots into the brush beside the water's edge. They could hear the natives running and yelling in their native dialect, their voices growing distant, fading into the jungle's interior. Feeling as though they had scared them off due to the silence that followed over the next few minutes, Odessa holstered her gun and sat back down to paddle their now slightly damaged boat, once again, to their next destination as Alec kept a steady watch, his gun still in hand. She had only just gotten situated and had picked up the paddle when an arrow flew from the brush into the boat, this time finding its mark in her left thigh.

"Aaaa!" Her fists clenched the paddle handles tightly as pain ripped through her inner thigh.

Alec quickly fired his revolver, striking the man dead. He fired a few more shots into the brush for good measure, anger now fueling him.

He looked back at her but scanned the area, afraid to take his eyes off the riverbank.

"Dee, are you all right?" Concern evident in his expression and in his voice.

Her voice was a bit shaky. "I think so. I don't think it hit the bone, but I can't be sure since it didn't exit the other side. We need to pull it out as soon as possible," she said through gritted teeth.

"We can't do it right now, I'm afraid you would bleed too much, I'm sorry. Can you hold on just another ten minutes or so? We should be nearing the encampment soon," he asked her, knowing she had no other choice anyway.

"I'll try. But it hurts something fierce." Her lips were turning white around the edges, and perspiration formed on her forehead and biceps.

Alec gave her his gun as she pulled hers from its holster. He sat and took over the paddling to ease some of her pain. He paddled as quickly as he could, looking back over his shoulder every few minutes to check on her. She held strong, both guns pointed upward, cocked, and ready to fire at the first sign of anything strange as her eyes scanned both sides of the river's edge.

Finally making it to the encampment, Alec began shouting for some of the men staying there to help him pull Odessa from the boat. Several men and women ran over to help him move her to land. She screamed in pain as they hefted her in their arms carrying her over to a tent and laying her on a pallet on the ground. Alec had to grab the packs from the boat and secure the lines before he could join her. By the time he headed for the tent he heard her scream in anguish. He took off running, reaching it in time to see the local medicine man place the arrow from her leg onto a small crate being used as a makeshift table. She had passed out from the pain. The man looked at Alec and, in his native tongue which Alec understood a little of, told him that the arrow had been tipped in poison, but that he had an herbal remedy that should help if they had caught it in time. Alec shook his head in agreement, and the man started applying the paste-like herb to her wound, binding it with bandages of ripped cloth and tying it with raffia string made from the nature surrounding them.

Alec sat watching Odessa as she rested, the rest of the people slowly thinning out as the medicine man finished his task, promising to check on her throughout the night. After he left the tent, Alec prayed hard. For the first time in his life he prayed to God out loud. Ready to accept and believe anything He wanted him to as long as He spared Odessa's life. Alec removed the bedroll from his pack and, lying down beside her, drifted off to sleep as he prayed.

For we wrestle not against flesh and blood,
but against principalities, against powers,
against the rulers of the darkness of this world,
against spiritual wickedness in high places.

Ephesians 6:12

Chapter 13

Jerusalem, 587 BC

Jason could barely keep up with Seth as he tore through the streets searching for who he believed to be Caroline. The man was fast, he had to give him that. He just wished that he knew what they were running toward. If his gut feeling was correct it wasn't going to be pretty once they found this mystery woman.

Jason tried to keep track of every twist and turn so they could find their way back to the inn. As he turned the last corner he nearly ran Seth over. Seth had stopped and was standing still, breathing hard as he watched a figure move about in the dim moonlight of the dead-end street.

"Caroline?" Seth spoke almost breathlessly, more from the intense emotion of the moment than from running through the streets to catch up to her.

The woman then turned and looked at Seth, her features still hard to see well in the dim moonlight. *It certainly resembled her, but was it her?* Seth wondered. *If it was Caroline why wouldn't she speak to him?* He started to walk toward her again speaking her name.

"Caroline, are you all right? Please speak to me."

"Seth, that isn't Caroline, it's demonic," Jason said, reaching out his hand to stop his friend's approach toward the unanswering figure before them. Just as he did, the demon ran toward them taking Seth by surprise. Jason pushed Seth backward out of the way knocking him to the ground, and stepped between him and the demon, sword raised, swinging at the dark, foreboding, creature.

The demon's appearance suddenly changed to a black ashen figure almost void of shape but then quickly changed into solid form. It had wings attached to long boney arms, and its form was of a skeletal type of appearance with muscles protruding out from the bones and receding back to nothing but bone at the joints. Its body appeared to be covered with a thin, black, skin. Its head was vulture shaped with a long beak protruding forward and what appeared to be sparse black feathers standing out over the back of the skull. It had ears shaped like a hound dog's that stuck out a bit more, then curved down, almost touching its shoulders. They were pointy, paper thin, veined, and boney. The body was that of a man's and its feet were cloven hooves. Seth quickly gathered his thoughts and composure and, standing, took up his sword to help Jason battle the hideous beast before them.

"Be careful Seth!" Jason yelled to him. "Demons are wicked tricky and hard to kill! Aim for the head or heart!" he yelled over the beast's screeching, taking a ready stance once more, watching as the demon flew about them. The air circulating around them from the force of the beast flapping its wings had a stench about it. Like the smell of death and rotting flesh.

Each man stood across from the other, the beast between them plotting who to attack. It turned its focus to Seth, screeching, and flying down to attack him, lashing out with gnarled, sharp, claw-like fingers, and biting at him with the sharp curved beak. Seth swung his sword at it, striking it in the arm and severing the appendage from the beast's body, but not before it scratched his forearm with its claws.

It screeched in pain flying upward as Seth watched it's every move, blood dripping from the deep scratch on his right arm. However, the beast's wound did not bleed, Seth noticed. The demon flew back toward Seth, its back to Jason. Jason took the opportunity and jumped on top of some wooden crates that were lying against a wall in the alley. He jumped, springing forward toward the demon, arms over his head, sword pointing downward. He connected with the beast in mid-air, landing on its back as he drove his sword down into the beast's thick skull. As he did, it suddenly stopped screeching and fell to the ground, sliding toward Seth and stopping just at his feet.

Jason pulled his sword from the limp body and stood, breathing hard as he bent forward to rest his hands upon his knees. Seth stood there looking at the dead creature before him, not sure what to say or think.

He looked at Jason and asked, "You all right?"

Jason stood and, still breathing a bit hard replied, "Sure. You?" he asked, motioning with the sword in his hand at Seth's forearm.

"Yeah, I'm fine I guess. Unless that thing was poisonous somehow?" Seth answered with a questioning look at Jason.

"Not to my knowledge," Jason answered.

As the two men stood looking at the dead demon, Seth questioned Jason.

"So, what now? Do we just leave this thing here? It's bound to stir up a commotion when people see it."

Jason gave a half grin. "It'll take care of itself."

Almost as soon as he finished talking, the body of the demon began to quickly decay and turn to dust particles. Just as it had before, the body turned to a black ashen substance that seemed lighter than air. The particles began to lift and float upward, swirling in the breeze that lifted it above the roof tops where it was swept away into the night.

"The more I learn about this new world I've been thrown into, the less I understand," Seth said, watching the last remaining particles disappear into the night sky. "I still don't understand why it took Caroline's form. How did it know? Can they read thoughts?"

"No, they can't. You've spoken Caroline's name so many times since you've been here. That's what demons do. They take your inner most desires to tempt, torment, and destroy you with them anyway they can. Satan is known as a deceiver, a trickster. He uses whatever means necessary to try to make us miserable, to make us fail our missions. That demon was after you tonight, Seth. It was focused solely on you," Jason said as they walked the streets to return to the hotel.

"Hey, Jason, I'm sorry. I should have listened to you, but reasonable thought wasn't an option earlier tonight. All I could think about was the fact that I saw Caroline."

"It wouldn't have mattered. Either way this encounter was bound to happen. I'm pretty sure it was the same one following us earlier today. At least it's done with for now. What you need to remember is there are forces pitted against stopping you anyway possible. And they wish to make it as though you're alone in all this. Just know that you're not. You have friends, Seth, and we won't turn on you. You have to trust us even when it seems like you shouldn't. They would like nothing more than to separate us and rip us apart. We are all in this together. Not only that, but God brought you here for a reason. He won't forsake you either. Now, let's get this mission over with and head back to Simon's."

Jason and Seth made their way back to their hotel with Seth pondering what Jason had told him. He wasn't used to trusting or depending on people. It was definitely a new skill set he would have to learn quickly. It could mean his life, or someone else's.

After entering their room, they cleaned and bandaged Seth's wounded arm. It didn't take Seth long to fall asleep this time around, his body and mind now exhausted from the events of the evening.

The next morning, several hours before sunrise, Jason and Seth woke. Without eating breakfast, they left the room key at the front desk and went in search of the secret tunnels that ran beneath parts of the city to certain locations inside the temple. There happened to be one entrance that they believed they could access easily that was said to start at the King's private stables. A place like that shouldn't be too hard to get into. As they reached the stables they noticed a large door leading into the main part where the animals were stalled. No one seemed to be around just yet, so they slowly and quietly made their way to the door. Jason cracked open the large wooden door just enough to peer inside. There didn't appear to be anyone inside the stables, so the two of them squeezed through the slight opening, and quietly secured the door behind them. The movement startled a few of the animals and they began to neigh and bleat their protests. Jason and Seth stopped moving to make sure the noise from the animals wouldn't attract anyone who might happen to be somewhere inside. With no appearance being made, the two men as quietly and quickly as possible, moved about the stalls in search of the tack room. They found the door and entered the room securing the lock behind them just in case. They didn't need any surprises while they searched for the hidden passageway the map said was located in this room. They made their way around the room searching the walls for any signs of the hidden tunnel's door.

"Jason, over here," Seth whispered as loudly as he could. "Feel here. There's air blowing through the cracks in the wood."

They ran their hands along the rough trim, Seth going left and Jason going right, tracing and feeling for the edges of the door that they were sure to find. Seth had reached the top edge of the wood when his hand brushed a small latch. He stopped and, feeling for the latch, pulled it to the right as a small dull click was heard and the door slightly gave way just enough to stick his hand in and pull it open. The men stopped moving, listening for any noise outside the tack room, afraid the clicking noise from the releasing door might have drawn some attention. Feeling confident that they were still alone, they pulled the door open just enough for them to squeeze through. They turned back and pulled the door securely closed behind them, hearing the click again signifying the door had latched.

Jason pulled a flashlight out of his pack as Seth brushed at the many cobwebs that had overrun the passage. Obviously, no one had been in this tunnel for many years. They continued walking forward stepping over rats, fallen stones, and dodging occupied spider webs until they came to a forked passageway. Seth pulled the tunnel plans from Jason's pack and they went over which direction they needed to take that would lead them to the temple. Turning left, they had to climb over rubble and debris from decay and lack of maintenance, where the tunnel had collapsed in some areas. These tunnels were obviously forgotten about, at least this one was. The map showed them to be about three hundred feet or so from the tunnel's exit, which appeared to empty into the Chamber of Secrets inside The Holy Place. They jogged as quickly as they could through the passage needing to get inside the Holy of Holies before the priests started their daily rituals. Soon they came upon another door, also covered in cobwebs and dust from years of unuse, and quickly found the latch located in the same place as the last door. They also found a small wooden peephole about the size of a twelve-inch ruler that appeared to slide along a small track enabling someone to peer inside the room before exiting the door. Jason slowly grabbed the small knob that protruded out from the latch. He had to wiggle it a bit to get it to move, being slightly stuck from the settled dust and webbing. He carefully slid the piece to the left and peered into the room. There was no one present and no light visible except for the moonlight pouring into the very small windows surrounding the top of the twenty-foot-high walls.

The two men looked at each other with raised eyebrows as to question each other to their sanity.

"Here we go," Jason whispered, taking a large breath and exhaling slowly. He pushed the latch, and the door made a small clicking noise before popping open. They quickly pushed the door open enough to squeeze through the opening and stepped into the room.

The Chamber of Secrets was a room where wealthy people could come and anonymously give of their excess provisions to help the less fortunate and the very poor. They would place their items in the room or give them to the priests or porters to be placed here for distribution at a later date or as needs were brought to their attention. They carefully walked around the perimeter of the large room toward a set of large double doors that graced every entryway in the temple. Again, being extra careful not to make noise, they slowly opened the doorway and looked out into the courtyard of The Holy Place. Still not seeing anyone, they slowly exited the room leaving the door slightly ajar and quickly slunk their way along the walls to the backside of the great room, stopping just to the side of the entrance to the Holy of Holies. Knowing no one would be inside yet they quickly opened the large doors as quietly as possible and headed toward the Ark of the Covenant.

Jason stopped and just looked at where he was. Gazing upon the actual Ark of the Covenant almost took his breath away.

"Jason!" Seth loudly whispered, gaining Jason's attention, while motioning him to the other end of the Ark. Jason shook himself out of his trance like state, and grabbing the handles meant to carry and open the container with, they lifted the heavy gold-laden lid up and over, trying not to flip the top-heavy Cherubim that graced the lid's top. After placing the lid of the Ark carefully upon the floor, they quickly looked inside, finding the staff immediately. Seth reached inside the Ark, his height and long arms lending ease to the task. He carefully hoisted the item and slid it into his robes, securing it to his back with the straps of his pack. He and Jason quickly replaced the lid of the Ark and made their way back toward the large doors. As Seth peered out the doors, Jason turned to glance back once more in awe at the one place where God Himself dwelt amongst his people. He offered up a quick prayer of thanks for this opportunity and for their safety for the remainder of their journey. They quickly made their way back to the Chamber of Secrets, sliding inside the room and closing the door just as the priests and ushers began opening up The Holy Place to early morning worshippers.

Returning to the secret passageway and stepping back inside securing the door and latch, the two men disappeared quietly into the walls and underground passages that led in all directions beneath the city streets, grateful for the ease of retrieving the Staff of Moses.

Seth peered at the map of the tunnels through the light of the flashlight. "We need to turn left up ahead. If we turn right, it will take us back to the stables. It shows on the map that by taking a left we should find another series of tunnels, one of which should lead us out into a cave at the edge of the city. An outside exit would be less risky than stepping out of a wall inside the city somewhere."

"You're right." Jason ceased walking and turned to look at Seth. "We need to find a place as far away from human contact as possible. Revealing these tunnels to anyone now could really stir up some trouble. Actually, come to think of it, I don't think it will matter much anyhow. Historically the temple is destined to be destroyed by Nebuchadnezzar within the year anyway. What a shame. I doubt this will be a mission I will ever forget."

"Yeah, I noticed you kind of went blank back there." Seth's voice posed a question, his focus turning from the map to his friend. "What happened?"

"Well, for a Christian like me to be standing where I was, it was just so…surreal. I could feel the presence of God and it was all I could do to keep going and not just fall to my knees. I really believe that's one of the reasons why you peregrinated at the particular time that you did, Seth. It was for this mission. You aren't yet a believer and I needed someone with a clear head; without a connection to God yet that would pull me out of it, and God knew that. I could have stayed in that room forever and been completely happy. We could have been caught if not for you. Thanks, Seth." Jason looked at Seth with gratitude.

"No problem." Seth was a bit uncomfortable about the conversation's turn toward belief in God and having a true connection to Him.

"Why do you think it was a provision from God though? I mean it could just all be coincidental."

"Perhaps, but I doubt it. You'll learn, Seth; the closer you get to God the more you see his hand in your life every day. He provides for us in ways you may never know or understand." Jason turned and continued walking in the direction the passageway was leading.

Seth placed the map into his pack after divining a pathway to take to lead them out of town. He and Jason traveled in silence the rest of the way, only speaking to give directions. They reached the end of the tunnel, found the door latch and, trying to open the door, realized it was stuck tight.

"What now?" Seth asked, looking at the stuck door.

"Well, the map shows this as a remote exit, so I say we push through and take our chances with whatever is on the other side." Jason looked at Seth and shrugged his shoulders.

The men pushed on the door to gauge just how stuck it was and noticed it giving way a bit. So, they both put all their weight into the door and pushed hard, giving a few lunges at it to push it the rest of the way open. Finally, the door released its hold, and the two men nearly fell through to the other side, stumbling over each other and the piles of loose rock that had been lying against the outside. They looked around at their surroundings, realizing they were in the woods on the outside of a mountain. The rocks blocking the door were probably from a rockslide from some point in the past and had been there for some years due to the moss and weeds that covered their surfaces. The door, although made of wood on the inside, had been camouflaged on the outside to look like part of the mountain to keep the passage hidden.

"Amazing that someone actually dug a tunnel through the bottom side of a mountain," Seth said, arching his back and straining his neck to look up at the high cliff side stretching into the heavens.

"Yeah, it's even more impressive when you think about the time period we are in. Way before modern conveniences like dynamite and big machinery," Jason supplied.

"How long before the storm blows through?" Seth pulled the map from his pack and glanced at it. The men started walking through the woods toward the open field that the map showed to be three or so miles north.

"I'd say we have about another four to five hours before it gets here and it's strong enough for the portal to open. We either find a safe place to make camp, eat lunch, and wait for the storm here in the woods, or walk back into town. According to the map, it should only be a few miles north. What do you think?"

"If we have that long to wait, I say we head back to town and grab a hot meal. We can catch the portal there, right?"

"Yes, the strongest part of the storm should move right into town. By the time we get there and grab a bite to eat, we shouldn't have too much more time to kill before it hits the area full force. It's supposed to be a quick-moving storm with a lot of lightning and even some hail, if I remember correctly from what Simon told us."

"So, how do you jump into a storm? I haven't gotten to experience that yet," Seth asked as they walked through the quiet woods, the morning sun shining through the tree canopies as woodland creatures flitted through the trees and underbrush.

"It isn't really something I can explain. You'll just have to wait for the actual experience of it." Jason glanced back at Seth and grinned.

"People don't see us time-jump?"

"No. I believe most are busy running for cover or seeking shelter themselves. Not many people roam around in the storm's eye waiting to see what happens. I've never encountered anyone who has ever had anyone ask questions. I'm pretty certain they don't see the portal open since they can't traverse them. If anyone does see us, I believe they just see two people kind of vanish. Most probably assume it to be a trick of the eyes or that we found some sort of shelter and ducked inside."

"That makes sense."

The two men made quick pace to town arriving within the hour. They grabbed lunch at a little out of the way diner with outdoor seating underneath a wood and stone pergola setting. They sat the majority of the time eating and discussing the trip. Seth had removed his robe on the walk into town and carefully wrapped the staff in it, tying it closed with some jute twine they had purchased off a farmer on the edge of the city. They didn't need anyone seeing the staff and possibly recognizing the artifact.

After eating, they still had about another hour or two to waste before the storm hit. So, they decided to walk the Souk area and see what they could find that they may want to purchase, or, just to witness a little bit more of the culture. That was one of the things about peregrinating. You usually had some time to kill between jumps. So, you found interesting and entertaining ways to do so.

The Souk, or market, as Jason explained to Seth what it was called, was a gathering place to farmers, merchants, and buyers. Anyone who wanted to sell or buy, came to the Souk. The majority of items for sale were fruits, vegetables, and animals. There were some carpet merchants, gold and silver jewelry, pottery, candles, incense and burners, clothing, and sandals. Anything that Seth could imagine was here. They managed to while away several hours walking the Souk when they noticed a change in the weather. Many of the merchants began quickly covering their merchandise and moving it indoors in anticipation of the approaching storm. The sky was quickly growing dark and the wind began to blow as the dark clouds rolled across the sky, lightning already visibly shooting from cloud to cloud, occasionally touching the ground across the other end of the field that lay just off the edge of town. Thunder cracked as lightning split a tree off in the distance making people scramble for cover even faster.

Seth looked at Jason who motioned with a shake of his head to a small canopy just off to the right of them. They jogged over to the small shelter taking cover from the storm as they watched the town people gather their goods and secure their products to deal another day. When the rain started, everyone disappeared inside a building or ran up a nearby street probably heading for home.

The winds picked up quickly, blowing with a gusting force that was hard to stand against at times. Lightning strikes became more frequent as thunder constantly boomed across the sky. Jason watched the storm intently, waiting to see the portal appear as the hail began to pound the ground and nearby Souk stands. It rained hard for about five minutes when Jason yelled to Seth.

"There! Do you see it, Seth?" Jason pointed into the wind, rain, and hail as a small light began to appear in the field just about three hundred feet from where they were sheltered under the small wooden canopy.

"Yes, I see it!" Seth's voice was barely audible, carried off by the gusts of wind.

"It's almost time! We just need to wait until the portal fully opens!" Jason yelled against the wind as rain pelted their faces and exposed skin, the small canopy being a feeble cover against the intensity of the storm.

Suddenly, a bright light split the air in the center of the field as Jason, and then Seth, took off at a full run into the brunt of the storm; rain and hail still pounding the earth; lightning striking trees and buildings behind them as they ran. Seth tightened his grip on the staff making sure not to lose the very thing they had come after. The intensity of the wind made it hard to run, making Seth wonder just how long they had until the portal closed. It didn't appear to be much further from what he could see through the rain. Reaching the portal, they both ran through, coming out the other side into Simon's charging station.

Simon had set their return point to the station knowing Jason would know how to shut down the equipment and exit the hidden cave.

The men took a minute to catch their breath from running against the strong wind and to shake off the rain; standing behind the large metal cage for protection. Jason walked over to the control panel turning off the coils and closing the portal. With the machine powered down, Jason and Seth made their way up the steps to exit the cave into the forest. Seth thought it was some magic spell that only Simon could do to open and close the cave. Apparently, it was much more simple than that, and Simon had already spelled it to accept certain people, making it unnecessary for him to be present should they need entry to or from the cave.

"So, all I have to do is say my name, touch it, and that's it?" Seth asked, rather deflated.

"Yeah. What? You wanted him to make it harder or more complicated?" Jason asked in amused disbelief.

"Well no, not exactly. Can someone else say our names and gain entry to the cave?" Seth asked as they made the short trek to Simon's

"No. I don't know how, but it recognizes your voice as well. Strange huh?" Jason looked at Seth with raised eyebrows.

"Yeah, just a bit." Seth felt a little unnerved by the prospect of an inanimate object recognizing his voice pattern. But he supposed it worked about the same way with the messaging grid when Simon sent out the messages via canister and barrier.

They reached Simon's in just under fifteen minutes, and realizing they were alone, decided to shower and catch a nap before getting dinner ready. They knew that Alec and Odessa would also be returning sometime today but were unsure as to when Simon would be back. Seth placed the Staff of Moses in Simon's office partly hidden in a corner for safekeeping, first removing it from his wet robe. He then went to his room, grabbed some clean clothes, and headed for the shower. His body was tired and ached from the recent peregrination, and his bed would feel mighty nice for a few precious hours of rest that he hoped he would be able to find.

Chapter 14

*Barrier's Edge, Reader's Island,
Bermuda Triangle*

Simon and Safra started to walk the four-mile distance from the charging station hidden beneath the old lighthouse that graced the rocky, steep, shoreline. They headed inland toward the main house, which sat near the interior of the small Island located within the center of the Bermuda triangle. Centuries ago, according to the Dragoman Archives, one particular Dragoman had a dream where God revealed the location of the Island. Reader's Island was completely hidden from view and detection. It took them some time to find the exact spot where the Island sat but it has been used as their central meeting place ever since. It was the most secure area in all the lands, planes, and time eras. It was the hub of the entire barrier and protected from any unwanted visitors. The barrier worked like a force field of sorts, a shield against all things natural and unnatural. Nothing could get through the barrier; not storm, demon, ship, plane, or person, unless God ordained it that way. Some ships, planes, and other craft that ventured into the triangular shaped area got lost or they simply vanished into thin air. Those particular vessels were actually transported into another realm or dimension. That was the reason there had been so many claims of missing planes and boats over the years because the vessel had come in contact with the barrier at certain times of the year. It had to do with many things, some of which were the tides, season, and the position of the sun and the moon. Many things played a part in whether a vessel sailed or flew away, sunk or disappeared.

The lighthouse was built as a beacon to Peregrines and Dragoman traveling by way of ship or plane. Later, after Tesla's coil technology was created a charging station was placed within a bunker beneath it.

Peregrines and Dragoman were able to see the island through the barrier but no one else was. This was the one location where demons could not cross the barrier. God had provided all Dragoman and Peregrines with their own little safe haven where they could completely step away from danger, if only for a little while, to recharge, regroup, plan, and commune with Him uninterrupted. The earlier Dragoman, realizing all of this, had built a small temple and worship center in the Island's interior with small separate rooms, located within a larger oval shaped stone building, with cloisters that opened up onto a courtyard, nestled within the natural island beauty and landscape. The center of the courtyard had smaller, fruit, nut, and berry producing trees, small flowering bushes and plants, and a natural circulating waterfall fed from a clean spring located beneath the center of the island. There were all sorts of animals that roamed peacefully across the island, living in harmony with each other. And the weather on the island was always perfect temperature, regardless of what that meant for each individual person. There were benches, hammocks, and chairs scattered throughout the courtyard and the surrounding area. Hammocks swung in the breeze near the water's edge on the sandy part of the beach. Adirondack chairs graced the shoreline in several spots beneath the shade of coconut palms, and small row boats and small engine craft were tied to several twenty-foot-long docks that jutted out over the water in several different areas along the coast. On the rocky edge of the shoreline where the lighthouse stood, were a series of underground caverns that, depending on the time of year and the position of the sun and moon, sometimes flooded with ocean water, creating a water geyser that shot into the air as the waves pounded the shoreline. Reader's Island more resembled a vacationer's paradise than that of a hidden safe zone. But all the amenities did make for a relaxing get away for those who spent their lives time-jumping, running from danger, and battling demons, all for God with no glory or appreciation to be seen or received from anyone else.

Reader's Island was approximately seven miles across from every direction, and with it being the central location of Barrier's Edge they were able to access any land, plane, or era from there. The grid for Barrier's Edge that surrounded the island was made up of layers, much like the longitude and latitude lines that help plot navigational points on the earth's surface. A Dragoman or Peregrine could simply spin any layer of the barrier with the flick of a hand to find whatever place or period they chose. Each grid line extended upward from the water level into the skyline connecting to each layer above or below it. Each horizontal layer of the barrier had a century located within its grid. Each vertical layer within that horizontal layer had a decade and, when spun, could access the years within that decade. This was the only location at the barrier where travel by storm was unnecessary, making it quicker, more easily accessed, and safer to time travel. This being said, only a small handful of the most trusted and devoted Peregrines knew of this place. The island itself being too much of a temptation to stop the peregrinations and the battle to save mankind, the Dragoman decided to keep it secret until the last of the Peregrines were found. The meeting, soon to take place in the council chambers, hopefully would give them the knowledge they needed to find the missing Peregrine. Simon hoped that one of the other Dragoman knew of this Peregrine already. If not, it could take them years to find him or her, and he wasn't sure they had years left before the Final Battle began.

Simon and Safra reached the main house within an hour and a half and were greeted by one of the house-keepers. The island, being forty-nine square miles, had quite a few amenities to offer. The main house was a large, Caribbean style dwelling, made with stucco, brick, and stone, and housed about thirty bedrooms, ten bath-rooms, several living rooms, and a huge dining room. The restaurant sized kitchen also had dining space as well. The house also had two offices, a room for council meetings, the archival library, and a large computer room, making communication, weather tracking, and charting easy, and helped to keep them up to date with the most current technological advances. The outside had a covered porch that wrapped around the bottom story, and a large balcony that also wrapped around the entire upper level as well with balcony doors leading in and out of every room and bedroom. The size of the house required help to run and keep it up, and so it sustained a few employees, of which were five housekeepers, three cooks, and four grounds-keepers, all of whom were retired Peregrines or Dragoman. People who just couldn't handle the intense lifestyle any longer, whether it was due to age or infirmity. Retirement and service on the island still enabled them to be useful to the cause. Besides, after leading the life of a Peregrine or Dragoman, returning to the ordinary world of man was not an option for them. They were content here on the island, living out their days as servants to any and all who came there. Plus, they still had input into the happenings since they were, at one-point, mission leaders themselves.

"Hello Simon, hello Safra," the older woman said with a bright beaming smile as she reached out to give them each a hug. "It's so good to see the two of you. It's been a while." She took their coats and packs.

"I'll just put these things in your regular rooms. You can go on into the kitchen and grab a bite to eat. Clancy has dinner ready."

"Thank you, Shannon, it's good to see you as well. It's kind of you to take our bags for us," Simon said, taking the woman's hands in his and smiling down at her.

After their hellos with Shannon, they ventured into the kitchen and were greeted by Clancy and Henry, the two men who acted as the resident chefs. They grabbed a quick bite to eat then went in search of Nuncio Agnusdei, the head Dragoman who resided on the island. Someone had to stay here and monitor Hub Central, and since he had suffered a hip injury many years before that prevented him from walking well, even with the use of a cane, he chose to stay on the island as keeper of the archives.

They found him in the archival library reading over some piece of important information.

"Nuncio, old friend, how are you?" Simon said as he walked into the extremely large room.

"Simon, Safra! I was wondering when you two would arrive?" Nuncio limped over to greet his two old friends, taking their hands in his and giving them a good shake.

"Yes, I'm afraid we are a bit late. We had a mishap at Safra's."

Safra answered, "Yes, quite so. Have him tell you more about it later. Now that I've said my hellos I believe I'm going to excuse myself for an hour or so to go to my room and rest for a while."

"Of course, Safra, I'm sure you're exhausted after the ordeal of the last few days," Simon said. "We'll send word with Shannon when the others arrive."

"Thank you. See you both a bit later." Safra turned and left the room.

"Simon, would you care for a cup of coffee while we sit and catch up a bit?" Nuncio offered as he sat down in a large, leather, wingback, chair located in the sitting area of the room.

"That sounds wonderful, thank you." Simon sat in another replicated chair across from Nuncio.

Nuncio spoke into the intercom, pushing a button on a machine located on the table by his chair. "Petra, could you please bring some coffee to the archival library?"

"Certainly, be there in just a bit," answered a voice on the other end.

"Has anyone else arrived yet?" Simon questioned.

"Only Malachai; and he is at the temple right now. We're still waiting on the others. Ryan should be in tonight sometime, and Prisca and Vashti should arrive tomorrow morning."

"Good...good. Then I suppose we'll have the meeting in the morning after the ladies arrive," Simon said as Petra entered with the coffee.

"What's with all the urgency about this meeting? Why call everyone together now?" Nuncio questioned as the two men thanked her for the coffee before she turned and left.

"The last Peregrine has been named." Simon paused for his friend's reaction.

"Is that so?" Nuncio said with surprise and a knowing sigh in response. "Well then, it begins."

"Yes, I suppose it does. But I don't recall hearing of an eleventh yet. Do you know of any recent Peregrines named since the tenth?" Simon queried Nuncio.

"No, actually, I don't." Nuncio rubbed his chin, deep in thought. "You're sure the Twelfth has been found?"

"Positive. He actually came through a storm with Jason Marshal from a completely different era and place."

"Well that's interesting isn't it? Have you found anything about a new Peregrine appearing in one storm with another Peregrine before in the archives at your place?"

"Not yet. None of the books I have revealed anything unusual in that yet. I was hoping the archives here would hold an explanation. Perhaps after the meeting we could spend some time searching through them? If we could convince everyone else to stay longer and help we could make short work of it."

"Sounds like a good idea, Simon."

They sat and visited with each other drinking coffee for the next hour, Simon regaling Nuncio with the tale of Aisha Kandisha's visit to Safra's Moroccan village, and the visit from the demon on the train ride to Marrakech. Each man wondering aloud the significance of that bit of information as well.

"Why would they try to stop you and Safra at this point? Demons generally seek out Peregrines. Their usually not so aggressive toward ordinary people such as Safra, unless it was just you they were after. Do you think they now know about Safra and her unique gifts, Simon?" Nuncio's mind whirled, deep in thought from the ordeal.

"Well, if that's the case, it won't be safe for her to return home. We'll have to discuss it with her tomorrow."

Deciding to call it a night, the two men went their separate ways, Simon heading to his room to rest as well. He truly enjoyed Reader's Island and the constant ocean breeze that blew across it. He opened the windows in his room to allow the breeze to blow through, and to be able to gaze out upon the very distant waves breaking against the beach on all sides of the shoreline. As he glanced out the window over the moonlit landscape, he suddenly got a heavy burden to pray for Odessa and Alec. Simon knelt before the open window and prayed to God about the urgency he felt, heavily beseeching the Lord to protect all of his Peregrines, but especially Odessa, as the burden was specifically for her. He stayed that way for about thirty minutes before going to bed.

The next morning Simon woke early, Odessa still on his mind. So, before anything else, he prayed earnestly for her and Alec once again, then dressed and headed downstairs for breakfast. Several of the others were already there eating and visiting when he walked into the kitchen.

"Good morning all," Simon said, entering the room.

"Morning Simon," everyone replied.

"Has everyone arrived yet?" Simon asked no one in particular as he glanced around the kitchen where people were scattered about, standing, leaning, or sitting at any available space. During breakfast time people preferred to hang out in the kitchen instead of sitting in the larger formal dining room.

"Not as of yet," stated Malachai Harel. "Ryan arrived late last night, but the ladies have yet to make an appearance." He walked toward Simon and placed his coffee cup on the counter before giving the man's hand a hearty shake.

"Good to see you Malachai." Simon smiled and returned the man's handshake with even vigor.

"Now what's this urgent meeting all about?" Malachai asked, never being one to beat around the bush.

"How about we wait till the others get here, hmm? I don't want to keep repeating myself." Simon looked over his glasses as he poured himself a cup of steaming hot coffee.

"Sure thing. I just hope they get here soon. The suspense is killing me." Malachai grinned.

Ryan Halloran, being a sort of recluse, watched the interaction between the two men with little interest. He was a brilliant young man who happened to be very high functioning autistic, and he did not like being around people. These occasional get-togethers, even as sparsely placed as they were, stressed him out. It was all they could do to get him to show. He only came because he knew they were of the utmost importance. He was happy sitting in his charging station waiting for Peregrines to come to him. He enjoyed spending his time working on his computer programs and designing software and hardware technology that was beneficial to their cause.

"Ryan my boy, how are you faring these days?" Simon asked pointedly, peering at him.

"I'm good Simon." Ryan feigned interest in his breakfast without looking at the man. He answered questions with a matter-of-fact attitude, but never offered more and didn't usually initiate conversations unless he needed to ask a question or offer a solution. His questions were direct, and pertinent to something, never making small talk. Everyone knew how he was, and didn't take offense to him at all, understanding him and letting him be himself.

"Good," Simon offered, turning to smile at Malachai and the rest of the staff gathered there in the kitchen.

Nuncio entered the kitchen and announced that Prisca and Vashti should arrive before noon and that he would like to have lunch on the covered terrace outside the archive room. Everyone agreed to the time and, after breakfast, all went their separate ways, enjoying the down time on the island until the noon hour.

The final two Dragoman finally arrived and, after eating lunch, the seven of them got down to discussing the reason they were there.

"The reason I called you all here today is because the last Peregrine has been named. The only problem is I don't know of an eleventh. Have any of you had a new Peregrine revealed in the last few months?" Simon asked, glancing around the table.

"No. I know of no such person," Vashti Mayer said, looking around.

"Nor I," Prisca Delacroix announced.

Everyone glanced around the table, all giving the same answer and all looking puzzled at the strange turn of events.

"Doesn't the archives state that Judah would be the last?" Ryan asked, staring down at his empty plate.

"Yes, it does, Ryan," Nuncio answered. "But Simon has found the last. And he came in an unusual way. He came through the same storm with another Peregrine from a completely different place and time."

"Isn't that a bit out of the ordinary?" Vashti asked.

Simon answered, "Yes, highly unusual. In fact, we want to search the archives later to see if we can find out what, if anything, that it could mean. And we would like all of you to help us search the massive system if you all wouldn't mind staying a few extra days to help?"

Everyone agreed to the request, that being only a few days for most. Simon filled them all in on the events in Morocco and the train ride to Marrakech, with everyone agreeing that Safra would be safer staying on the island for the time being.

"Another matter we need to address, since no one knows who the eleventh Peregrine is, is to find this person. The archives were clear that Judah would be the last, so that means there is a Peregrine out there somewhere who is untrained and probably has no idea what is happening to them. It has to be a terrifying experience without anyone to explain." Simon looked around the table at the others.

"That is the reason I brought Safra here with me. Her unique gifts should help us to at least get an image of the Peregrine, and perhaps, God willing, a location as well."

"Why would God allow this lost Peregrine to travel untrained? He has always led them to a Dragoman or vice versa," Prisca inquired.

"I'm not sure Prisca. It is quite odd that it happened this way." Simon scratched his head as he thought about the strange circumstances.

Safra stood, looked around the table, and spoke.

"I will prepare myself to speak with God this evening. I will go up into the temple house to a prayer room to do this after cleansing myself in my room."

She excused herself to shower and don her prayer robes, ready her incense and prayer mat, and to confess and pray to God to cleanse her soul. She never entered the presence of the Lord unclean. Whether it be in body or spirit, claiming that to do so would hinder her walk and how she heard from God. Her robes were made of the finest silks available to her in Morocco as was her prayer mat. The incense she used was an ancient blend her father taught her how to make. She used only her finest and best to enter God's presence.

Everyone watched her go and excused themselves as well, the meeting being completed until after Safra communed with God and hopefully received the answers they desperately needed. Simon decided to use this time to send a message back home to his Peregrines explaining his need to stay longer.

They all gathered together again to walk the short distance up the hill to the temple area with Safra as she silently walked swinging her incense holder in front of her. The others also walked in complete silence following behind her. When they arrived at the temple, they all sat or knelt around the open courtyard outside the center prayer room to offer up their own prayers as Safra entered, closed the door, and commenced her ceremony.

Safra placed her burning incense holder upon the ornate hanger located against the back wall. She then placed her mat on the floor, kneeling upon it as she pulled the long scarf up over her head and down around her forehead. She bowed to pray and ask God for His favor in finding His lost warrior, placing her hands and face against the mat in reverence. She stayed this way for the better part of an hour before she emerged from the prayer room. The others stood to receive her, again in silence, knowing not to disturb or break her concentration until she was ready. They all walked back to the main house waiting for her to emerge from her room, hopefully with good information.

Safra met with the others in the main living area where everyone was having coffee. She took several pieces of drawing paper and colored pencils and began drawing the vision that God had given her. She drew the place she saw first, quickly sketching the image and the few words that she saw. She then began sketching an image of a young girl. None of the Dragoman in the house recognized the young woman or the place that she drew. Petra, the house maid, took the pictures and made colored copies of the image for each Dragoman to take with them and handed them back to Simon.

"We're giving each of you copies of the images for you to distribute to your Peregrines." Simon handed out the images to each person. "We need to issue a wide-spread search for this girl, utilizing all available resources. Safra says that the location is Dover, England, but it doesn't show which time period or where exactly. Only what a certain street looks like but without street names. This street could be where she resides. This could take a while people. Time we really may not have, so pull out all the stops, tricks, and techniques you have to try and figure this out. Ryan can run a computer diagnostic of the streets located within or around Dover to try and match this image with one from the satellites. But this will only work on newer time periods. We may not get proper readings for older eras. The other word given is *Trials*. What this word means or how it is to help is unsure as well. We can also run a historical word search through the databases to see what comes up, then everyone can take separate categories and research time periods that relate to the word. I cannot stress enough how important it is we find her immediately."

Malachai looked down at the sketched photo in his hand. "Sure thing, Simon. When we all get back to our places we'll contact all our people and send them out as soon as possible. We'll find her, whoever she is."

"Good. Now that we've discussed this, what say you to getting started on the archives?" Simon asked, glancing around the room.

Everyone agreed with each person tackling a section in the Events in History part of the archival library. Hoping to find something, they spent the better part of the evening and some well into the night, searching for clues to the mystery of the peculiar way Seth Jager had appeared to the peregrination lifestyle.

Chapter 15

*Niamey borderlands, Niger River Encampment,
North Africa, 1795*

Alec awoke before dawn checking to see if Odessa was still breathing and that her heart was still beating within her chest. She was still feverish, and he tucked the blankets even tighter around her shivering body. He had gotten little to no sleep the night before, worry keeping his mind and body from relaxing into a state of rest.

Odessa had made little noise throughout the night. The only sign that she was still alive was the fever in her body and the occasional shaking fits that she took from it. He had applied cold compresses to her face and forehead throughout the night trying to bring her fever down. The tribal medicine man checked in on them during the night as well, changing the dressing on her injured leg and informing Alec of what to do and watch for. The poultice the man had applied to the wound to draw out the poison from her body was black in color when he removed it for changing. He stated that meant the salve was doing its job and extracting the poison from her body. Alec just hoped that it had not gotten too far into her system since the arrow had stayed in her leg for the better part of fifteen minutes before they could remove it.

Some of the tribal women arrived to take over sitting with Odessa and sent Alec to clean up, rest, and eat, mumbling in broken English that it would do them no good if he too took ill from lack of tending to his own needs. He hesitantly agreed to their wishes but made them promise to come and find him should her condition change at all. He stepped out of the tent into the morning air. The sun was just starting to peak out over the tree canopy across the river from their encampment. Alec stretched his tired back, legs, and arms, and rubbed his sleep deprived, bloodshot eyes. A few of the other women walked toward Alec, bringing him some food and water, and directing him to sit upon a stump near a campfire located beneath another of the village tents. Alec gratefully accepted the food and quiet reprieve they offered him. He hungrily ate the meal not realizing how famished his body actually was. The food also began to alleviate the nagging headache that had started to plague him sometime during the night. He sat on the stump by the fire after eating, offering up another prayer on Odessa's behalf. Alec had decided he would completely turn his life over to God if He would just spare Odessa. While he prayed he felt a calming sense of peace fall over his body as if someone had reached out and wrapped his entire body in a warm blanket. He now knew what Odessa meant when she said that God gave her a peace about many things. He sensed His presence all about him, especially when he prayed. Alec now understood what it meant to have a personal relationship with God. He had a peace about Odessa, even though it still did not keep him from worrying, he just knew she would be okay.

Alec busied himself helping the other village men and women tackle some of the daily chores to be done in the encampment, taking his mind off their current situation, but only slightly. He never strayed too far from the center of the encampment where the healing tent was just in case Odessa's condition changed. As he worked he busied his mind as well, thinking about their mission and where they should be by the day's end. He knew that even if she awoke today she would be in no condition to travel, meaning they would probably have to stay here in this river side village for the better part of a week. And that was after she came to. He had no way of contacting Simon to explain what had happened, and he knew the man would be beside himself with worry. They would just have to make do until she came out of it and they could find a storm large enough to peregrinate home. Once they reached Simon's, Alec would make sure that Dee took it easy for a while. If Simon had anymore missions for them, Alec would do them alone or quite possibly team up with Jason and Seth to tackle them.

Either way she would be out of commission for a while. The medicine man had told Alec during the night that the poison that had been on the arrow was a very potent one, and even if she survived it would possibly take her body months to fully recover from it and that it could even cause permanent damage of some sort. They could only wait to see. Dee was relatively young, healthy, and in excellent physical condition. These all played a strong part in her favor but still was no guarantee for survival. All Alec could do was pray that God was not finished with her yet and that He would spare her life.

It was around noon when the women who were sitting by Odessa's bedside tending to her needs came in search of Alec. Odessa had awakened only slightly and seemed to be more restless. Alec nearly ran to the tent bending down beside her to try to get her to speak to him.

"Dee, please wake up. Can you hear me? Dee, if you can hear me, please, squeeze my hand," Alec pleaded with her as he held her right hand gently in his, but got no response from her.

Just then, the medicine man entered the tent and felt her skin, realizing she was still way too hot. He stood, yelled out the flap of the tent, and went back to her side, uncovering her body. Just then, several of the larger young men in the village entered the tent and picked Odessa up, following the medicine man as he continually gave them orders.

"What's happening? What are you doing?" Alec desperately questioned them, following their every step trying to get the men to stop and speak to him. He continued to yell at them as the women who had been tending to Odessa turned to look at him, grabbing at him to try and stop him. One woman began speaking to him quickly in her native tongue trying to make him understand something, but he was too distraught to understand her or make out the native Hausa language she spoke. He only caught the ancient French dialect of the language and that was sparse. She said something about fever and cool. Alec pushed at them desperately trying to reach Odessa.

Breaking free of their hold on him, Alec raced to catch up with the men and Dee, still yelling as he went. Suddenly, he realized what they were doing. Breaking past the men, he tried to enter the chilly running water of the Niger River, but the sentries wouldn't allow him to pass. He stood watching, holding his breath as the two younger men submersed her entire body from the neck down into the waters. The other village men stood watch over the waters, keeping a keen eye and a ready bow and staff searching the moving water for approaching crocodiles or hippopotami. They held her there for about five minutes when her body took to shivering uncontrollably. The medicine man instructed them to return her to the tent where the village women had already changed the fever-soaked bedding. The women ushered everyone out of the tent except for Alec and the medicine man, then commenced to undressing her down to her under garments and wrapping her body in clean robes. The medicine man then returned to the tent and changed the dressing on her leg once again, after which, they tightly bundled her up in blankets stoking the fire in the tent to warm her still shivering body. Alec just sat and watched every move they made, constantly searching her face, hoping to see some sign of awareness in her. Still, after all of that, she lay motionless except for the slight still shivering of her body. Alec again fell upon his knees, clasped his hands, and beseeched his heavenly Father above to bring her back to him.

Finishing his prayer, Alec leaned forward, softly brushing the hair back from her forehead and lightly brushed her skin with his lips as he whispered.

"S'il te plait mon amour, s'it te plait retour a' moi."

Odessa, slightly coherent for just a brief moment, could hear Alec speaking to her, only he sounded so far away. She wasn't sure what was happening to her, only that she felt very cold and that her leg hurt badly. She tried to open her eyes and call his name, but she could only briefly make out small slivers of dim light. She thought she heard Alec's voice telling someone 'Please my love, please return to me.' She didn't understand what he had meant by that or who he was speaking to. For some reason she was unable to speak. She slipped back into unconsciousness as the quiet darkness overtook her thoughts.

Alec thought that for a brief moment he saw her move her eyelids, but it must have been a figment of his imagination because there was no movement at all now that her body had stilled from the shivering. He scooted in as close as he could to her, wrapping her cocooned body in the protective circle of his arms. He would not leave her side again until she awoke, no matter how long it took. He lay there, silently praying to God and softly singing French nursery songs and love songs to her on and off throughout the remainder of the evening into the night, until sleep overtook his worrisome body and mind.

Barrier's Edge at Garganthera, Simon Lane's House

Seth woke around four in the evening. He pulled himself from his bed, opened his bedroom door, and realized that the house was quiet. Jason must still be asleep, but where were Odessa and Alec? Perhaps he had misheard their return time? They must be due back later. He padded through the living room into the kitchen to start some dinner. He removed one of the precooked frozen dinners that Simon kept in the freezer for such times as this and placed it in the oven. Then he pulled a few cans of vegetables from the pantry, placed them in pots, seasoned them, and turned the burner to simmer.

He then filled the coffee pot, set it to brew, and went to sit at the table and wait for it to finish. As he sat in the quiet of the house, he suddenly heard something begin to beep. He listened to try and trace where the sound was coming from. He got up from the table and walked toward the sound coming out of Simon's office. He opened the door, walked inside, and noticed a light blinking where the canisters for the messaging grid system sat. He pushed a button sitting next to the light which turned it off. He thought a minute about what it could mean and decided to walk through the mapping room and out the front door. Once he reached the barrier, he noticed a canister sitting on the grid system. He removed the canister and opened it to reveal a written message inside. He pulled the letter from within and opened it to read as he walked back toward the house.

It was a letter from Simon addressed to him and the other three Peregrines, stating that he would be away longer than predicted but hoped to return within the next three days, and that he would explain everything to them once they were all together again.

He walked back to the kitchen placing the letter and canister on the table, after which he poured himself a cup of coffee and returned to the table to sit down. He wondered what would keep Simon longer than he had originally planned on being away. As he sipped his coffee and pondered the question, Jason entered the kitchen. They sat drinking coffee and discussing the letter from Simon as they waited for dinner to finish.

It didn't take long for the meal to warm, and as they ate, they both wondered when the original arrival time had been for Alec and Odessa. It was close to six p.m. now and they both thought that they should have returned by then.

"Perhaps they missed their returning storm?" Jason gave by way of an explanation.

"Maybe," Seth replied, "no need to worry I guess. They have been at this a lot longer than I have."

"Yeah, Odessa for sure knows what she's doing." Jason grinned slightly. "I guess we'll just take it easy tonight and head to the training fields tomorrow morning while we wait on everyone to get back."

"Sounds like a plan. Besides, I need a bit more work on defense. The scratch from that demon is one nasty cut. I want to avoid that in the future as much as possible."

"Yeah, they aren't deadly, at least to my knowledge, but they are so full of bacteria and who knows what else. Make sure you keep it clean, medicated, and bandaged well so nothing else aggravates it. The last thing you need is a nasty infection setting in. I have seen what happens when a Peregrine neglects a wound from a demon. There was one man, years back when I first started, that lost a leg due to infection from a demon wound. Even with all the technology, medicine, and magic now a days, it still isn't always possible to heal that sort of thing," Jason replied, looking very serious.

"You're serious? He actually lost a leg?" Seth asked, worried now that maybe he should tend to his wound more thoroughly, never being one before to make a fuss over such things.

"Nah, I'm just kidding." Jason burst out laughing at the sheer look of terror and worry on Seth's face.

"Man. That was wrong." Seth sighed in relief and grinned from ear to ear, slightly sniggering as he watched Jason roll with laughter. "Come on." Seth motioned Jason to the map room. "Let's go see if we can find another storm that maybe Alec and Odessa would be returning in, that is if you can bring yourself upright from laughing at my expense?"

Jason, still laughing, answered Seth between breaths. "Sorry, I couldn't resist. It's been a long time since I was able to mess with a new Peregrine like that."

"Yeah well, that will teach me not to be so trusting in the future," Seth replied grinning as they walked into the mapping room by way of Simon's office, depositing the canister in its rightful place and laying the letter on his desk.

"Do you remember where they were supposed to make camp their last night?" Seth questioned, entering the map room, and busying himself looking through the storm archival books for anything else that would enable them to return should they have missed their storm.

Jason cleared his throat. "Yeah, I think so." He spun the globe positioned in the middle of the large table in the room's center, stopping on Niger Africa. "Riiight...here." He pointed to a spot on the globe. "A small river encampment in Niamey, Niger is where they were to make camp last night. They may have run into some kind of trouble. The Niger River was a very dangerous place in that time era. Lots of untrusting, angry native tribes that weren't too keen on the white man's visits, except for the fresh meat it provided. Most tribes were cannibalistic."

"Well, that sounds very reassuring!" Seth choked out, giving Jason an incredulous look. "Pulling my leg again?"

"Afraid not. Not this time. I'm *very* serious." He gave Seth a tight-lipped grin.

"Well, if they aren't back by the morning, what do we do?"

"There really isn't anything we can do, Seth. Just wait and see if they show up. If they aren't back by then we'll send Simon a grid message. Maybe he'll have an idea."

"How long does it take for the grid to deliver a letter anyway?" Simon hadn't shared that bit of information with Seth when he explained how it worked.

"Not long, maybe an hour or so, depending on where or how far it has to travel. You saw how fast it moves out there."

"Do you know where Simon went?"

"Probably Reader's Island. That's where they hold all the Dragoman council meetings," Jason replied. Not willing to tell Seth anymore about the island just yet. He was one of the few trusted Peregrines who knew about the island's location and amenities. Simon would inform the others when he was ready. Jason was sure that Odessa knew about it as well, but not many others. Each Dragoman probably had one or two of their most trusted Peregrines that they imparted with the finer details. But it was up to them to divulge information about the island, not the Peregrines. The Dragoman had insights into their mentored people that others did not. They alone chose who they thought was trustworthy enough. Luckily, Seth seemed satisfied with his reply and didn't ask any further questions. He seemed to be coming along well in the trust department and Jason didn't want to set him back any by making him think he had things to hide or things he didn't trust Seth with yet.

"Here we go," Seth said, looking down into a book. "There is another thunderstorm that blows in on the same front right after the one they were supposed to catch today. It hits Niger early in the morning, just north of the encampment where they should be now. Surely they won't miss this one seeing as how it should blow right through where they should currently be."

Jason thought a minute about Seth's remark before answering.

"They probably already know about it. Odessa usually has a backup plan. Alec is a ready fellow as well but tends to fly by the seat of his pants a bit more than she does." He smiled at Seth.

"Yeah I've gathered that just from talking to him. He has spoken to me about how things, *"always seem to just work out."* Making the quotation marks in the air mimicking Alec's accent.

Both men laughed at Seth's attempt to portray Alec's character, which he did well. They decided to retire to the living room and attempt a game of chess while they waited for bedtime; neither of them particularly sleepy, whether it was due to the nap earlier upon arriving, or the nagging feeling of worry over their friends. Hopefully, the morning would settle the uneasy feelings and their friends would make an untimely return.

Alec awoke to a heavy thunderstorm brewing just outside the tent. He looked down into the still unconscious face of Odessa. He felt her head and it seemed as though the fever had broken, his arm that had lain underneath her and his shirt front drenched with sweat, as well as the blankets that were tucked around her. He pulled himself up to look outside.

The storm was definitely large enough to create a portal but there was no way he could move Dee yet. They would just have to wait until she could at least walk well enough on her own before they could try to leave. They might be better off just staying where they were until Simon sent Seth and Jason to search for them. Alec knew that if they failed to return by today that Simon would do just that. He now understood why Odessa was so diligent about keeping to the schedule and letting Simon know their every move if possible. If it wasn't for that, they may never make it home.

Alec turned back to the tent's interior, stoked the slowly burning coals of the small fire that had been built the day before to warm Odessa, and sat next to her on the pallet. He pulled the blankets from around her injured leg and removed the bandages. The packing seemed to be clearing up some, the blackness of the ooze not quite as dark, which lent him to believe that the salve was doing its job and pulling the poison from her body. Or, they didn't get to it in time and that was all it was able to pull out. He set about reapplying the salve and clean bandages, and as he sat there, he wondered where his usual peppy, *it'll be fine*, attitude had gone? Reality had finally set in and he realized that they weren't guaranteed a tomorrow, even if they were working for God and had the mark of one of the Twelve. Surely God still needed Dee? Alec prayed that it was true.

Seth woke early again, another nightmare about Caroline pulling at his subconscious. It was just around four a.m., so he decided to grab the Bible from his nightstand where he had left it before their time-jump and picked up reading where he left off. He read through chapter three of Genesis before he laid the book down and went in search of some coffee. Entering the kitchen, he wasn't surprised to see Jason already there, coffee cup in hand.

"Morning. Another nightmare?" Jason asked when Seth entered the kitchen just around five.

"Yep, you too I suppose?" Seth watched Jason confirm with a shake of his head. "Think the dreams will ever end, or at least get better?" Seth sat down at the table with a steaming cup of coffee in hand.

"I don't know. I guess that all depends on whether or not we ever come to terms with our feelings. Me, I need to forgive myself which is a lot easier said than done. You, I'm not sure what *you* need. I guess we're both still a bit traumatized by the memories of past happenings." Jason somberly stared into his coffee cup as he swirled the dark liquid around the mug in his hands.

"If it's based on need, then my *need* is Caroline. That will never end until I get her back. The last thing I heard before blacking out and waking up here was her screaming my name amid all the noise and chaos from the earthquake. Now, I have the added thrill of her changing into a demon added to the dream. That's really messing with my head."

"I'm sorry, Seth. But you're just going to have to learn to figure out how to live without her. I have to tell you that you'll likely never see her again. I know it's hard and it hurts, but those are the facts. The sooner you come to terms with it, the better off you'll be. And you'll eventually get used to the demons messing with your life in any way they can."

Seth looked at his friend. He understood what Jason was saying and he knew he meant well, but Seth would never give up hope. No matter if it took the rest of his life. Even if it meant she had survived and moved on to marry someone else. As long as he knew she was all right, especially after that whole demon thing back in Israel. If demons could mess with his head like that, he'd have to be very careful in the future and keep his wits about him.

The sun started to rise in the sky, streaming rays of light across the treetops of the forest that stood on two sides of Simon's home, dappled light streaking across the kitchen table from the east facing window. Seth and Jason had breakfast, cleaned up, and decided to head outside to the charging station to see if there was any sign of Alec and Odessa. Hearing only the wildlife that roamed the forest floor and treetops surrounding the house, and no activity in the hidden charging cavern, they decided to head back inside and write a note to Simon informing him of Alec and Odessa not showing up at the allotted time. Speaking Simon's full name and placing the container on the barrier's surface, they watched in awe as it took off like a bolt of lightning heading straight upward and disappearing into the clouds high above the surface of the ground. They looked at each other, and realizing there was nothing left to do, they shrugged and went inside to dress for the training fields planning to work the majority of the day; hoping beyond hope that when they returned, Alec and Odessa would be back from their mission. They packed lunch and water and set out for the almost hour-long trek across the mountains.

Simon,

Our mission was successful. The Staff of Moses is secure. However, Alec and Odessa have not yet returned from their mission. They have missed both returning portals. What would you like us to do? We are worried and feel something may be wrong.

Jason

1 Thessalonians 5:17

Chapter 16

Reader's Island, Bermuda Triangle

It was the second morning of the third day on the island when Simon received a return message on the grid. He and the other Dragoman had already been combing through the Historical Events section of the archival library without any luck so far, when around 8:00 am, Shannon brought him a canister with his name iridescently glowing upon the outside.

"Simon, grid mail for you. It just came across not a few minutes ago." She handed him the canister.

They could tell who received a message when they were all gathered together because Simon had spelled the canisters to glow the name of the named. Of course, only Peregrines and Dragoman could see the lightly glowing name for protective reasons. Shannon, who once was a practicing Dragoman herself knew exactly which of them to deliver it to.

"Thank you, Shannon." He took the cylinder in hand.

"You're welcome." She smiled and left.

Simon opened it, reading the message with a heavy heart. He knew God had been moving him to pray for Odessa, but he didn't realize that they both hadn't returned.

Did that mean she had been hurt on the mission? Simon turned to the others in the room.

"I'm sorry, my friends, but I seem to have an emergency back home. I'm afraid I must leave at once. I'll use Barrier's Edge for faster traveling. Please send me a message should any of you uncover anything in the library here, will you?" Simon immediately left the room and headed upstairs to pack. He returned downstairs to the library about ten minutes later, and after saying his goodbyes, went outside to Barrier's Edge. He swiped his hand west to east along the barrier sending time backward until it landed on his century. Then, he swiped his hand on the century north to south until it landed on his decade, and with a simple thought as to the day and location, he stepped through the barrier and into his charging station back home within minutes. Traveling by Reader's Island barrier made quick work of peregrinations, but you never got to see much of the countryside that way.

Simon peeked outside of the caves hidden doorway, looked around carefully, and headed to his home making the short walk in record time. Walking through the door and finding no one there, he assumed that Seth and Jason had headed to the training fields to get in a good workout. He went into his office in search of the Staff of Moses and placed the empty canister on his desk. Finding the staff, he transferred it to the artifacts room for safe keeping. He then went into the kitchen checking the pantry for supplies. Finding they did indeed need a few items, he decided to head into Garganthera to market until the men returned. It shouldn't take him long and he would be back in time to have dinner ready when they returned. Just in case they returned before he did, he scribbled a note for them placing it on the kitchen counter and left the house for the barrier into town. He only prayed that Odessa was all right. During his walk into town, he would have to think about what to do and pray they could find them.

Seth and Jason spent the morning and afternoon sparring and working on Seth's abilities to avoid being struck when in battle. They decided to call it a day around two p.m. and head back to Simon's just in case he had sent them a return message. When they returned, they realized that someone had come back because the smell of food cooking wafted throughout the whole house.

"Hello?" Jason yelled as he entered the long hallway leading into the living area but received no response.

"Maybe Alec and Odessa finally made it back? Where do you think they are?" Seth asked as they both walked into the kitchen. He spotted a note on the kitchen counter and walked over to read it. The letter was from Simon, and it said that he had returned around eight-thirty that morning and was currently in the artifacts room cataloging the current items they had brought back.

"Simon's back. How did he get back so quickly after the message you sent?" Seth asked, offering a thought in answer to his own question. "Maybe the grid mail and Simon crossed ways and he didn't get it? He says he's in the artifacts room. Where's the Artifacts room?" Seth laid the note down on the counter.

"Travel from Reader's Island is faster than other places," Jason answered, and quickly changing the subject answered Seth's next question. "The Artifacts room is located on the other side of the wardrobe room in a secret, hidden, area. We forgot to show you that one. That would explain why he didn't hear us come in. Let's get cleaned up, and if he isn't out yet, afterwards, I'll show you where and how to find it."

"Sounds like a plan." Seth felt grimy from the workouts and was ready for a hot shower.

Simon sat in the artifacts room cataloging the Scroll of Rubric, the Staff of Moses, and several other items that he hadn't had the time to log as of yet. After putting them into the books, he would find them a temporary place to keep until they were needed. As he sat there writing, he had another overwhelming urge to pray for Odessa and Alec. *Where could they be?* he wondered. He offered up another quick prayer for their safety and return, after which an idea struck him. He would contact Ryan Halloran and have him build a small device that Simon figured would allow them to track the Peregrines in case anything like this happened in the future. He would send Ryan a message as soon as he finished cataloging the items which took him about fifteen minutes, and as he was walking through the wardrobe room headed for his office to send the message to Ryan, Jason and Seth were walking in.

"Hello there boys," Simon said joyfully, glad to see the two men.

"Simon," Jason replied, "I figured you were still in the artifacts room. I was taking Seth to show him where it was."

"Yes, we never got around to that did we?" Simon smiled as the three of them reached the center of the room. "You two go on ahead. I need to send a message to someone, after which, I'll meet you in the kitchen. We can discuss the dilemma with Odessa and Alec while we eat an early dinner."

"Sure thing. We'll meet you in about thirty minutes," Jason replied as he continued walking to the back of the room, Seth following behind.

Seth watched as Jason stopped at the archway in the center of the room. He walked to the right side and pushed the maroon curtain back, revealing the edge of the stone wall inset. Reaching out, where the curvature ended into strait stones that went to the floor, he grabbed the bottom stone on the edge of the archway, pulling it out of the wall. The stone looked just like the others but was hollow inside, covering a lever in the wall. He twisted the lever and the middle of the archway released and swung ajar inward. Jason replaced the fake stone, pushed the door open, and they walked inside. He turned and closed the door, which when it closed and latched, automatically turned on the lights within the room.

The entire room lit up in sections one at a time, starting closest to them and continuing outward from the center on both sides. The room was approximately sixty feet long and forty feet wide. It was an archaeologist's dream room. There were x-ray machines, tables, cleaning stations, tools, computers, shelves of books, and of course, artifacts. Simon had quite the collection.

"Why all the secrecy and high security?" Seth asked, curious to the reason the room was hidden.

"According to Simon, during the final days and the Final Battle, several of these artifacts will play an integral part in helping us to accomplish whatever it is we're to do," Jason explained as they walked around the room looking at the displays.

"All right, but why is it hidden? Didn't you tell me the demons weren't interested in the artifacts, just from stopping us?" Seth asked again, his question only half answered.

"Yes, but if they happen to find Simon's place and get through the enchantments, they could easily find the artifacts and destroy them. If some of these are crucial to our winning then destroying them could decide the final victory." Jason sat upon a stool positioned at one of the tables.

"Good point." Seth looked around at all the artifacts. "I suppose the Dragoman know how to use these things?"

"Yeah, I guess so." Jason wasn't really sure about the truth of it. "I guess I just never thought about that. Either they do or someone they know does. The Dragoman and Peregrines are the only people I know of who are in this battle, except for one other person, Safra Driscoll."

"Who is Safra?" Seth settled onto a stool across from him.

"She's a healer and a sort of...mystic who resides in Morocco in the 1900s. She's the only regular person that I know of that helps all the Dragoman and Peregrines on their missions. She can also peregrinate with any one of us."

"I thought that was impossible. For regular people to time jump I mean?" Seth asked, confused.

"It is, for everyone except Safra. I believe it's just one of the gifts she's been given by God. She's also a Seer. She finds the lost; whatever or whoever that is, sort of like seeing the future a little. She also interprets dreams. She's extremely wise and knowing, and, she has a very unique way of communicating with God." Jason stood as he finished speaking.

"How so?" Seth stood as well, following Jason from the room as the two men headed toward the kitchen to join Simon.

"It's in the way she worships and hears from God. He gives her visions through her special prayer time."

Seth thought it was very curious. He only offered up brief prayers to God, not really knowing if he listened or answered. But this woman Safra, God gave visions and information. He thought about her ability to peregrinate as well and couldn't help thinking that if Safra could do it, there may be hope for Caroline as well. Perhaps he could find Caroline and she could join him here. He would nonchalantly ask questions whenever he could with this line of thought in mind. Maybe, just maybe, he wouldn't have to live without Caroline after all. If he could figure out this time traveling thing exactly, perhaps he could jump back before the accident and convince Caroline somehow about all of this. Then again, she may think he's lost his mind. He would likely think the same of her if the situations were reversed.

They reached the kitchen and Simon was standing at the stove stirring the contents of a large stock pot.

"The soup's finished and I just took the rolls out of the oven. There's green salad and dressings already on the table, along with a pitcher of iced-tea," Simon said, ladling soup into three large bowls, handing them off to Seth and Jason who carried them to the table and sat down. He grabbed the plate of rolls and carried them to the table to join the others.

The men quickly ate their food, pushing their empty bowls to the center of the table, ready to discuss finding Alec and Odessa.

Seth started. "Well, Simon, is there anything we can do about Alec and Odessa?"

"I'm not sure. The two storms that blew through Nigeria in the last day were the only ones close to the area that they should have been camped at. We may need to retrace everywhere they went. Odessa gave me a tentative route they were going to follow depending on where they walked out of the storm, so we can start there. We'll need to find a storm as close to Niamey as possible." Simon reached over and picked up the storm archive book he had placed on the table earlier, thumbing through the storms for that year.

"What about returning? There can't be that many storms in the same area at the same time," Seth said.

"Well, I may have to generate a storm to return through."

"What do you mean by 'generate'?" Seth asked curiously.

Jason replied, "Simon can magically create a storm."

"Really, how does that work?"

"Well, it takes a great deal of my strength to generate a storm large enough to create a portal, and I am considerably weaker for several days after. Which means, depending on what has happened to Alec and Odessa, you and Jason would be responsible for whatever needs that may arise for a few days. It really zaps me, and I'm afraid I'm quite useless for a while." Simon tried to act as natural about it as possible, but Seth noticed the small exchange of looks between the two men.

Seth had a feeling there was more to it than Simon was letting on, and that option may come with consequences. "Maybe there's another way. We can plan as best we can and then wait and see what happens. That should be a last resort attempt."

"I agree with Seth. We can't risk your health, Simon. Let's just see what the storm archives hold. Africa is a big place. We may be able to catch a storm just with a bit of traveling."

Simon looked at Jason. "Yes, but if one, or both Alec and Odessa are injured, travel may be nearly impossible. So it must be kept open and receptive as a viable option. I won't risk either of their lives just to avoid creating a storm." Simon's stern expression brooked no argument.

"All right, we can deal with that," Seth answered, looking at Jason who was slow to agree.

Jason picked up one of the books and leafed through it. "Now, let's heavily search these books here and see what storms we can catch a ride on."

The three of them sat at the table for the next few hours plotting routes on a map of Africa for the years 1794-1796, locating storms, laying out travel options available during that era with time allotments between different selected documented storms, and making possible necessary plans for traveling with an injured person or two.

Once they had their plans laid out, they decided to pack and get ready to leave as soon as possible. They would leave tonight, traveling until around midnight when they would make camp, then set out around five the next morning. They met up around five p.m. in the living room and left Simon's for the cave to peregrinate. After saying a prayer for safety and success, they leapt through the portal into the southern central part of Africa in search of their friends; hoping and praying along the way they would find them both alive and well.

Chapter 17

Burkina Faso, Africa, 1795 AD

Simon, Jason, and Seth exited the heavy thunderstorm, just catching it on the backside before it diminished. They had been fortunate enough to find the same storm that had blown through Niamey earlier in the day still going strong and moving slowly into lower Africa. They were able to time-jump to the territory of Kantchari located in central Burkina Faso, almost straight south of Niamey in Niger. They sought the shelter of a portico attached to the outside of a local store to wait out what little of the storm was left.

When the rain stopped about ten minutes later, they went in search of some horses to buy for the near ninety-mile journey through the interior of the African jungle. To reach Niamey, where they hoped that Odessa and Alec had made it to for the last leg of their journey, it would take them twenty-four hours of straight travel to make the distance. They would need to rest at some point, especially due to the fact that none of them had slept since the night before. The journey would be hard and dangerous, traveling through the jungle and having to cross the river. They would need to travel further west to be able to exit the river at Niamey. If Alec and Odessa weren't there and hadn't yet been there, they would backtrack to Timbuktu where they would have started their peregrination.

It was just past six in the evening when they acquired some horses and supplies, after which they headed north trying to stay out of the thickest parts of the jungle and stay on the travel paths as much as possible. As long as the paths stayed due north and didn't turn too much east or west. They traveled into the early morning hours, deciding to make camp around two a.m. They were all about to fall out of the saddle from sheer exhaustion, and their alertness to their surroundings was all but nonexistent. Seth and Jason made camp while Simon cast a protection spell on the area around them, making it possible for all of them to sleep instead of someone staying up as watchman. They would rest until sunup and head out again after eating a quick breakfast.

Dawn seemed to come early with none of them feeling particularly rested, but at least they hadn't had to fear being mauled by something wild during the night, thanks to Simon's protection spell. They ate quickly and headed out again, being on high alert since protection spells only worked if you were staying put. Jason took point, Simon in the middle, and Seth pulling up the rear as they moved as quickly as possible. They should reach their destination close to midnight as long as they didn't have any trouble.

The morning sun was already heating up the air around them, the bugs swarming in the balminess surrounding their already perspiring bodies. They did have the sense to put on mosquito spray or they would have already been eaten alive. It did offer some protection but would not keep them completely safe, especially from the dangers of malaria.

There was no breeze to be found anywhere, and it was only eight a.m. The dark coolness of the jungle was looking more and more tempting, threatening to lure them in as they traveled. They would eventually have to travel the jungles interior soon enough. They certainly didn't want to risk the dangers any earlier than necessary.

They trekked on until almost noon when they came upon a small village nestled on the outside of the jungle's edge. They stopped to water the horses, eat some lunch, hydrate, and rest both themselves and the animals. They had traveled about thirty-five miles so far leaving about fifty-five to go. It would take them about another twelve hours of straight travel, putting them there after midnight, not adding in the necessary breaks. That would put them traversing the dangers of the Niger River past midnight and that would be unacceptable. Simon decided they would travel until they reached the banks of the river and camp there until morning, then they would trade the horses for a boat and head downstream until they reached Niamey.

Since they would spend the night on the river, they took a bit more time to replenish their bodies with both food and sleep. They all took about a two-hour nap after lunch, being able to relax in the protection of the village. When they awoke, it was almost two p.m. They saddled the horses, climbed on once more, and set out for the third leg of their journey.

By the time night began to fall, they had just entered the thickness of the jungle where they would have to travel the interior the remainder of the way to the river village. They kept close together lighting torches to illuminate their way through the dark night and thick underbrush of the forest floor. The horses would alert them to anything that they sensed as dangerous, and the fire from the torches would, hopefully, ward off any animals who thought they might make a good meal. They traveled in silence, trying to avoid making as little unnatural noise as possible, whispering to each other, or whistling to gain the others attention. This only worked on the animals however, the natives would be drawn to the light of the torches, but it was a chance they would have to take.

The path started to narrow and become nearly invisible, making it apparent that no one had come this way for some time. As they pressed on, they did have to remove a couple of smaller felled trees to allow the horses room to pass.

Seth said, "It may have been a better idea to ditch the horses earlier in the day in one of the villages we passed. Traveling without them might have been easier."

"Perhaps," Simon answered, "but we are making much better time with them, even with the obstacles we have to remove."

They pulled and prodded the horses on, even having to dismount and walk for about an hour. They had finally stumbled onto a clearing and were just about to mount the animals once again when the horses began to get jittery and began dancing around, lowly whinnying.

"Sh...," Jason whispered to Seth, Simon, and his large brown mare, taking the reins, and tying them off around a tree branch. He stepped carefully forward, holding the torch out in front of him and slowly scanned the clearing. Seth followed suit, backing up to Jason to cover the area behind them. Simon tied off all the horses to keep them from bolting in case of an animal attack and joined the two men in the center of the clearing. Just as he reached them he heard it. It was definitely animal. He could hear the low growling sound, although he was unsure where it was coming from. Scanning the canopy of branches above them, his eyes landed on the source of the sounds.

Simon tapped Jason and Seth on the shoulders and pointed to a branch approximately forty feet above them on the edge of the clearing. A rather large panther was making its way from tree to tree through the lower hanging branches. Its' glasslike eyes illuminating like small light bulbs against the darkness of the forest's lower canopy. It watched them, and then the horses, surely sizing up which would be the easier target. It hunkered down on the branch once it realized they had seen it, taking a stance to pounce. Seth, realizing the animal was going to jump the horses, pulled his sword from its sheath, and slowly walked over to where they were tied off. Jason and Simon did the same to help him should a battle arise. Instead of pulling his sword, Jason slowly slid his bow off his shoulder and grabbed an arrow from the quiver on his back. He loaded the arrow and slowly pulled the bow strings taut, ready to let go at any moment. Just then, movement caught his eye from the underbrush to the far left of where the panther sat watching them in the tree. Jason, keeping his arrow trained upon the panther, alerted Seth to the movement.

"Um...Seth."

Seth looked at Jason who motioned over his shoulder with his head.

Seth looked over to see the underbrush move, and he could hear the noise growing louder by the second. Unsure what to expect, the three men braced themselves for battle against a treed panther and whatever larger animal was coming at them on the ground.

Just as the brush began to crunch loudly, Seth's nerves grew ever more taut, his heart beginning to race in anticipation of what was to come. The animals broke through at the clearing's edge, and a small herd of elephants lumbered toward them. Several mature adults and two smaller calves walked past them. The men quickly stepped to the side behind the horses, still trying to keep an eye on the panther which had suddenly disappeared, apparently unwilling to take on an elephant herd for his supper. However, it hadn't seemed too daunted by the three of them and their horses. The men tried to keep as still as possible while the herd passed as to not frighten them into stampeding. They watched as the great beasts passed them by, seemingly uncaring as to their presence.

Once the last elephant had lumbered past, they quickly mounted the horses and rode as quickly as possible without full out running the animals. It would be treacherous to run them through the jungle, as one could step into a hole and break a leg. They kept their eyes and ears peeled, listening, and watching the jungle shadows passing all around them. They only had about an hour before reaching the village, and they prayed to God that it would be an uneventful one.

Just as they were coming close to the jungle's edge, a dart whizzed past Simon's head and imbedded itself in a nearby tree trunk.

"Run!" Simon screamed, triggering the flight response in all of them including the horses that sensed the fear in the men. The horses bolted as the men urged them on as fast as they could through the underbrush. They could make out the village lights ahead through the edge of the tree line, but they were still a-ways off. As the horses trudged through, the men continued to dodge arrows and darts being flung their way from an unseeable adversary. It was dark and almost impossible to see past the horses nose. They had to keep hold of the reins to guide the horses, and the torches to see where they were going, making retaliation impossible. A few of the arrows found their way into the thick part of Jason's saddle and into the rump of Seth's horse.

Just a few more hundred feet or so and they would break through the edge and into the open. Knowing the history of the area, they knew there would be several sentries standing guard at the village's edge with rifles. Also knowing that they could hear the commotion of the running horses and see the light of the torches coming at them, they would be ready to fire. Jason and Simon both began yelling in their best Hausa.

"Don't shoot! Friends! Natives attacking!"

Ready to take their chances with the guards instead of the headhunters, they burst forth from under the canopy into the clearing surrounding the village which stood several hundred feet from the jungle's edge for safety. They could hear the tribal screams of their attackers; angry they had missed their targets. They could also see the outlines of the sentries, rifles aimed and ready to fire.

They sped on as fast as the horses could go, knowing full well they could still be hit by an arrow or dart at this distance, still yelling 'friendlies' as they quickly approached. They wouldn't be safe until they reached the village. The natives would not venture out toward the village for fear of the guns the sentries carried. They knew their arrows, darts, and spears were no match for the guns. These river villages were swarming with traders from every corner of the world, and so the three of them knew they would be welcome and safe.

They didn't rein in the horses until they sped past the guards at the village edge. Once safely inside the small encampment, they dismounted the horses, almost as out of breath as the animals which they had escaped certain death upon. They took the horses to the water to drink and tended to the wounds that had been afflicted upon a few of them by the arrows and darts. The injuries weren't life threatening as long as the arrows which had found their mark weren't poisonous. Simon took the arrows they had pulled from the horse's flesh and holding them in his hand by the feathered ends, took his other hand and waved it slowly over the edge of the arrows, careful not to touch them, his eyes closed as he whispered silently into the star filled heavens.

"I don't sense any poison on the tips, thank God. We need to do a thorough check of the animals and ourselves while we unsaddle them, then find a place to bed down for the night. That was a very close call Gentlemen. I'm not against feeding the locals, but I don't wish to do so with my own hide," Simon said, shivering at the thought of almost being caught by the headhunters as he wandered off in search of a place for them to sleep.

Seth and Jason looked at each other and grinned at Simon's description of their narrow escape as they pulled the saddles and bags from the horse's backs. Once finished, Seth took a deep breath of the night air as he stood gazing out across the surface of the slowly moving water of the Niger River.

"What's going through that head of yours?" Jason asked, coming up to stand beside Seth, also looking out over the water.

"I was just thinking how simple these people's lives are, and yet how dangerous it is for them living here. Looking out over the water, it seems peaceful, but I know how deadly that river can be. It just really makes you think about your own life and how fortunate we are. Yet at the same time, I sort of envy their way of life. Does that make sense?" Seth asked with a sort of a chuckle.

"Yeah, it does. I felt the same way the first time I experienced something like this. Aside from the deadliness of the jungle, natives, panthers, and malaria, it all seems pretty perfect in ways. But I have to say, I'm partial to air-conditioning." Jason smiled and Seth looked confused by his answer.

"What's air conditioning?" Seth asked earnestly as Jason laughed loudly at his own realization.

"Sorry, I didn't realize you had yet to experience that as well. I had forgotten that it wasn't invented until 1902 and probably wasn't mass distributed yet. It is a type of cooling device that regulates the temperature of your home or automobile to whatever setting you like." Jason explained as best he could, smiling at the luck of being paired with someone who didn't have all the comforts that he was so use to and had taken for granted most of his life. It certainly made him think about how to reply when answering questions.

Hearing someone approaching, Seth and Jason turned to see Simon walking toward them.

"I've found a place for us to bed down for the night and spoken with one of the village men who has a boat. He'll take the horses as trade for some provisions, a place to sleep for the night, and a lift to Niamey encampment in the morning." Simon stopped just in front of the two men. "I don't know about you two, but this old man has had enough excitement for one evening. I'm turning in. If you wish to follow me, I'll show you which hut we're in."

"I'm with you Simon," Seth said, pulling his hand over his tired eyes. "I could do with a good night's sleep, especially since this isn't over yet. And we have no idea when it will be."

"I agree. That run through the jungle did me in. Plus, we just got back from a previous mission we hadn't fully recovered from yet," Jason added, following Simon to the small grass and mud-built hut that they were graciously given all to themselves to rest for the night. They rolled out their bedrolls with sleep quickly finding their tired bodies.

The next morning as the sun topped the tree line, they stirred from their slumber, realizing that both Seth and Jason had slept without being stirred awake by their constant nightmares. Figuring it was due more to sheer exhaustion than anything else they didn't get too excited to believe it would be a permanent occurrence.

As Seth and Jason packed the bags and bedding, Simon went in search of their river guide. When he returned several minutes later with the guide and some extra provisions, they headed toward the river's edge to board the small boat that would take them downriver, hopefully straight to Alec and Odessa. Simon, after speaking to some of the locals the night before, decided to hire a few more boats and men with guns to ride downstream with them as bodyguards. Simon related what he had learned to Seth and Jason.

"It seems, after speaking to several of the villagers last night, that there was a boat that traveled past here just two days ago. It had a man and a woman in the boat that fit Alec and Odessa's description. The villagers here heard distant gunfire about ten minutes after they passed this village. They say they were probably attacked by native headhunters. The Niamey Encampment is approximately a thirty-minute boat ride from here. And we have to pass the same tribe that may have attacked Alec and Odessa, so we need to be alert and ready. Since we have a local guide, and the extra two boats with armed men, perhaps they won't attack but we need to be prepared just in case."

They all climbed into the boats; their weapons ready at the slightest noise from the river's banks as they headed downstream to Niamey. Simon prayed earnestly for their safety, and that they would find Alec and Odessa well. As they floated downriver they saw a few natives standing at the river's edge, spears in hand, watching the passing boats. The men in the boats held their guns where they would be easily seen. The natives turned and disappeared into the thick brush that lined the river's edges. The men in the boats still stood ready, knowing full well that just because you didn't see them, it didn't mean they weren't there. They were masters at hiding, knowing the area very well. They could still mount a full-scale attack at any moment.

Fortunately, the boat ride to Niamey was a quiet one, and as they pulled up to the shore to exit the boat, the villagers were all a buzz with the arrival of the three boats full of men, especially when they looked at Seth. Most of these people in this region, men included, were small people. Simon could make out that they were calling Seth a giant and were very interested in him. Seth appeared a bit uncomfortable by all the attention, making Simon smile.

The loud murmuring of the villagers outside the tent caught Alec's attention and he pulled the tent flap back to see what the ruckus was about. At first he thought he was dreaming, but there was no mistaking the giant of a man looking very uncomfortable standing amidst all the villagers gathered tightly around him, all vying to touch some part of him. He then noticed Jason and Simon in the crowd as well pulling up the rear.

"Seth, Simon, Jason!" Alec yelled, running from the tent.

His voice caught the attention of the three men who smiled brightly at the image of their friend who appeared to be quite disheveled but well.

"Alec, I am so glad to see you're all right," Simon said, grabbing the man and hugging him tightly, Seth and Jason doing the same.

"Yes, I am fine. But Odessa is not. Come, I will show you." He led them to the tent where she lay, still unconscious.

"How long has she been like this Alec?" Simon asked, concern lacing his voice and demeanor.

"For two days. We were attacked by headhunters on the river, and she took an arrow to the leg. It was in her leg for about fifteen minutes before it was able to be removed. It had been tipped with a powerful poison. Her fever broke only last night, and she has stirred a few times, but she has yet to fully awaken."

"How's the leg?" Simon watched as Alec pulled back the covers to reveal the injury.

"The poultice the medicine man placed on it has pulled out the majority of the infection, but I am not sure if it is all out of her system. I have never seen her so sick, Simon. I am truly worried," Alec replied, his heart heavy, the worry visible on his face and in his body language.

"I believe she will be fine. She's a tough woman, and she's made it this far. But we need to get her home. Safra could tend to her much better than they can here. We have a route planned, and there is another large storm that will be coming through within the next few days toward Egypt, but we must hurry. I'm not sure how quickly we can travel with Odessa like this. We'll have to make a pallet to carry her on. We haven't any time to spare. Alec, go inquire of the villagers if they have anything we can use to take her out on. Jason, see if you can procure some horses and maybe a cart of sorts. Seth, you help me bundle her up and gather all of Alec and Odessa's supplies."

Simon dished out orders and the others obeyed without hesitation. Odessa was breathing but her skin was pale, and her leg appeared to have infection settling in. The poison may not be a threat any longer but an infection in her weakened state could kill her. They would have to get her home quickly and Simon would have to send word to Nuncio to bring Safra to Garganthera. Odessa's life may well depend upon it.

Chapter 18

Simon sat watching Odessa, keeping an eye on her vital signs. *What to do?* he thought. The nearest recorded storm due to hit anywhere around them was to be in Egypt, 1600 and some odd miles away. A trip like that would take them approximately two weeks to make, and straight across the desert. Not the safest route to take. He feared Odessa may not make it for the next few days without proper treatment. They had to get back to Barrier's Edge at Garganthera. Two weeks was completely unacceptable. As much as he didn't want to have to create a storm, it may be necessary to get them home safely, and to save Odessa's life.

Seth busied himself gathering what equipment and supplies they had while Simon tended to Odessa's wound. Alec returned about thirty minutes later with a few other men to help lift Odessa onto a makeshift stretcher fashioned from animal skins and small trees, lashed together with vines. They carried her outside, placing her in the back of a small, open, wagon hitched to the back of two of the three horses Jason had managed to acquire through bartering. The tribe that stayed in this particular encampment was extremely friendly and helpful. If it had not been for their medicine man, Odessa would surely have died.

Once they loaded the wagon, Alec and Seth drove while Simon stayed in the back with Odessa with Jason riding point on the other available horse. Alec waved goodbye to the people who had taken care of both him and Odessa over the last several days. He would be eternally grateful for God's provision of these people at their hour of greatest need. Were it not for them, Odessa would be dead for certain, Alec having no idea how to treat or tend to her wounds because of the poison that had started its course through her ailing body.

The trip northeast toward the desert would be safer due to most of the headhunter tribes living closer to the river within the jungle's borders. The closer you got to the desert, the scarcer food and water became. The tribes tended to stay as close as possible to their food and water supply.

They had traveled for about an hour when Simon yelled, "Stop the wagon! Odessa's temperature is beginning to spike again. She can't take much more of this jostling around back here."

"Okay, what do you want to do, Simon?" Seth asked, watching the man for a reply.

"The only thing we can do. I have to generate a thunderstorm." Simon jumped down from the wagon and made his way in front of the men.

"Simon, you can't..." Jason started saying when Simon interrupted him.

"I can and I will, Jason! We have no other choice! I didn't say this before, but if we don't get Odessa proper medical attention quickly, she could die. Infection is settling into her leg," Simon yelled a little too forcefully, worry settling into his mind and heart.

"When the storm opens up and the portal forms, Seth, you'll have to help me back into the wagon. Then, Alec, drive the wagon and horses through."

Not understanding why Simon would need help, Seth jumped out of the seat and went to stand next to him.

"Will the horses and wagon make it through the time jump?"

"I don't know, Seth, we've never tried before now. I suppose it's time to find out." He looked at Seth with a sideways glance. Saying a prayer and standing facing the open plains of the land, Simon grabbed his staff with both hands and raised it into the air, his face pointed to the sky. He began chanting a spell into the air, his voice growing in power and strength as he began circling the staff above his head.

Clouds began forming out of nothing, billowing quickly across the sky toward one pivotal point in the center. They quickly turned dark and thick as they circled the sky, obeying Simon's commands. Thunder started to boom, and lightning skittered from heavy cloud to heavy cloud as Simon chanted and swayed ever more strongly.

Soon the wind was howling across the grasses and sands, blowing up little dust storms here and there. The lightning grew ever stronger, echoing thunderous booms across the ground in front of them as the rain began to pelt down thick, heavy, drops. As the skies opened up and the clouds began releasing their fullness, the portal began opening and Simon literally dropped to his knees, catching himself with his staff before dropping full out onto the ground in front of him. Seth, in total awe watching Simon create a massive storm out of nothing, just caught the motion out of the corner of his eye. He rushed to Simon, picking the man up and literally carrying him to the wagon, depositing him in the back. He quickly jumped back up into the seat as Alec flicked the reins urging the skittish horses on into the thick of the storm. Jason stayed close to the wagon as he sat astride his horse, not willing to get too far away from everyone else just in case the horses couldn't peregrinate. No one had ever tried taking an animal through a time-portal. They all prayed earnestly and audibly as they raced their animals toward the portal. As they reached the edge, they all seemed to close their eyes, unsure if this would be the end of them or if they would be thrown through to the other side, either from the animals dying or the wagon completely disintegrating beneath them.

To their complete and utter surprise, they all made it through safe and sound, exiting the storm on the other side directly beside Simon's home.

Seth and Alec seemed surprised to have ended up where they were. There was no storm at Barrier's Edge. They weren't in the cave and they were in the fourth dimension. Jason and Simon seemed grateful to be alive as Jason whooped and hollered at their making it home in one piece.

They pulled the horses to a halt as Jason, Seth, and Alec jumped from their seated positions and rushed to the back of the wagon. Alec and Jason grabbed Odessa's stretcher, and took her into the house to her room, while Seth grabbed Simon and carried him inside, laying him on a couch in the living area. Simon was coherent but very weak, and strangely enough he looked older somehow. He appeared to have a few more age lines, and his hair appeared to be a bit more salted than peppered now. Seth shook his head at that last observation thinking it must be due to Simon's sudden weakness and exhaustion.

Seth ran into Simon's office scrawling a message onto a piece of paper and stuffing it into a canister. As he did so, he realized he only knew one person's name, and that was Safra Driscoll. He didn't have her full name.

"Jason, I need you!" Seth yelled across the house as the men exited Odessa's room, Jason looking at Seth and Alec running to the bathroom for supplies and medicines to tend to Odessa's needs.

"Yeah, what's up?" Jason asked as he quickly went to check on Simon on the couch, who lay nearly unconscious.

"I need a name, man. Please tell me you know a full given name of whoever we need to contact at Reader's Island?"

"Yes, I do. Give me the canister." Jason took the canister speaking Safra Pilar Driscoll against the outside and handed it back to Seth.

Seth bolted down the hallway and across the yard, placing the canister upon the grid and watching it speed away.

"God," he spoke into the air, "If ever we needed you, it's now. Please let that thing get there faster than ever before." Seth breathed deeply and slowly, trying to calm his frazzled nerves. He turned, realizing they had forgotten all about the horses which patiently stood and waited, and ran back inside heading toward Simon.

"How's he doing Jason?"

"He'll be okay. It just takes an awful lot out of him when he has to do that. It may even take him a few days to recover," Jason said, looking at Seth.

"Let's get him to his room, get him changed and into bed. We surely don't need him catching a cold or pneumonia on top of all of this."

He and Jason each gathered an arm around and under Simon and carried him to his room. After they tended to him and got him settled, they went to check on Odessa.

"Alec, how's she doing?" Jason asked as the two men poked their head through the door, entering her room and walking over to the bedside.

"I'm not sure," Alec said as he pulled the covers up tight to her chin, tucking them around her already nearly stripped-down body, using the cool water and clean rag to wipe her face and neck.

"Hey, she'll be all right," Seth said, placing his hand on Alec's shoulder for reassurance.

Alec turned to look at him. "I hope and pray you are right, my friend," he said, turning his attention back to Odessa.

"I'll take over here for a while, Alec. You should get some rest as well," Jason said, offering his assistance. "Besides, I do have some medical knowledge."

"You can check the wound if you wish, but I'm not going anywhere until Safra gets here. Thanks all the same." Alec only briefly took his eyes off Odessa to glance at Jason.

Jason pulled the covers up from the edge of the bed and looked at the wound on her leg. Simon had been right. It did appear that an infection was beginning to set in.

"Have you given her anything for pain or fever yet? I saw you grab some things from the bathroom earlier."

"No not yet. I want to, but I'm not sure what Safra will want to do. We should wait to hear from them. How long do you think it will be before we hear back?" Worry evident in Alec's voice.

"Well, the message we sent a few days back seemed to get there quickly, because when we returned from the training fields, Simon was already here. We sent it before we went up that morning and we came back at two. He had already gone to the market and started dinner. So, I'd say it's pretty quick," Jason answered, certain they would get a quick reply.

"Fella's, I'm going to check on Simon," Seth announced. "But after that, I have a few questions I'd like answered, Jason. You can do that while we tend to the horses we left in the front yard."

"Oh yeah, poor animals. I had completely forgotten about them. I'm not used to having them around." Jason stood. "I'll come with you, Seth, to check on Simon. Then we can go take care of them."

"We'll let you know, Alec as soon as we hear anything," Seth reassured him as they left the room.

They peeked into the room to check on Simon who seemed to be sleeping peacefully, then headed out the front of the house to where they had left the horses and wagon. Jason checked the horses over, making sure they hadn't suffered any trauma from the time jump as Seth unhitched the two from the wagon.

"All right, man, talk," Seth said, not looking at Jason as he pulled the yolk off the horses and separated them from the wagons tongue. "It didn't go unnoticed how you were totally against Simon creating that storm. And now, the man is near unconscious and was limp as a wet noodle when I picked him up and put him in the wagon."

"Speaking of that...Seth, I knew you were strong, but you picked Simon up like he was nothing. He's not a small man. I have to say, that was a very daunting image," Jason said, appreciation evident in his voice, smiling at Seth who returned one. "As for what happened to Simon, he can do a lot of things. Amazing things. But some of them come at a price. When he uses that kind of power, it takes its toll on his body. Creating a storm is always a last resort. He's only done it twice before today."

"Why is it so hard on him? I couldn't help noticing he seemed a bit more haggard afterwards, almost like he had aged somehow." Seth looked sideways at Jason as he walked the horses around to let them graze.

"That's because he has." Jason walked his horse to meet the others, stopping in front of Seth. "Every time Simon generates a storm, his body ages about five years. He's actually only forty-three years old. Since he became a Magus and has created three storms, he is fifteen years older. He was fifty-three when we left this morning. Now his body has aged another five years in just a matter of minutes. Putting him at about fifty-eight years old now. Sometimes, cheating time has a price. Natural peregrination, what we do, doesn't affect time like what Simon did today does."

"I can't believe that's possible but, there are a lot of things that I would have found impossible just a few weeks ago." Seth shook his head at all he had learned. "Isn't there some way to avoid that in the future? I mean, with all the things that are possible here between the magic and the technology, surely there is some device that can be invented to generate a storm instead of Simon literally shaving years off his life?" Seth looked at Jason with a questioning expression.

"I don't know. But I do know who to ask about that. There is this brilliant technological whizz who happens to be a Dragoman. His name's Ryan Daniel Halloran, for future reference. He's an odd kind of guy but wicked smart, especially when it comes to any kind of technology. I believe he is high-functioning autistic. It's a more recent disability diagnosis," Jason explained at the questioning look on Seth's face at the mention of autism. "I'll send him a grid message later tonight and ask him about that."

"Sounds like a plan to me. One more question though. What is a Magus?"

"It's just a singular form for Magi. They were known in past years as people who had supernatural powers, such as Simon."

"You mean, like a wizard?"

"Sort of. But Simon doesn't like the term. It's often associated as dark, and the Bible talks about witchcraft being evil. Simon's abilities are God given gifts. So, he prefers to be called a Magus."

Seth seemed satisfied with the reply, shaking his head in thoughtful speculation. "Now, what do we do about these animals? We can't just leave them out here to roam freely." Seth looked over the vast alternating landscape surrounding Simon's place.

"You're right. How about we start building a fence and a barn while we wait around on everyone else?"

"Sure, that will at least keep us busy." They entered the house to change out of the still rain-drenched, 1800 period clothing, into something easy to work in.

Just as the two men ventured outside to start on the fence and barn, they noticed two people coming out of the woods behind Simon's home. They were walking from the direction where the hidden cave was located. At first they were startled by the sudden unannounced appearances, but then Jason seemed to recognize who they were. He pulled the gloves from his hands and walked toward them. One man was older and walked with a cane and a limp. The other person, a tiny, older, Arabic woman followed closely behind.

"Nuncio, Safra, are we ever glad to see you two!" Jason said as he pumped the man's hand and gave Safra a large bear hug.

"We really need your help. I'm not sure what all Seth mentioned in the message, but Odessa is pretty bad off, and Simon, well he had to generate another storm." Jason filled them in as they approached the house introducing them to Seth as they passed him by.

The four people entered the house, stopping to peek in on Simon once again, and then heading straight to Odessa's room where Alec still sat, ever attentive to any sound or movement she might make.

"Safra, I am so happy you are here!" Alec stood to embrace the tiny woman who smiled warmly at him. Alec filled Safra and Nuncio in on what had happened, after which she ushered everyone out of the room, much to the chagrin of Alec.

"You need to rest as well, Alec," she admonished him. "We already have two people to tend. We do not need a third. I will take good care of her. She will mend well, I promise."

Safra closed the door against Alec and the rest of them. Jason and Seth talked Alec into taking a nap in his room, and Nuncio spent the better part of the afternoon traveling back and forth between Simon's and Odessa's room, reassuring Seth and Jason that they had everything covered. The men returned to the chore of fence and barn building to give the new residence of Barrier's Edge some shelter, certain that their friends were in good hands.

Chapter 19

"Jason! Grab the side wall there will you and push up hard!" Seth yelled, needing help lifting the large, framed wall he had just built into place.

He and Jason had spent the remainder of yesterday afternoon and well into the night building a wide fenced area for the horses to roam and eat grass. Seth had dug and set all of the poles while Jason nailed the cross boards, attaching them all together. This morning they had gotten up at the break of dawn and started on the barn.

They had ventured into Garganthera yesterday before noon with two of the horses and the wagon to purchase the wood to build with. They had plenty of trees around Simon's place, but nothing was cut or dry and it would take months for them to do it that way. Plus, they would have needed a sawmill to cut the boards. The wood purchased from the city was dried, and the pieces were large, so the wood went further.

"All right, got it!" Jason yelled in return. The two men lifted the last wall into place and began securing it together with a hammer and some nails.

"I have to say, I never thought I would be using a hack saw, hammer, and nails to build anything. With all the modern conveniences of 2017, a nail gun, screws, circular saw, and a battery powered drill would have made all this go *way* faster," Jason said, shaking his head as he thought about what was missing.

"I've never heard of any of those things. Hammer and nails is what I'm used to," Seth said smiling.

"It shows." Jason smiled back. "You almost work faster with these things than I could with the modern tools. What say we take a break after we finish this wall. We need to eat lunch anyway, and see how Simon and Odessa are doing?"

"Sounds like a plan. Besides, we've actually gotten a lot done today so far. Maybe we can coax Alec out to help us with the barn after lunch. It'll help occupy his mind for a while."

"Yeah, I've noticed he's taking Odessa's illness really hard. I knew they were close partners, but I didn't think they were that close," Jason said, thinking about Alec's reaction yesterday, and earlier when he had offered to sit with her.

"I don't know how she feels about him, but I can promise you that Alec is in love with Odessa," Seth said, hammering in one more nail before breaking for lunch.

"How do you know? Did he say something to you?"

"No. But I've felt the same way he does, and I can tell when a man feels like that about a woman." Seth finished and laid the hammer and bag of nails on the back of the wagon.

"I have to say, I never really had time for relationships. Between the military and then college and vet school, I was one busy guy. Then, after school I was only a few years in business when I ended up here."

"There wasn't anyone here that caught your attention?" Seth asked as they walked toward the house.

"No. This life is a tough one. It's kind of hard to form relationships doing this. Everyone's always going off in different directions for weeks at a time. I don't even think

I've met all the other Peregrines, and I've been at this for eight years. Besides, pickings are slim you know. There aren't a whole lot of age-appropriate women doing this." Jason chuckled as they entered the long hallway heading toward the living area.

Alec stuck his head out of the kitchen archway when he heard the men coming down the hall.

"Hey guys, I have some lunch ready here in the kitchen after you wash up." Alec wiped his hands on a dish towel.

"Thanks Alec, we appreciate that. How is Simon and Odessa doing?" Jason asked.

"Simon is awake and regaining his strength pretty quickly. But Safra and Nuncio won't let him out of bed yet." Alec's slightly crooked grin spread across his face. "Dee is conscious, but still not completely lucid. Safra said she had the infection in her leg under control and it is starting to heal. She seems to think Dee will make a full recovery, but it will take her body time to recover from all the stress of the poison and infection."

"That's great Alec. I'm glad everyone is on the mend," Seth offered. "I think I'm going to head to the bathroom and wash up, see you in a bit." He crossed the living room and disappeared into his bedroom.

"Yeah, I should too," Jason said. "You want me to stick my head in the rooms and let the others know lunch is ready while I'm headed that way?"

"Yes, that will work. I will finish up in here and it will be on the table by the time everyone comes in to eat." Alec turned to enter the kitchen once more.

Jason informed everyone that Alec had lunch on the table and that he and Seth would join them shortly. Safra said she would take her lunch and some broth and water for Odessa in the room. Jason informed her that one of them would return shortly with a platter. He then stuck his head in the kitchen to tell Alec of Safra's wishes and headed to wash up. It wasn't long before they all met in the kitchen. Simon insisted on having lunch at the table with the others, stating that he felt fine enough to venture a brief walk to the kitchen table.

Seth offered to take the platter into Safra and Odessa, seeing as he had been the first to enter the kitchen. He carried the food laden tray across the living room and into Odessa's room, placing the tray on the bedside table.

"How's she doing?" Seth asked the small, attentive woman sitting beside Odessa's bedside in one of the small armchairs that each room was equipped with.

Safra looked up from her patient at Seth and she seemed to stare at him briefly before speaking. She smiled at him and answered.

"She is doing much better. Her fever broke just a while ago, and the color in her leg is returning to normal. The infection and poison have both vacated her body, and she should feel much better by tomorrow morning."

Seth noticed how thick her accent was, and that she still looked at him a while longer, grinning strangely at him again. Seth, feeling a bit nervous wiped his slightly sweaty palms on his pant legs as he cleared his throat to speak.

"Well, I think I'm going to head back for lunch. Is there anything else you need before I go?"

"No," she said bluntly as she continued to look at him. "You don't remember me do you?"

Seth looked at her in confusion.

"Of course, I realize I was much younger then," she said.

"No ma'am, I'm afraid I don't. Should I?" Seth asked, a bit apprehensive. He was sure he would have remembered her if he had met her. She must have him confused with someone else. Besides, how could she possibly have been much younger?

"Well, perhaps," she said, walking around the bed to stand in front of him. "I was a young girl of about sixteen when I last saw you. You, however, don't look much different; only about seven or eight years older now I gather. Time travel is a strange thing," she said with a slight chuckle. "You were all of three or four years my senior when I last saw you. You were with a few other young men when you stumbled into my father's shop in Morocco." She smiled, a twinkle glinting in her eye.

"What? No! You...you can't be that same little girl who talked me into getting my tattoo?" Seth exclaimed incredulously. "The one who told me I had a great destiny!"

"Yes," she said with a giggle. "One in the same. And I see I was right." She smiled broadly again. "You are the last-named Peregrine, are you not? The tribe of Judah?"

Seth collapsed into one of the other chairs that were available and fortunately positioned directly behind where he had been standing.

"How...how did you know? Would I have had a choice of a different life if I hadn't gotten this tattoo?" He knew it was a stretch, but he needed to hear it anyway.

"God had your future planned way before He created you. The mark would have appeared in another form if not a tattoo. He also gave me a great gift. I am known as a Seer. I can see certain things, people, places, and some-times...someone's destiny. Yours was very clear that night. You had a definite aura about you. When I looked at you, I saw the mighty lion roar. God led you to me. And knowing the rash behavior and decision making of a young, inebriated man, you were easy to convince." She giggled.

"Wow, this is a bit surreal," Seth said, gaining his bearings again. "What about your age. How were you younger than me then, but now you're considerably older?"

"As I said, time travel is a strange thing. Simon brought me to Reader's Island from the year 1950. So, naturally, I am sixty-nine now," she said, still smiling at him.

Seth stood, still kind of in a daze with where this conversation had led.

"Um...I uh, I had better let you get to your lunch before it gets cold. And...get back to Odessa. It's been very interesting speaking to you, Safra. Maybe we can continue this conversation at a later date?"

"Certainly, whenever you are ready with more questions, I can always be found by grid mail if I am not close by." She smiled at him once again, lifted the tray from the bedside table, and walked to the other side of the bed.

Seth looked back at her one last time before he shut the door and returned to the kitchen, his mind reeling from the conversation with her.

"Hey man, where have you been? We were fixing to come looking for you," Jason said as Seth entered the kitchen.

"Just speaking with Safra," Seth replied quickly, not wishing to elaborate on the conversation just yet. "Simon, it's good to see you up and about. You gave me a bit of a scare." Seth reached the table and gave Simon's hand a shake.

"I'm fine, my boy. It just takes a little time to recover, that's all," Simon said with a tight-lipped grin as he peered over the rim of his glasses.

"I hear it's more than that Simon." Seth pulled a chair out and sat down.

"Yes, well...we won't be telling Odessa about my creating that storm, will we?" Simon looked around the table, his statement more of an order than a question.

"I'm pretty sure she'll notice the changes in your appearance. They aren't dominant, but they are a bit evident," Seth replied matter of factly.

"Yes, well, if she doesn't notice then we won't tell her, all right?"

Everyone agreed to keep it a secret as Simon wished. It was evident that he didn't want her to feel bad about the effect it had had on his health. Odessa had been at peregrinating for fifteen years. She had witnessed the effects herself long ago when Simon had been in his thirties and the effects were visibly noticeable, adding some streaks of gray hair to his head and beard in an instant.

They all ate lunch, and while Simon had them all together, he decided to fill them in on Safra's vision and the hunt for the missing Peregrine.

"Safra had a vision from God. She was able to get an image of the girl, the city and country which is Dover, England, and the word *Trials*. Alec would you mind grabbing my satchel from my desk in my office? I want to give you all copies."

"Sure thing, Simon." Alec stood to retrieve the bag. Once he returned, Simon continued talking.

"Now, Odessa won't be able to peregrinate for a while so Alec, you will travel with Seth and Jason for now until she's better. This is the street Safra saw in her vision." He handed them the sketch of a street somewhere in Dover. "It didn't give the street name or the time period, but hopefully the word *trials* will cross reference in the databases. Ryan Halloran is also running map image searches hoping to find a match to the street image. It must hold some historical significance or else I don't believe God would have shown it to us."

"What happens if the map image search isn't successful?" Seth asked, unsure to exactly what they were talking about when mentioning a map image search, or how they went about it other than utilizing the public library system.

"Well, I'm not sure. We discussed each peregrination team taking a decade or so and searching the country of Dover, England, until we find the young woman pictured here." Simon handed each one of them a sketched image of the woman Safra had seen. She had long, waist-length, sandy-brown hair, dark brown eyes, was about five foot four inches tall, weighed about one hundred pounds, and looked to be around the age of sixteen.

"It is of the utmost importance. We believe, since no one knows who she is, that she has peregrinated, and she isn't sure what's happening. You all know what it was like to wake up in a strange place and time surrounded by strange people. She's had no one to explain anything to her. She's very young, probably frightened, confused, and any number of other things."

"Do we have anything else to go on other than this picture?" Jason questioned.

"I'm afraid not, Jason. These images are the only things the Lord provided to us. We will have to make do and pull out all the resources available to us and see what we come up with. Several of the other Dragoman are searching for all available information in books, maps, satellites, internet, old historical archives, such as newspaper clippings and the like, to try and find her and this street."

"When do you want us to get started?" Seth asked.

"Well, in light of the week and a half that we've all just had, I say we rest here for the next week or so. Besides, we need to see if the data searches reveal any important or useful information. We may not need to send you all off blind." Simon looked around the table.

"That will give us time to finish the barn at least," Seth replied.

"Barn, what barn?" Simon asked curiously.

"We needed a place for our new residents to live," Jason replied. "You know...the horses that came through the portal with us."

"Oh my goodness! I had completely forgotten about them. Of course, I wasn't really coherent when we came through. You mean to tell me they survived?"

"Yes, completely unscathed. I checked them all over and they are just fine."

"Well, well, will wonders never cease?" Simon smiled. "God just keeps revealing little miracles all around."

Simon then looked at Alec. "Oh, by the way, Alec, did you and Odessa find the Goddelikheid Crucible? With all the excitement I forgot to ask."

"Yes, we did. It is in her pack. Although, I'm not sure where that is. We just rushed you two inside and forgot about everything else," Alec answered, seemingly deep in thought as to where it could have been placed.

Jason answered, "Yours, Alec's, and Odessa's packs are in your office Simon. Seth and I unloaded everything when we unhitched the horses and wagon. Tonight, after we do some more work on the barn, I will take the crucible to the artifacts room, put it in the books, then find it a place to sit until needed."

"That sounds good, thank you, Jason," Simon stood up from the table.

Nuncio stood up from the table as well while he spoke.

"Well, Simon, it appears you're in good hands here and I am no longer needed. Safra can stay here to tend to Odessa, but I'm afraid I need to return to Reader's Island to continue the search for the information we discussed when you were there. All the other Dragoman returned to their own homes when we received the urgent grid message from Seth."

"Oh Yes, Nuncio, thank you for coming so quickly old friend. When Safra is no longer needed we will either return her to the island, or she can stay here, whichever she prefers. Jason, can you go with Nuncio to the cave and see him off? I believe I'm going to head back to my room for a brief nap." Simon suddenly appeared very tired.

"Certainly, Simon, you get some rest. We have everything under control here. Alec, Seth, and I will spend the rest of the day on the barn and then later make some dinner."

"Thank you, boys, I owe each of you quite a lot. I'll see you all at dinner." Simon left the kitchen and went to his room to rest.

After they cleaned up the kitchen and informed Safra of Nuncio's departure, Jason took Nuncio to the cave while Seth and Alec headed outside to work on the barn. Jason returned shortly and the three of them managed to get two sides of the building completed before heading inside to clean up and have a late dinner.

Safra had already prepared their evening meal, and Simon and she were in the kitchen drinking a beverage when the three of them walked in.

"There you are. We were just discussing whether or not to come find you," Simon said.

"How is Odessa doing?" Alec asked, her well-being still his main concern.

"She is doing much better," Safra answered him. "She is coherent and talking, but still weak and needs plenty of rest. You may go in and see her if you wish but try not to tire her out."

"Thank you." Alec smiled and almost skipped out of the kitchen. He headed to shower first before going in to visit with her.

Seth and Jason went in to clean up as well, deciding to try and finish the barn tomorrow. When they returned, Alec had taken his and Odessa's dinner to her room, allowing Safra a break to eat with the rest of them.

"In the morning before we start on the barn, Seth and I will head into town and get some horse feed and supplies for the animals. Is there anything else we need?"

"I will need some more medicinal herbs to continue to treat Simon and Odessa. I will make you a list if you would pick them up for me?" Safra asked.

"Certainly Safra, whatever you need. We are grateful you are here to tend to Odessa and Simon. You can give them much better care than either of us ever could. Thank you for your help," Jason answered, sincere appreciation shining in his eyes.

"You are very welcome. This is why God called a simple herbalist such as me to the cause. Simon is a beloved friend. I would do anything for him." She patted Simon's hand and smiled up at him. "It is my duty to tend to all of God's warriors and seekers." She smiled at Jason and Seth, referring to them and the others as she spoke.

"Well, we are fortunate to have you," Jason offered the kind, older woman.

Seth watched his friends as they sat at the large wooden table chatting. What a strange life he had come to live. It was definitely interesting, and there was always a new surprise around every corner. But Caroline's memory would never leave him or let him completely let down his guard. He still held out hope of getting back to her, hopefully someday soon.

Chapter 20

The next week at Barrier's Edge at Garganthera was spent finishing up the barn and paddocks for the horses to graze, stocking the tack room and barn with supplies and feed, and preparing the plans for the next peregrination to find Eleven; which is what they had all taken to calling the missing Peregrine.

Odessa's health was returning slowly, and she was allowed to get up and move around the homestead, but she wasn't allowed to participate in any sort of activity. If she did too much she would tire easily. Needless to say, she sometimes was a bit grouchy due to the fact that she was normally a very active and fit woman. She did however understand, and knew that her body couldn't tolerate too much, so she resigned herself to helping Simon in the artifacts room and doing internet, map, and archival searches that may help the men with their upcoming journey.

Safra decided she would stay there with them to aid Odessa and Simon with any further health needs. And, since Seth, Jason, and Alec would be leaving soon she would be beneficial to Simon and Odessa, helping with the meals and household chores.

"Simon, grid mail just came in," Seth said, bringing the canister into Simon's office and placing it on his desk.

Simon was at his desk going through some of the information they happened to scrape together giving them a few leads on finding Eleven.

"Thank you, Seth." Simon opened the container and read its contents, which also contained a small package. "It's from Ryan. He has developed something for me that I requested." Simon lifted the package out of the canister and tucked it inside his shirt pocket.

"Seth, why don't you call everyone together in the living room and I will explain then." Simon walked across the room to the bookshelves on the other side, searching for something.

"Sure thing, Simon." Seth exited the room and went in search of everyone else to tell them of Simon's request for their presence.

All of them, including Safra gathered into the living room. Simon was already there waiting on everyone to sit down before he started.

"Week before last we had a little scare with Alec and Odessa going missing. I didn't want to take that chance again so, I contacted Ryan Halloran, whom most of you already know, and had him invent something for me."

Simon lifted a small box from the chairside table and opened it. He plucked out a small device that was the circumference of the head of a pencil eraser but flat. It was opaque in color and round in shape.

"This...is a tracking chip. Each one of us will receive one. It will sit just behind the right ear and take on the exact color shade of whoever's skin it touches so it won't be visible. You won't be able to feel it, it will be permanent, and will allow us to track you wherever you are." Simon finished, handing the device to Seth who looked at it and passed it on to the next person.

"How does it work?" Seth asked him.

"Well, at this point it is only theoretical. We aren't quite sure if it *will* work yet, but it is electronic and should send a signal across time and space, in theory. It essentially works off your heartbeat. It tracks the speed of your heart and sends back the waves via radio. It will also allow us to track your pulse rate and several other functions in your body to determine whether you're under extreme duress, such as Odessa experienced." Simon looked at her with affection. "Perhaps it will allow us to get to anyone who's injured, faster."

"That is really cool!" Jason fingered the small device in the palm of his hand, flipping it over to examine it closer. "It amazes me how they can put so much into something so tiny."

"How do they stay attached?" Odessa asked.

"It has small barbs, kind of like Velcro, that grabs the skin. But you won't feel it because they are so small. We will attach it by simply pressing it to the skin, and it will do the rest by pulling itself tightly."

"How do you know it will stay where you place it?"

"We don't yet," Simon replied. "We need to test the devices. I will attach them, then I want everyone to go about your normal activities. I want to make sure they don't detach with physical contact such as in battle, showering, sweating, bathing such as in rubbing the area they are on and so forth. Odessa and I will set up a tracking center in the artifacts room. I believe that will be the best place from which to track everyone, plus that is where all the modern technology is anyway since we use computers for it. I also will make a handheld device that will allow me to keep up with all of you as well when we are on the move. Now, let's get these attached and Odessa and I can get to work on installing the tracking program that Ryan sent along with the chips."

They all walked into the artifacts room to make sure the chips worked. First, they installed the program onto the computer and set everything up. Then, Simon took a chip from the box and applied one to every one of them. As he pushed the chips into the skin of each person, the computer automatically connected to the sensors in the chips. A blinking light appeared on the computer screen with each one of their names appearing beside it. The program also graphed them on a map and in the proper dimension.

"You are right. I can't feel a thing. Are you sure it's there?" Alec asked.

"Oh yes, it's there," Simon said. "The computer is already tracking you. Now, everyone get busy and let's test these little gems, shall we?"

Jason said, "Seth, Alec, and I, could do with some physical training. We'll head up to the fields after lunch and get a workout in. You can tell us how the chips did when we return." They all left the room, except for Simon, Odessa, and Safra, who spent the next hour working with the new program to learn how it all operated, then watched as it tracked the men while at the training fields.

The chips worked well so far, but they had only gone a few miles away. Simon decided to take a walk into town to see if it tracked him in the third dimension, and Odessa confirmed that it had worked fine. Now, to test it over time and space. Which is what it was intended for in the first place.

By the time the men had returned from the training fields, grid messages had been coming in from all over and going out in reply. Dragoman who found information were all sending and sharing what they had found out in the great search for Eleven. They had gathered enough information to whittle the time period down to approximately a fifty-year span. They discovered that the word *trials*, they believed, referred to the witch trials that took place in Dover, England, more heavily around the years 1540-1590.

Jason also received a return message from Ryan concerning the handheld storm generators that he asked Ryan to try to design. Jason tucked the canister under his arm taking it to a quiet location around the back side of the barn to open it. He wasn't ready to share the information with everyone yet until he knew it would work. He and Seth had agreed to secrecy until hearing from Ryan. The letter stated the following.

Jason,

I have had success in designing the requested device. However, I am still having issues with making it small enough to make carrying it convenient. The power needed to generate a 4.0 or higher storm is hard to design in such a small device. However, I will not give up. It will become very handy to use once designed. I will contact you soon about the finished product. When completed, I will send one for each Peregrine, including Eleven.

Ryan

The letter was very reassuring. He would send Ryan a thank you back and pray it was something he completed quickly. If anyone could make such a device in a short period of time, Ryan Halloran could. The kid was a genius with electronics. Proof that God uses people from all walks of life.

Jason tucked the letter away to show Seth later, hurried into the map room, scribbled a thank you letter, and quickly sent the reply off before anyone saw him and asked questions, especially Simon or Odessa. He surely didn't want

Odessa asking questions or she may find out about Simon's condition.

With the message sent, it was getting close to dinner time and the whole crew was supposed to meet to discuss the next mission and look over all the collected information on how and where to find Eleven. As he rounded the corner of the house, Seth appeared, exiting the barn.

"Seth!" Jason trotted to catch up with him, looking around to make sure no one else was within earshot. "I just received word from Ryan about that device we were talking about."

"Great, what did he say?"

"He said it was in the works and looked promising. Here's the letter, you can take a look at it later when you're alone." Jason removed the folded sheet of paper from his pocket and handed it to Seth who quickly stuffed it into one of his own.

"That's really good. This Ryan fella' seems like a great asset to this whole storm, time-jumping, process. Seems like he can make just about anything."

"He is and can. He's around twenty-nine, and he's been at this for about eight years now. As I said before, he's a bit odd, probably due to his autism. He doesn't like crowds, is a straight-forward as they come, doesn't do conversations unless the information is pertinent, and hardly ever makes eye contact. With all that being said, he is a Dragoman and the most technologically intelligent person I've ever met."

"Sounds like my kind of guy. I can identify with several of those same qualities, specifically the ones about being straight forward and not being much on idle conversation." Seth chuckled and Jason laughed along with him.

"Yeah, I feel you man, I have the same sort of issues." Jason laughed.

The two men chuckled as they went inside to join up with everyone else at the kitchen table. Everyone was grateful that Safra had taken over the cooking, freeing them up to concentrate on the missions, paperwork, and dealing with the new tech that they were putting into play.

With all the information on Eleven pretty much being had already, they devised a plan. Simon had heard from the other Dragoman about the time periods that their Peregrines were going to search through. Seth, Jason, and Alec would take the 1575-1580 periods. Knowing where they were to look from the map images, all they had to do was match the street with the picture Safra had drawn. If they found it in one of the years, it would be easy to search the others, knowing the name and location by then. The hardest thing would be locating storms to time jump through to reach the next year. Seth thought about how much easier that part would be if Ryan had only finished the storm generators before they had to leave.

Once they found what area or street was pictured then they had to find the girl. That may pose to be the largest problem of all. They would be looking for someone who was likely scared, and more than likely hiding. Seth just hoped she would be receptive to what they had to tell her once they found her. He knew what a hard time he had had when they first told him. A young kid may have a harder time understanding, believing, and adjusting to this kind of life. What he didn't understand is why God would call one so young to live a warrior lifestyle. The fighting, training, and even killing that was required of them was really tough. He just didn't understand bringing young kids into it, but God must have His reasons. Seth had been spending most nights before bed reading the Bible in his room. He was really starting to learn quite a bit, he just wondered if it would afford him any understanding as to why God does some of the things He does.

After dinner and travel plans were made, the men went to shower, and Simon and Odessa went to the artifacts room to check that the chips were still sending signals. They wanted to make sure nothing glitched or stopped working due to the presence of soap and water. So far, every one of the chips seemed to be holding up and functioning per its designed purpose. Simon was relieved that he could better keep track of his Peregrines. He was sure the other Dragoman were grateful as well. Certain that Ryan had sent the technology to everyone. Ryan may not be a mentor to Peregrines, but his abilities well made up for his lack of leadership skills. He was the only Dragoman who didn't lead any Peregrines. He simply ran his charging station full time; which was another brainchild of Ryan's; and created amazing technology.

Everyone decided to meet in the living room for a brief prayer time and discussion concerning tomorrow's peregrination. After they were finished, Alec, Jason, and Seth, made sure to search the wardrobe room for appropriate time period clothing, and pack everything they would need for the trip. They would be heading out at first light to catch a storm, dropping them in the heart of Dover, England in the year 1575 AD.

He guides the humble in what is
right and teaches them His way.

Psalm 25:9

Chapter 21

Dover, England, 1580 AD

Bridget pushed back the thick burlap curtain that served as doors in her small, three-room house that she had lived in the majority of her sixteen years. Her mother had died when she was one year old, and her father had been killed when she was fourteen. She had no other known relatives and had lived on her own since his death.

Walking over to one of the small beds that sat against the wall, she picked up the damp rag from the small bowl of water that sat on the tiny table by the bed. She rang out the cool rag and wiped it across the face of the woman she had found in the ditch just outside her place almost a week ago.

A massive earthquake had hit Dover and surrounding areas the week before, and Bridget, like everyone else in town, had been out after the shocks wore off assessing the damage it had caused. She hadn't gotten too far from home when she all but tripped over the woman lying in a ditch.

Interestingly enough, the woman didn't appear injured, at least not outwardly. But something was wrong with her because she wouldn't fully wake up. She stayed completely unconscious for the first three days after Bridget had found her, put her on a piece of burlap, and drug her into the house. Over the last three days, Bridget was able to get her awake enough to get some fluids into her system. She never stayed awake for long, and when she was slightly coherent, she mumbled someone's name, but Bridget couldn't quite make out what she was saying.

As she sat looking at the woman, she tried to think about whom she might be and how old she was. She didn't appear too much older than Bridget, and she was obviously married because she wore a wedding band, a really pretty one too. Nothing like she had ever seen before. Her clothes were a bit odd as well. Women here didn't dress this way, especially in trousers, so she must be from another country. She was a really attractive woman with long hair, high cheek bones, a slim nosed slightly turned up at the end, long lashes, and a thin figure.

Could she be one of them? Bridget wondered. *One of the people that her father occasionally had very secretive visits from?*

Her father had been in a type of secret society of sorts. One which he never included Bridget. Her father had kept these secret books that were labeled Dragoman Archives, some very detailed maps, and a book about all sorts of different storm history. Bridget had asked him about them several times and he had dismissed her. He told her the last time she asked; she had been about 11 years old; that she should forget about them. That they could only cause her pain. She didn't understand how books could cause pain, but he made it clear that she should never ask him about them again.

Bridget had quit asking but she had always paid very close attention to everything her father said and did. He had been very different from the people here. He had lived a simple, peasant-style life, but they never wanted for anything of basic need, and he was much more educated and well-spoken then the other people around them. He had educated her very well, and she knew a lot about other places, people, history, writing, reading, numbers, all sorts of interesting books, the Bible, and God.

Her father had never let her have any friends because she was so different from the other kids. The parents of other children thought her odd to know so much about everything, or they accused her of telling lies because some of what she knew they had never heard of before. Fearing that these uneducated people might think her a witch, her father told her it was best just to keep her distance and so she had.

Life so far since her father's death had been very lonely. This stranger was the first person she had had at her home since then. She was very curious and prayed that God would allow the woman to wake up soon. Bridget was growing more worrisome, but she couldn't risk bringing a doctor here. They would put her in an orphanage if they knew she was alone. At least her father had left her with a considerable amount of money, which she used very sparingly.

Bridget barely remembered traveling once when she was little. What she remembered though couldn't be real. She must have dreamt it, although it felt very real. She was three years old at the time, and she remembers her father running with her in his arms. She couldn't remember what he had been running from, but she knew he had been very frightened. She remembered a very bad thunderstorm, a very bright light in the middle of the storm, and then they were here, in Dover, England. And she had been there ever since.

"Mm...S...e...," the strange woman moaned again.

"Sh....you are fine. I am taking good care of you," Bridget tried reassuring the woman as she wiped her head and face once more.

Caroline Jager slipped in and out of consciousness, only waking long enough to see what appeared to be a young girl standing over her. She couldn't quite make out the girl's appearance or what she was saying, but her voice was calm and soothing. The only thing she was sure of was the pain in her head and her body every time she gained any type of consciousness. She slipped back into a deep sleep thinking about Seth once again.

Bridget watched her slip into unconsciousness once more. She looked out the window just above the bed. It was growing dark outside and so Bridget readied the house to go to sleep. She secured the windows and doors, stoked the fires against the cool, damp, night temperatures outside, and sat on the bed that sat parallel to the one the stranger was using. She knelt to pray, just as she did every night, again saying a special blessing over her injured guest and praying that she would soon wake. She needed more nourishment than what little Bridget could force down her when she briefly woke. She checked on the sleeping woman one last time, tucking the blankets securely underneath her. Blowing out the lantern, she climbed into her own bed and drifted soundly off to sleep.

Caroline awoke in the early morning hours, a blinding headache pounding within her head and her whole body ached. She could barely move her arms and legs, and she couldn't open her eyes for the pain searing through her skull. She was terribly parched and desperately needed a cold drink of water. She pulled herself up into a sitting position and felt that she was on a small cot like bed. She had thick blankets wrapped around her body which aided against the cold she could feel radiating from the wall beside her. There seemed to be a type of fire or heat coming from somewhere in the room, so she swung her legs over the edge of the bed, finding the floor. Dizziness shook her body and almost made her fall over backward onto the bed. She wrapped the blanket tighter around her and leaned against the cool stone wall, waiting on her head to clear some so she could move. The cold from the wall tried to find its way through the thick blanket making her pull it even tighter around her. Why was it so cold? It must be from her body feeling so terrible. Perhaps she was running a fever and it only *felt* cold.

Think Caroline, think. Where was she? Last thing she could remember were rocks falling, and a loud rumbling sound like that of an earthquake. Good grief! Is that what had happened? If so, where was she and where was Seth? Was he here as well in the same condition as her?

She tried standing, losing her balance, and falling back against the wall and onto the cot, making a bit of a racket in the process. At least the blanket had shielded her back against the hard stone.

"Goodness are you all right?" Caroline heard someone say. She tried to speak, but no sound came from her lips.

"You must be very thirsty? Here, let me get you some water."

Whoever she was, she sounded quite young but very concerned and friendly. Caroline felt a cold glass pressed into her hand and she drank thirstily from it, draining it quickly. The girl guided her glass to a pitcher and refilled the glass once more. Caroline drained it again.

"Would you like some more?" she heard her ask.

Caroline shook her head no as pain seared behind her eyes, bringing on another dizzy spell.

"I'm sorry, try not to talk or move. You seem to be in a great deal of pain. Can you motion to me what hurts, I will try and give you something to ease your suffering?" Bridget asked, carefully watching the woman.

She pointed to her head and made motions that it was throbbing, and she was dizzy. She also pointed to her throat and signaled that she couldn't speak.

"Don't worry, I will help as best I can. My name is Bridget by the way. I found you outside after the earthquake that hit the town. I brought you here to my place to tend to you. I am sorry but there was no doctor available. But, on the good side, you don't appear to be injured except for your headache and the other things you are experiencing. There isn't so much as a scratch anywhere on you that I can see." Bridget talked to her while she stoked the fire, adding plenty of wood to heat the house, then placed a tea kettle of water on the swinging handle.

"I'm sorry I'm talking so much, but I'm sure you're wondering where you are. I noticed you have a wedding band on. I'm sorry, but if you were with anyone else I didn't find them, only you. But, I haven't left the house really since I found you, so surely your family is here within the city somewhere. I will stop talking now, for surely I am making your headache worsen. I will make a nice pot of tea for us."

Caroline appreciated everything the, obviously, young girl had told her. Surely Seth was somewhere in San Francisco Bay. Caroline prayed that someone just as kind and caring had found him as well. *God, please let Seth be all right?* she prayed her silent prayer, finishing just as she felt the girl come closer to her.

"Here, I have a cup of tea for you. It is slightly hot, but the cup isn't very full. I didn't want you to spill and burn yourself. When you have emptied it, I will refill it again if you'd like?" Bridget watched the woman sip the hot tea hungrily. "I also have some bread and butter, if you would like a piece of that as well?"

Caroline drank the hot liquid as quickly as she could, nodding yes to the offer of the bread and butter. She could hear the girl get up and move about the room, returning abruptly and placing a small cold plate in Caroline's hand as she gently took the cup to hold for her.

"Here you are, I'll just hold your tea for you. I'll refill your cup while you eat the bread. I must say, I'm very glad you finally woke. I was beginning to worry. I prayed God would wake you soon and sure enough, He did," Bridget said, brightness warming her voice as she spoke. Evidence of her excitement that her guest had finally woken up.

Caroline could feel the effects of the hot tea and the buttered bread ease some of the pain in her stomach and help with the headache and dizziness as well. Perhaps most of what was wrong with her was from sheer hunger pangs. The girl seemed very genuine, and she was glad that God had led the kind stranger to find her. She tried opening her eyes once more and quickly shut them to the brightness of the fire that caused instant pain.

"Oh my, I'm ever so sorry! I've forgotten the medicine for your headache! Please forgive my thoughtlessness. Here you are, just place this under your tongue for a bit. It should dissolve and aid in some relief very soon."

If Caroline didn't feel right horrid she would have laughed out loud. The young woman named Bridget had to be the most proper person she had ever met. Poor thing was apologizing for taking care of her improperly! *Lord, bless this dear, sweet child.* Caroline could feel herself smile slightly as she placed the medicine underneath her tongue.

"Oh, you must be feeling a might better already, for I do believe I just saw a tiny smile grace your lips!" Bridget said excitedly.

Caroline could only shake her head yes very minutely, but she knew the very observant young woman would catch it.

"I'm so very glad. Now, I am sure you would like to rest a bit until the medicine takes hold. When you've finished your bread and tea, I'll take them from you and help you lie down again."

Caroline finished the tea and bread and handed the cup and plate to Bridget, who afterward, slowly, and carefully guided her still achy, dizzy, body back down onto the cot, tucking the blankets around her once again. She felt herself relax and slowly drifted off the sleep.

Chapter 22

Caroline woke several hours later to dimmed brightness that was possible to make out through her quickly blinking eyelids, as dappled sunlight filtered through what must be a window. She closed them tightly again. The sounds of Bridget moving about the room obvious. She lay there with her eyes closed, trying to assess if her body would allow her to move without much pain this time. So far, it seemed as though everything had stopped hurting, so she tried fully opening her eyes. The brightness caused some light sensitivity and pain, but other than that she could see fine. A small headache pulsed at her temples, but it was nothing like before, and the dizziness and nausea seemed to be gone now. She tried sitting up, taking things as slowly as possible. *So far so good.* She slowly tried opening the thin slits of her eyes a little more, still having to blink them occasionally against the brightness of the cool, damp-feeling room.

The movements about the room stopped, and she assumed that meant that Bridget was aware of her being up and was watching her.

"Good morning. You appear to feel much better this morning. Do you?" Bridget asked earnestly.

Caroline, still unable to find her voice, answered by slowly shaking her head yes.

"Oh...does your throat still hurt?" Concern evident in her voice.

Caroline made a sign with her hands trying to tell Bridget that it only hurt 'a little', but also tried to convey to the girl that it was more nonexistent than painful.

"I'll make us another pot of tea. Perhaps a bit of lemon and honey will help with that. I also have some nice blueberry scones on the stove heating. I purchased them from the baker just down the street just this morning, so they are nice and fresh. I ventured out after I gave you the drought for your illnesses earlier when you woke. I wasn't gone long I assure you. Just in case you woke while I was out, I didn't want you to be frightened all alone."

Bridget had returned to the cot and had sat down beside Caroline on the bed as she spoke.

"Would you like to try and stand? Perhaps sit at the table to have your scone and tea? It might make it easier for you to handle the cup and plate all at once that way."

Caroline tried opening her eyes further to look at the girl, shaking her head yes in reply to Bridget's questions.

"Here, let me help you." Bridget took hold of both of Caroline's hands and pulled her to her feet.

Caroline swayed just as a small wave of dizziness took hold of her body.

Bridget reached out to steady her, placing both hands on Caroline's shoulders.

"I've got you. Try taking about, oh, ten steps straight toward me," Bridget instructed her.

Caroline followed the instructions, opening her eyes as much as possible to try and see where she might be going.

"All right, you're doing just fine. Now, turn to your left and take about twenty steps more and we should be at the table."

Caroline and Bridget reached the table with little mishap, and Caroline found the chair to sit down. Bridget placed a cup of tea and a plate with the blueberry scone in front of Caroline, adding some lemon and honey to her cup for her and stirring them in.

"I hope you like lemon and honey in your tea. It should do wonders for your throat."

Caroline nodded yes, forming the words thank you with her mouth. Her vision was beginning to clear, and the light-sensitivity was easing up quite a bit.

"You're ever so welcome." The smile in Bridget's voice was apparent.

Caroline could make out the bright toothy smile the girl gave her as Bridget's face began to come into focus. She was a very pretty young woman, with long brown hair, and big brown eyes. She was a petite little thing. She appeared to be around fifteen years old, but it was hard to tell really.

Caroline sipped from the steaming cup of delicious tea and took wonderful big bites of the glorious tasting scone. They ate in silence and Caroline was grateful for it while she concentrated on feeding her hungry body. Bridget watched her, and each time Caroline looked over at the girl, Bridget would beam her big, closed-mouth grin as she too chewed on her scone. Obviously just tickled pink that Caroline was there, no matter what the reason.

Caroline finished her tea and Bridget offered her more. Caroline graciously accepted, adding more honey and lemon to her cup. The hot liquid seemed to be working wonders on her throat as she cleared it, trying to speak.

"My name...is," she cleared her throat again, "...Caroline."

Bridget grinned from ear to ear this time.

"I'm so happy your voice has returned. Hello Caroline, my name is Bridget Burke. I'm very pleased to officially meet you."

"And I you." Caroline continued to sip her tea and clear her still hoarse throat as they conversed.

"Jager is my last name. Can you tell me where I am exactly? Your home seems a bit...different, then anything I've ever seen."

"Oh, certainly. I'm confused though. How could you not know where you are?"

"Well, this all looks so different than where I live. I really don't know how to explain it," Caroline said carefully, not wanting to hurt the girl's feelings. She glanced around the room, taking in the fireplace with the swinging arm tripod which held a pot and kettle above the flames. The walls were rough stone and the doorways were rough wooden square beams with no doors except for burlap. The windows didn't appear to have glass in them, only shudders. And the furniture was very sparse. Could she be in one of the shanties down on the waterfront in San Francisco Bay? If so, how did she get that far from where they had crashed?

"Well, this is my home and I live in Dover." Bridget wasn't really sure what Caroline was asking.

"Dover? Where exactly is that? I've never heard of a Dover here in California."

"Where is California? I've never heard of that place before. This is Dover, England."

Caroline suddenly sat bolt upright, her senses all on high alert as she looked about the room. Did she hear Bridget correctly?

"What do you mean, Bridget? How long was I sick for?"

"I'm not really sure what you're asking, but you were out for about a week. For three whole days you were completely unconscious. For the last three days I was able to get some liquids into you. Are you all right Caroline? You're looking rather peeked."

"I don't understand." Caroline tried to stand and make her way to the door. "Last thing I remember was crashing the motorbike in an earthquake or a land slide."

"Yes, there was an earthquake. It was quite a shaker too. But I'm not at all sure what a motorbike is." Bridget stood also, following the still slow-moving Caroline to her front door.

Caroline reached the one solid door in the whole small house and opened it, peering outside. She was stunned to see the image before her. Yes, it appeared that this town had been hit by an earthquake, but this was not California. It didn't even appear to be the year 1902. Everywhere she looked people were dressed in period garb, like in a play, and there were people pushing carts and horses pulling carts. Vendors lined the streets and filled every street corner.

Her head began to reel from everything rushing through her mind at once. She stumbled backward, and Bridget caught her.

"Goodness! Are you all right? You're as white as a crisp linen sheet." Bridget helped Caroline back to the table.

"I just need to rest a bit. I...I...mu, must be having delusions," Caroline stammered. "Bridget, wh...what year is this?" Unsure she really wanted to know the answer.

"Why, it's 1580." Realization began to set in. This woman *was* like the people who used to come around her father when he was alive. But why didn't she know that herself?

Caroline's head reeled again, and the dizziness began to worsen.

"I think I need to lie back down for a while." She felt almost breathless, as though panic were going to set in. As she tried to stand, her legs wobbled, trying to give out as she sought the comfort of the cot.

"Wait, I'll help you." Bridget quickly grabbed hold of Caroline, and practically carried her the rest of the way. After depositing Caroline on the cot and covering her back up, Bridget went into her storage room and pulled the old wooden box from underneath the shelf. She carried it into the kitchen and placed it on the table, thinking she might have read something about this type of confusion somewhere in the Dragoman Archive book. She would look through them again to see if there was any information to help her new friend when she awoke again.

Caroline lay there, her head swimming and spinning with what Bridget had said to her. Her head began to pound once more, and the returning dizziness began to turn her now nauseated stomach. *This can't be right. Bridget must be mistaken, or I must be having a very real, very intense, dream. That's it, I'm hallucinating. I probably have a head injury, and I'm just not seeing or hearing things clearly. Rest.... I just need some rest...everything will be clear when I wake.* Caroline began to relax, her once tense and stressed body relaxing more as she drifted further into sleep, certain that things would be back to normal when she woke again.

As Caroline slept, Bridget read through the books trying to find something that would explain what was happening. She spent the rest of the morning reading over the books and marking pages to show Caroline when she woke. Now that she had actually met a Peregrine, as the book called Caroline, a lot of the things she had read before were starting to make more sense. Such as why Caroline was so sick. And why she had been out for so long, and why she had no idea when or where she was. Bridget never thought she would ever have a chance to actually meet one of them. Now, not only had she met one, but she was the only person who could help her. Bridget now understood why she was here. It wasn't to just eke out a meager living here, alone in this world. She had a greater destiny. One that her father didn't want her to know about. She didn't know or understand why, for he had led the same life. Why try to keep her from her own similar destiny? Bridget decided to spend all her free time reading and learning everything she could from her father's old books. She had always read them, even though she didn't understand much of the information. But now, with God's help, she would do the very best she could, for God had called her to it.

"Dear Lord, help me to guide her in the right direction as you guide me, show me what it is you wish me to do, and teach me the proper ways to do it." She looked back at the sleeping woman who was in for another huge shock when she awoke once again.

Caroline tossed and turned in a fitful sleep, her dreams plagued with unnatural things. She caught a glimpse of Seth gazing at the stars, calling her name. *Caroline.* Then he was looking out a window screaming her name. *Caroline!*

"Caroline?" Bridget peered down at the woman tossing and turning in her sleep, becoming more and more agitated.

"Seth!" Caroline jerked awake, suddenly unaware of her surroundings.

"I'm sorry to wake you, but you must have been having a nightmare and you were growing increasingly more fitful, so I thought it correct to wake you," Bridget said, a bit contritely.

"Oh...um, no...no, it's all right." Caroline realized where she was. *So, it hadn't been a dream.*

She sat and swung her legs over the edge of the bed and stood. It seemed as though her body had finally righted itself. There was no more dizziness, headache, or nausea. And her voice seemed to work just fine a moment ago.

Caroline walked to the door of the small house and opened it. The air outside was warm and breezy, and there was a lot of muddy rain puddles dotting the ground, apparently from a recent shower, and the fact that the street was unpaved. The village, although it had apparently just sustained an earthquake, was bustling with activity as people roamed back and forth going about their daily lives, now having to add cleaning up the rubble from a few collapsed buildings to the list of daily chores. She shivered against the breeze blowing against her sweat dampened clothes.

"Here, wrap this quilt back around you until we can get you some proper clothing. You're drenched right through." Bridget walked up behind her and wrapped the thick blanket around her shoulders.

"Thank you, Bridget." Caroline accepted the blanket but didn't say much else. She knew Bridget was watching her, curious as to her behavior. But at the moment Caroline had nothing to say. She didn't *know what* to say. Standing in the doorway it felt like a different world she was seeing, and she was only looking at it like a living picture. But as she stepped out onto the muddy street, her world became real again. She was actually walking around in Dover, England, in the year 1580! How in the world had this happened? She heard the door behind her close, certain that Bridget was following close behind.

"Caroline, please be careful. These people here aren't used to seeing strangers who look and dress like you. They may become curious and cause all manner of troubles. Please come back inside before you draw to much attention to yourself."

Caroline turned and looked down at Bridget, fear and pleading evident on her face. She wasn't sure what she had to fear, but Bridget had been very kind and helpful, and since she didn't really know anything about where she was, she decided to heed Bridget's warning. As the two of them walked the short distance back to Bridget's home, Caroline looked over her shoulder one last time before entering the small stone home and closing the door. She was unsure of everything she had ever known to be true in her entire life. She had lived her life inside a library the majority of her years, pouring through book after book. Never had she come across anything like what was happening to her in any of the non-fiction books.

She had also read hundreds of fiction novels. Maybe the authors that had written those novels actually experienced the very things they had written about. Her perspective of what was real and what wasn't was a bit shaky at this point, and not trusting herself, she sat down at the table ready to ask all manner of questions to the young woman who seemed to be unaffected by Caroline's strange behavior. Caroline returned to her seat at the table.

"I know things seem very strange to you right now, but I believe I have an answer for you, that is, if you are what I think you are," Bridget said with a mixture of excitement and apprehension.

"Do you? Do you possibly know what happened here? Because I am thoroughly confused and a little frightened right now." Caroline's voice escalated in pitch and speed as she spoke. "I have no idea where I am, how I got here, what I'm supposed to do, how I'm going to get home, or where my husband is!" Caroline slumped onto her resting elbows and placed her face in her hands as the blanket fell to the floor.

"It is a normal reaction you are having. Everything I have read has stated as much." Bridget cautiously spoke, trying to find the right words to comfort Caroline, clutching the book she had picked up to her chest and peering over the top edge of it.

Caroline raised her head and looked at Bridget. The poor thing was doing her best to help her and Caroline was acting like a spoiled child, stomping her feet in protest. Bridget wasn't responsible for Caroline's situation, she just happened to be the one to find her. Caroline sighed, sat up straight in her chair, and grabbing the quilt, wrapped it back around her shoulders.

"I'm sorry, Bridget. I don't mean to sound ungrateful or angry at you because I'm not. You have been a wonderful person to take care of a complete stranger the way you have. Thank you, from the bottom of my heart. If you have any ideas about this," she said, gesturing all around her, "please, go ahead and explain."

"Just remember to keep an open mind, all right? First, let me explain why I think I know what is happening to you. You see, my father; I think; was what is called a Dragoman. I'm not certain you see because he never really let me in on that part of his life. But I watched and listened when I could. From what these books say, a Dragoman is a sort of leader or guide to other people called Peregrines, which is what I believe you are. A Peregrine is a person chosen by God to time-travel through storms. I think that's how you ended up here."

"You think God chose me to time-travel through storms? You're serious? Well, all right...why now? I've been through many storms in the past and this has never happened before." Caroline was unsure what she was hearing was on the up and up.

"Perhaps it just wasn't your time until now?"

"What about Seth?"

"Is he your husband?"

"Yes. By one night, until we were separated," Caroline said sadly.

"Oh my, I'm so very sorry for you! I'm not sure where he is or what happened to him. I haven't found anything in the book that tells anything about that yet. It simply says that The Chosen can storm travel via a portal that opens up when a storm reaches a particular strength."

"So, does it say why I was so sick for so long?" Caroline asked, curious for answers.

"Yes, actually it does." Bridget flipped some pages before speaking. "It is called Peregrine Sickness. It says here that the first time you peregrinate, or storm jump, your body has to go through an adjustment period. You shouldn't experience it again it says."

"Yay for that," Caroline stated bluntly and a bit sarcastically.

"Yes indeed." Bridget smiled brightly.

Caroline smiled at that. She had to admit, this girl made everything seem much better than it actually was. Her personality was one of pure joy. Just realizing something Bridget had said earlier, Caroline asked the next question.

"Bridget, you said your father had been known as a Dragoman. Where is he now?"

"He's dead. He was murdered two years ago. I think by demonic forces. I read about them in Father's books." Her demeanor turned a bit sad.

"I'm so sorry your father's dead, but why do you think he was murdered by demons? And where is your mother? I just realized that I haven't seen anyone else."

"Well, because Father's books say that the demons are the main enemy of the Dragoman and the Peregrines. It says that the minute you are chosen by God they seek to destroy you. As far as my mother, she's dead as well. Died when I was just a wee child. I have no other relatives here. I believe that my father peregrinated here, just like you did. Why he stayed and never left I'm not sure. I only know he was very sad, always nervous, and got angry when people like you showed up."

"I'm truly sorry, Bridget. You mean to tell me you've been on your own for two years? How do you possibly live here alone? How do you survive, get food, clothing, the necessary items for everyday life?" Caroline asked, astounded by one so young being left all alone. As far as demons seeking to destroy her, that was a discussion for later. Right now, she needed to find out about Bridget. Besides, Caroline's Christianity taught her that demons sought to destroy people's lives every day. What was so different about that here?

"Well, my father left me quite a considerable amount of money, but I am very careful with how I use it. I don't want to draw to much attention to myself. The authorities would come and take me away putting me into an orphanage. Plus, there are people here that are witch crazy. I must be very careful not to seem very different. There are men who would float me in an instant. No matter how young I am."

Caroline had heard the term 'float' before. She had read about it through the library books that her father allowed her to read. It was an old practice of divining whether someone was a witch. They threw you into a lake, or river, and if you sank you were innocent. If you floated then they considered you a witch and then either hung you or burned you at the stake.

Good grief! Where in the world had God sent her? Caroline looked at Bridget. Perhaps God had sent Caroline here specifically for Bridget. Maybe they were to make whatever journey God had planned for them together.

"Bridget, did you ever wonder if you were meant to be a Dragoman?" Caroline asked her, watching her face for sincerity when she answered.

"Well, I remember traveling once when I was about three years old, and I think that traveling, or peregrinating may be why Mother died. I think that is the reason Father didn't want me to do this. Even though I survived the time jump, I think maybe he was still unsure and afraid for me. I've always known I was meant for something different than what I am now. I'm very different from the others here and living here makes me afraid sometimes. I have no one else, no friends or family here. I think that is why God brought you to me. I believe we were destined to find each other."

"You know, Bridget, I do believe you are correct. I too believe that God brought me here at this time, to find you. I'm still not sure, however, how much of this peregrination thing I believe in, but I am willing to try anything right now to get back to Seth. Do you think maybe you could help me find a way back to him?"

"Oh Yes!" Bridget replied enthusiastically. "I'm ever so happy to help you any way that I can. Especially if it means I get to help God. Leaving this place would just be a bonus!"

"Well that should be our first order of business. How do we go about leaving here? Do you think you can find a way for us to time jump again?" Caroline asked, not believing what was coming out of her mouth.

"I'm sure it is in one of Father's books somewhere. He has several volumes of archives. Some of them have different titles. One book is *Historical Events*. One is a *Book of Codes*, kind of like a rule book I think. Another talks about *Geography* and has lots of maps and charts, and the other I believe is a *History of Storms*, whatever that means. Surely we can find the answer in any one of those books," She said, blinking at Caroline.

"Well then, I say we get to it, Bridget. Now, where is the book labeled *History of Storms*? That sounds like a good place to start. Let's see if we can find us a way out of this place."

Caroline, determination setting into the very bones of her, took the book and began reading. Hopefully, these Dragoman books held some answers to finding her way home to Seth.

Cast your cares upon the Lord and He will sustain
you; He will never let the righteous be shaken.

Psalm 55:22

Chapter 23

Dover, England, 1579 AD

Seth, Jason, and Alec had been traveling for about three weeks through Dover, England, in search of Eleven. It had taken them the better part of four full days to find the proper street to match the drawing that Safra had given them. Especially since things can change quickly from year to year. And, since they didn't quite have the proper year to begin with, it took a lot of comparing and quite frankly, having a visionary eye. Once they had the street matched, then they just had to search for the girl.

They walked all of Pickfurt Street the remainder of the time, showing the drawing of Eleven to everyone they met. No one they had spoken to, in any of the years between 1575 and 1579 had seen the girl.

"Well, I guess that leaves us with just one more year to search. How much longer do we have before our storm blows through?" Seth asked Jason, who kept up with all of the travel plans.

"Believe it or not another full day," Jason said drudgingly.

"What are we going to do for another twenty-four hours?" Alec asked, looking around the village with raised eyebrows and exhaling loudly.

"Well, since we're sure she isn't here, and there isn't a lot of local culture around this place right now, we do what we always do. Find a place to sit and wait. I say we duck into that little pub over there and rest. We can have a cool drink or two, get a hot meal, and then find a place to sleep," Jason suggested to them.

"Sounds good to me," Seth said, standing instantly and walking the short distance down the street as Alec and Jason followed closely behind him.

They entered the establishment and found a remote corner table, as always, just in case discussions led to places they didn't want anyone hearing. They ordered a few pints of ale and a few hearty lunches of pork with potatoes and gravy with beans on the side.

"What do we do if no one finds this number Eleven?" Alec asked.

"Surely someone will find her. Why else would God reveal what he already has? He gave us her picture, where, and almost when. I don't think He would send all of us on a wild goose chase." Jason stretched his tired back against the back of the chair.

Seth took a long drink from his tall thick glass. "Besides, without Eleven, we can't win or even fight the final battle. Right?"

"I suppose so," Alec said as he sat thinking about almost losing Odessa. "I think though, that none of us is guaranteed a tomorrow." He looked at the other two as they shook their heads in agreement. "So, if she is not findable, then He will either lead her to us, or raise another to take her place. I realized when Dee became very ill, that God does not need any of us. He uses us, but we are not needed. He can call another to replace us, we are not immortal,"

"Sounds to me like somebody may have found God recently," Jason said, observing a slight change in Alec's attitude about life in general.

"You would be right my friend," Alec answered soberly. "When Dee lay there and I could do nothing to help her, and she wouldn't respond to anything I said or anything anyone did to her, I thought, surely God could take her if He chooses. We are all replaceable, even as one of the Twelve. But Dee, she knew where she would go. I did not know about myself. At first, I just prayed to God to heal her and I would do whatever He wanted. But since I was already doing whatever He wanted, I realized it was a heart thing. He wanted my heart, not just my actions. I surrendered to Him right there on the Niamey River Encampment. After, I had such a peace about Dee. I just knew she would be okay, but that it was God's choice whether to save her. He isn't in the bargaining business. I just had to trust that He knew what He was doing."

"That is really deep stuff, Alec. And I'd say He knew exactly what He was doing. God knows how to reach all of us. He knew Dee was your 'reachable moment', and to what extent it would take." Jason's smile began to spread across his face as he looked at Alec. "Welcome to the family brother!" Jason grabbed Alec and hugged him as the two smiled at each other infectiously.

Seth noted the exchange, and that Jason had called Alec brother. Did he refer to him as such because they were close working or traveling partners? Or did it have to do with Alec's new-found faith in God?

"So, does that mean no more flying by the seat of your pants when it comes to missions?" Jason asked teasingly.

"Of course not! Now, I can fly free as a bird. God is in complete control!" The Frenchman raised his glass to the ceiling and laughed heartily. "But I will try to make sure I plan better in the future."

Seth couldn't help laughing along with the other two men as he sat and listened to their exchange about Alec's faith and what it meant. Seth had to admit, Alec seemed a bit different. He was always a jolly, free spirited kind of fellow, but his demeanor had changed somehow.

They sat in the pub for another hour or so as they ate and talked about all manner of things. After which they exited the pub and went in search of a place to sleep for the night. The thunderstorm that they needed would come through just before noon tomorrow, and they actually needed to travel just a bit north to catch it.

They found a place to rest and clean up, all of them desperately needing baths since the last time they had had one was six days ago. Men may have used to live this way, but Seth, Jason, and Alec, were used to daily showers. The only water that touched their skin lately had been in the form of hard rain as they peregrinated between time periods. The village hostel only had two tubs for bathing in, and since one was taken already by another guest, it was a mad dash, and an all-out battle to see which of them would get to bathe first. Of course, Alec, being the smaller and the fastest of all three of them, won out, but it was a fun shoving match to see who would get there first.

"Alec, you're lucky you're so small of a man and I like you. You popping me with that towel will probably leave a blood blister," Seth said, smiling and wincing at the same time. "I think you broke the skin."

"Oh, poor baby, I will kiss it for you when I come out if you like?" Alec said with amusement in his voice.

Seth stood, grabbed the water pitcher from the side table against the wall, walked over to the short, half wall that surrounded the bathing area, and dumped the cold water over the top of Alec's head.

"AAHH!!! That was dirty Seth! That water is very cold!" Alec gave him a dirty look.

Jason, who also sat in the waiting area, watched the scene unfold before his eyes, laughing so hard he almost fell off the small, wooden, four-legged chair he was sitting on.

"You can go next Jason. I'm waiting until the Frenchman is sleeping before I jump in." Seth grinned at Jason who laughed even harder.

It had been a very long time since any of them had the time to just relax and goof off, even for just an evening. Seth never had any brothers growing up, and they were beginning to grow as close as brothers could be. He was growing very comfortable around these people. But he reminded himself daily that his main mission was Caroline. He did as God asked, but with his own purposes in mind. He didn't think he would ever turn over complete control to God the way Alec or Jason had. God apparently had different plans for his life and future, but Seth's was somewhere in 1906. He wasn't sure where God's was, but he *was* sure that if it didn't include Caroline, he didn't want any part of it.

The next morning, they woke at dawn, had a hearty breakfast, and headed north in search of the storm that would blow through in a few short hours. It took them longer than expected to make the six-mile hike, and they reached the center of the storm's peak just in time to see the portal open. Doing as they always do, they ran straight into the center of the storm that would take them into 1580 Dover, England, just one week and one year into the future from where they currently were.

Caroline and Bridget had spent the last six weeks pouring over the Dragoman books, learning everything they could about what Dragoman do and what Peregrines do. They looked closely at the geographical maps and the storm listing in the *History of Storms* book, finding out that a storm has to be a certain strength to time-jump, and that they would see a portal open within the storm's center. But it wasn't clear where they would end up when they did walk through. The book mentioned having something called a charging station located at several different places throughout time and space. And it even gave some coordinates for their location, but it didn't mention how or what they had to do to find them.

Caroline still wasn't so sure that all this was going to work, but it beat sitting around here reserved to living a life in the year 1580.

When they ventured outdoors to town, Caroline told anyone who asked that she was Bridget's aunt visiting from another country. Not that many people asked except those that lived close to her, and not many of *them* inquired. They just simply watched them. Caroline couldn't wait to leave this time period. The clothing was bulky and itchy and was actually starting to cause a slight rash in places. She missed the weaves that she was used to wearing. She made sure to pack what she had come here in so she could put it back on once they left.

After weeks of waiting and searching, the storm they would jump through would blow through this very day. They spent yesterday and this morning, packing supplies needed for their journey. It was supposed to blow through south of town just after noon, and it appeared by the coordinates that they needed to walk a few miles south of town to actually catch the portal there, if there was no such portal, then they would just keep going. If all this time-jumping stuff was just a theory or the mad writings of a delusional individual, then Caroline and Bridget would head anywhere but here. Caroline would take care of Bridget as best she could in this strange new world God had dropped her into. But regardless, she would never stop searching for a way back to Seth. Caroline went in search of Bridget, ready to leave, both of them a bit anxious over this new journey life was about to take them on.

Seth, Jason, and Alec exited the storm in almost the same place they had entered. They would need to make the now five-mile walk south back to town to search for Eleven. Storm traveling was a hard business. It seemed they spent about thirty percent of their time drenched from rain or covered in sand. They hadn't traveled by earthquake yet, not intentionally anyway, since they were much less frequent. Seth wasn't at all sure he wanted to attempt it anyway, his last experience with one tearing him from his just acquired, happy life.

With all the storm traveling, they had to have special waterproof packs and bags to keep their stuff from staying wet and mildewing. It also kept the drawing that Safra had made of Eleven from dissolving from constant contact with water.

"Just a few more miles and we'll be in town." Seth looked over the landscape they had come to know by heart. They had peregrinated in this same village six times now over the last three weeks.

"I'll be glad when this trip is over. I'm ready for some real down time." Alec adjusted his pack on his back for better comfort. "I think I have blisters where my pack straps rub my shoulders."

Jason and Seth chuckled at Alec's remarks feeling the same way he did. Although they both new the real reason he wished to return. He was used to traveling with Odessa, and they were sure he was missing her. Seth understood that feeling all too well.

They made it to the edge of town and, leaving nothing to chance, they occasionally showed someone the picture asking if they had seen her or knew her. As they walked the slightly progressed streets of Dover headed for Pickfurt Street, they continued showing the photo to anyone who crossed paths with them. Reaching Pickfurt Street, they stopped to take a break and drink some water.

"You know something I don't understand. If she were here, wouldn't she have been in the past years as well? I mean she would be a younger version of herself, but she would still be there," Seth stated. "If we didn't find her over the last five years, I doubt seriously that she's here in this one. We have to have the wrong time period. One of the other groups will likely find her in another decade."

Jason filled him in on some brief Peregrine history. "Well, that depends. Like we said, she's a new Peregrine. She apparently hasn't been around for long, so we really aren't sure which one she's in. And people likely don't know her yet, especially if she's been hiding out. Technically, she only came on radar after you appeared. Since Ten was named just two years ago, at the most she's only been around for a few years. They usually happen a year or more apart."

"That makes sense." Seth stowed his water. "Well, let's get back to it." He stood and headed along the street.

As they walked up Pickfurt Street, they passed the drawing on to several of the merchants that were located on the street, getting nowhere. They were about mid-way up when they walked into the baker's shop, realizing it was a new establishment. It hadn't been in this spot over the last five years. Seth ventured inside the small shop, the smell of baked goods permeating the air making his mouth water and his stomach growl.

"Excuse me sir, have you by chance seen this girl?" Seth asked, handing over the drawing.

The short, round man took the paper from Seth, looked at the picture, and quickly looked back at him.

"Who's askin'?" the man questioned, not looking too friendly.

This caught Seth's attention instantly. "Please, if you know her, I believe she may be in trouble. I'm here to help her, my friends and I mean her no harm."

The portly man eyed Seth, sizing him up. "Well, you seem like you're on the honest. She lives just up the street in a small shack at the other end."

"Thank you so much, you have no idea how grateful I am." Seth quickly took the picture from the man and headed outside. "She's here," he told the others, excitement almost stealing his breath away.

"Where?" Jason asked.

"Just at the end of the street."

They took off running up the street, reaching the end where several small houses sat, spread apart from each other by a few small businesses and a bit of muddy ground.

"He didn't say which house but there are only a hand-full here. It can't be that hard to find her." Seth started knocking on doors.

A small, frail little woman answered the door and almost jumped back inside when she saw Seth's huge, daunting, figure taking up her doorway.

"Excuse me ma'am, I'm sorry to bother you, but would you happen to know which house this girl lives in?" Seth felt as though he were about to crawl out of his skin. Not sure why he felt so anxious.

"Yes, she lives in the last one down there on the right," the woman said pointing brusquely.

"Thank you!" Seth began to walk away.

"But you won't find her there! She and her aunt left down the road that way, just a while ago. They were carrying bags with them. Pretty sure they were headed somewhere," she said, closing the door.

"Did you hear that, guys? We need to go, quickly. We could lose them anywhere along the way," Jason chimed in.

"Guys, take a look at the sky in that direction," Alec said with concern in his voice.

The blackening sky revealed there was a storm about to hit in the very direction the two women had walked. If they somehow knew about peregrination they could jump to who knows where, and they may never find them again.

"We need to hurry!" Seth said, and they all took off running.

Caroline and Bridget continued walking in the direction which the storm was supposed to blow through. True to its listing in the storm book, the weather had darkened, and clouds rolled in heavily as distant thunder began booming. They hurried their steps as lightning began streaking across the sky and rain drops began to sparsely pelt the earth beneath them.

"What now do you think?" Caroline asked Bridget.

"Well, I guess we wait. I assume that storm-jumping is a wet business," Bridget said in her matter-of-fact tone.

"I suppose you're right." Caroline wasn't sure she wanted to smile or cry right now as apprehension began to form in the middle of her chest.

The thunder increased and lightning bounced from cloud to cloud as the rain began falling much harder now. As they stood watching the storm's power increase, they both noticed a small light forming in the center. Not sure if it was what they thought it to be or just a bolt of lightning that had touched the earth there, they both looked at each other and squinted against the pouring rain.

Sure enough, as they stood there being completely drenched to the bone, it appeared. Bright as the sun, in the dead center of the open field, a large, pointed, oval shaped light hovered and just touched the ground. They looked at each other and smiled as they began quickly walking toward the light, now believing the information in the books and what they said to be fact.

Seth, Jason, and Alec ran as fast as their feet would allow toward the storm, watching as it began to gain strength and start to rain. As they rounded the bend in the road, it opened up onto a large field where the full force of the storm had dropped its load, and a portal. There in the middle of the field facing away from them were two figures, quickly jogging toward the portal.

"Wait!" Seth yelled, even though he knew they probably couldn't hear him over the roar of the thunder and rain. All three of them began yelling as loudly as they could, waving their arms wildly in the air. But the figures kept moving ever closer to being lost again.

"Hey!!! Stop!!!" Seth's loud voice boomed through the air as Jason and Alec yelled right along with him. They were gaining ground but were still a-ways off from them.

With one last thunderous boom and a flash of lightning that lit the entire sky, the two figures disappeared into the portal. Before the men could reach it, the portal closed, and the three men collapsed to the ground breathing hard and filling their lungs with deep breaths of the damp air. The rain still pelted hard against their skin soaking them through and chilling them to the bone.

"Well," Seth gasped, "that's that! I suppose we should head back to Simon's and try again later," He looked to the other two men. Alec leaning upon his knees and Jason kneeling upon the ground next to Seth.

"Yes, I believe so." Jason breathed hard, taking great breaths between words. "Surely God will lead Safra to find them again. We found them once, and now we know a little better about who we're looking for. Even though we didn't get to see the other woman we know Eleven doesn't travel alone. And apparently she has some knowledge of peregrinating."

"I say we get out of this rain. Let's head back to the town and see if someone can give us a description of the other woman," Alec offered.

"Good idea." Seth stood and offered Jason a hand to stand. "Maybe we can find out a name also to go with that picture."

They walked back into town, found a room to rent and dry out, and waited for the storm that would lead them home. They inquired throughout the village about the name of the younger girl, which they discovered was Bridget Burke, but got little information as far as a description went as to her aunt. It seems that few people had really gotten a good look at the other woman. They had kept to themselves pretty much the whole time the aunt was visiting.

It seemed very strange to Jason, Seth, and Alec that a family such as an aunt and a niece would both be peregrinating. There was more to this story than they knew. They would have to wait until they returned to Simon's to concur with the rest of their friends. Surely they could all come up with some sort of explanation. They all hoped and prayed that they could find them both again very soon. Simon had made it very clear when they left as to the urgency of the mission. This girl was important. She was the last of The Twelve to be found; and finding her again was important to the salvation of all mankind.

Book 2 Teaser

Caroline and Bridget walked out of the portal to find themselves in the middle of an intense storm, worse than the one from where they had left. The wind was whipping wildly around them, and the rain was blowing side-ways. They held onto each other so as to not get separated, making their way to a standing of trees outlining the field where they had been deposited. They made it to the shelter of the trees and happened upon a cave that was lying just inside the edge of the hillside. Caroline hesitantly peeked inside to make sure there weren't any wild animals taking up residence.

"Goodness, what a storm!" Caroline entered the cave and shook the rain from her cloak, motioning Bridget to follow her inside. "We need to build a fire to dry our clothes and warm ourselves."

"Yes, I agree," Bridget said in her always cheerful voice. "But wasn't that exciting Caroline! I wonder where we are now? I haven't yet found any information in the books on knowing where we end up. Do you suppose we just float around through time, just landing wherever God chooses?" Bridget questioned, gathering some leaves and sticks lying about the edge of the cave's floor.

"I'm not really sure Bridget. Surely God has a hand in where we go since He is the one who chose us for this life." Caroline bent forward using the flint and steel they had packed from Bridget's to light the fire.

"What do you suppose we do after this?" Bridget found a place to sit by the fire after laying her cloak across a large rock to dry beside the fire's heat.

"I suppose the books have no answers on that either?"

"I'm not really sure. Perhaps when the storm lets up and we have more light to see by, we can look and see if there are any answers."

"I wonder what time it is? It's hard to tell with the storm still raging like it is." Caroline peered out of the cave's opening into the pouring rain.

"I suppose there's no way of knowing."

Caroline went to sit by the fireside with Bridget to dry her soaked hair and clothing. As they sat there in relative quiet, they heard a noise stirring just outside the cave opening. Just as they turned to look, a giant of a man stepped into the cave, giving them both a start.

He held up his hands in an attempt to show them he meant no harm.

"Sorry, didn' mean to frighten ya' none. Don' worry, I mean no harm. I noticed you two come out a' the storm there an' I came to warn ya' a' the dangers. There be people 'round here that search fer those like you two that *will* do ya' harm. If'n you two wan' ta' survive 'round here, I suggest ya' be followin' me right now. Normally, I wouldn' get involved, but that one there be awful young." The giant of a man pointed toward Bridget.

"And who might you be?" Caroline asked the man.

"Most folks call me Oz. Let's jus' say I know what you two are, an' there's quite a few others 'round here; that if'n they saw ya; know too. An' they won't be as friendly as I am. So, if ya' want to live, I suggest ya' put that there fire out and folla' me," Oz said, waiting for an answer.

Caroline looked at Bridget with raised eyebrows and a questioning look in her eyes. Bridget, ever the optimist, shrugged her shoulders and smiled. She stood and grabbed her bags and cloak as Caroline poured some of the water they had packed onto the fire to douse it.

Caroline stood and looked at the man.

"All right, Oz, lead on."

With that, they all exited the cave into the still pouring rain and headed up into the mountains. Where he was taking them, they had no idea. Neither of them were any match for the huge man regardless, and if he had wanted to harm them wouldn't he have already done so? Caroline could only hope and pray that God had sent this man to help them. If not, they would surely soon find out.

About the Author

S.G. Boudreaux is a stay-at-home mom who has home-schooled her three children for the last twenty years. She has been married to her husband for twenty-three years and they reside in Louisiana where her husband was born and raised. They, surrounded by three dogs and a cat, live in the country. Her idea for the books called the Peregrination Series were inspired by the constant and recurring storms that seem to be escalating in number and severity. God gave her the vision in the summer of 2017 to write a five-novel fiction series based on biblical values, Christian morals, and fun, true-to-life characters. Her family is very active in their local church where they serve in an array of areas.

For more on her life and current events that she is involved in, visit her website at www.sgboudreaux.com or her amazon authors page at amazon.com/author/sgboudreaux

You can also find her at:

www.facebook/s.g.boudreaux

instagram at sg_boudreaux,

twitter at SGBoudreaux@shawna20202917

and Pinterest at SGBoudreaux

Peregrination Series Book 1: Earth

Other Books in the Series

Book 2: WIND

Book 3: FIRE

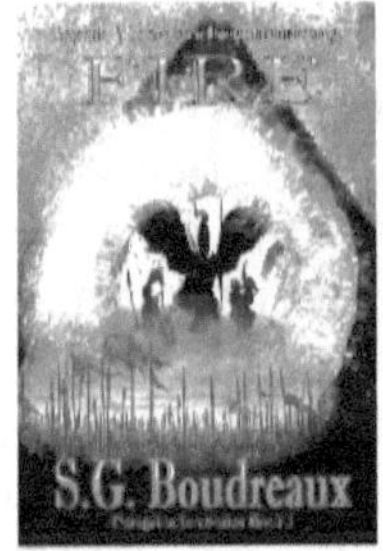

Book 4: WATER

Book 5: The Final Battle;
Battle of the Beasts

9 781733 963664